'Wickedly funny...
Ottessa Moshfegh has been hailed in America as a saviour
of literary fiction who...specialises in anti-heroines who
won't jump through the usual hoops of womanhood'

Evening Standard

'A deliciously dark and unsettling modern fairy tale...
The boldest literary statement of passive resistance since
Herman Melville's scrivener famously declared "I would
prefer not to"'

Financial Times

'Moshfegh's blackly funny new novel...hits multiple marks
at once: as an art-school prank, a between-the-lines tale of
displaced grief and pitiless anatomy of gender injustice, it
also offers...a dark state-of-America fable'

Observer

'You'll emerge from this darkly hilarious novel not
necessarily rested or relaxed but more finely attuned to
how delicately fraught the human condition can be'

Marie Claire

'Ottessa Moshfegh pulls off an unlikely premise, demon-
strating once again the unsettling energy, daring plotting
and biting observations that have earned her literary prizes
and praise from the start of her career'

Time

OTTESSA MOSHFEGH

Ottessa Moshfegh is a fiction writer from Boston. She was awarded the Plimpton Prize for her stories in *The Paris Review* and granted a creative writing fellowship from the National Endowment for the Arts. Her first book, the novella *McGlue*, was recently published by Vintage. Her novel *Eileen* was awarded the 2016 PEN/Hemingway Award and was shortlisted for the Man Booker Prize. Her collection of stories, *Homesick for Another World*, was published in 2017.

ALSO BY OTTESSA MOSHFEGH

McGlue
Elieen
Homesick for Another World

OTTESSA MOSHFEGH

My Year of Rest and Relaxation

VINTAGE

12

Vintage
20 Vauxhall Bridge Road
London SW1V 2SA

Vintage is part of the Penguin Random House group of
companies whose addresses can be found
at global.penguinrandomhouse.com

Penguin
Random House
UK

First published by Jonathan Cape in 2018
First published in Vintage in 2019

penguin.co.uk/vintage

A CIP catalogue record for this book is available from
the British Library

ISBN 9781784707422

Printed and bound in Great Britain by Clays Ltd, Elcograf S.p.A.

Penguin Random House is committed to a sustainable future
for our business, our readers and our planet. This book is
made from Forest Stewardship Council® certified paper.

For Luke.
My one. My only.

If you're smart or rich or lucky

Maybe you'll beat the laws of man

But the inner laws of spirit

And the outer laws of nature

No man can

No, no man can . . .

"THE WOLF THAT LIVES IN LINDSEY,"

JONI MITCHELL

MY YEAR

OF REST

AND

RELAXATION

One

WHENEVER I WOKE UP, night or day, I'd shuffle through the bright marble foyer of my building and go up the block and around the corner where there was a bodega that never closed. I'd get two large coffees with cream and six sugars each, chug the first one in the elevator on the way back up to my apartment, then sip the second one slowly while I watched movies and ate animal crackers and took trazodone and Ambien and Nembutal until I fell asleep again. I lost track of time in this way. Days passed. Weeks. A few months went by. When I thought of it, I ordered delivery from the Thai restaurant across the street, or a tuna salad platter from the diner on First Avenue. I'd wake up to find voice messages on my cell phone from salons or spas confirming appointments I'd booked in my sleep. I always called back to cancel, which I hated doing because I hated talking to people.

Early on in this phase, I had my dirty laundry picked up

and clean laundry delivered once a week. It was a comfort to me to hear the torn plastic bags rustle in the draft from the living room windows. I liked catching whiffs of the fresh laundry smell while I dozed off on the sofa. But after a while, it was too much trouble to gather up all the dirty clothes and stuff them in the laundry bag. And the sound of my own washer and dryer interfered with my sleep. So I just threw away my dirty underpants. All the old pairs reminded me of Trevor, anyway. For a while, tacky lingerie from Victoria's Secret kept showing up in the mail—frilly fuchsia and lime green thongs and teddies and baby-doll nightgowns, each sealed in a clear plastic Baggie. I stuffed the little Baggies into the closet and went commando. An occasional package from Barneys or Saks provided me with men's pajamas and other things I couldn't remember ordering—cashmere socks, graphic T-shirts, designer jeans.

I took a shower once a week at most. I stopped tweezing, stopped bleaching, stopped waxing, stopped brushing my hair. No moisturizing or exfoliating. No shaving. I left the apartment infrequently. I had all my bills on automatic payment plans. I'd already paid a year of property taxes on my apartment and on my dead parents' old house upstate. Rent money from the tenants in that house showed up in my checking account by direct deposit every month. Unemployment was rolling in as long as I made the weekly call into the automated service and pressed "1" for "yes" when the robot asked if I'd made a sincere effort to find a job. That was enough to cover the copayments on all my prescriptions, and whatever I picked up at the bodega. Plus, I had investments. My dead father's financial advisor kept track of all that and sent me quarterly statements that I never read. I had plenty of money in my savings account, too—enough to live on for a few years as long as I didn't do anything spectacular. On top of all this, I had a high credit limit on my Visa card. I wasn't worried about money.

I had started "hibernating" as best I could in mid-June of 2000. I was twenty-six years old. I watched summer die and autumn turn cold and gray through a broken slat in the blinds. My muscles withered. The sheets on my bed yellowed, although I usually fell asleep in front of the television on the sofa, which was from Pottery Barn and striped blue and white and sagging and covered in coffee and sweat stains.

I didn't do much in my waking hours besides watch movies. I couldn't stand to watch regular television. Especially at the beginning, TV aroused too much in me, and I'd get compulsive about the remote, clicking around, scoffing at everything and agitating myself. I couldn't handle it. The only news I could read were the sensational headlines on the local daily papers at the bodega. I'd quickly glance at them as I paid for my coffees. Bush versus Gore for president. Somebody

3

important died, a child was kidnapped, a senator stole money, a famous athlete cheated on his pregnant wife. Things were happening in New York City—they always are—but none of it affected me. This was the beauty of sleep—reality detached itself and appeared in my mind as casually as a movie or a dream. It was easy to ignore things that didn't concern me. Subway workers went on strike. A hurricane came and went. It didn't matter. Extraterrestrials could have invaded, locusts could have swarmed, and I would have noted it, but I wouldn't have worried.

When I needed more pills, I ventured out to the Rite Aid three blocks away. That was always a painful passage. Walking up First Avenue, everything made me cringe. I was like a baby being born—the air hurt, the light hurt, the details of the world seemed garish and hostile. I relied on alcohol only on the days of these excursions—a shot of vodka before I went out and walked past all the little bistros and cafes and shops I'd frequented when I was out there, pretending to live a life. Otherwise I tried to limit myself to a one-block radius around my apartment.

The men who worked at the bodega were all young Egyptians. Besides my psychiatrist Dr. Tuttle, my friend Reva, and the doormen at my building, the Egyptians were the only people I saw on a regular basis. They were relatively handsome, a few of them more than the others. They had square jaws and manly foreheads, bold, caterpillary eyebrows. And they all looked like they had eyeliner on. There must have been half a dozen of them—brothers or cousins, I assumed. Their style deterred me. They wore soccer jerseys and leather racing jackets and gold chains with crosses and played Z100 on the radio. They had absolutely no sense of humor. When I'd first moved to the neighborhood, they'd been flirty, even annoyingly so. But once I'd begun shuffling in with eye boogers and scum at the corners of my mouth at odd hours, they quit trying to win my affection.

"You have something," the man behind the counter said one morning, gesturing to his chin with long brown fingers. I just waved my hand. There was toothpaste crusted all over my face, I discovered later.

After a few months of sloppy, half-asleep patronage, the Egyptians started calling me "boss" and readily accepted my fifty cents when I asked for a loosie, which I did often. I could have gone to any number of places for coffee, but I liked the bodega. It was close, and the coffee was consistently bad, and I didn't have to confront anyone ordering a brioche bun or no-foam latte. No children with runny noses or Swedish au pairs. No sterilized professionals, no people on dates. The bodega coffee was working-class coffee—coffee for doormen and deliverymen and handymen and busboys and housekeepers. The air in there was heavy with the perfume of cheap cleaning detergents and mildew. I could rely on the clouded freezer full of ice cream and popsicles and plastic cups of ice. The clear Plexiglas compartments above the counter were filled with gum and candy. Nothing ever changed: cigarettes in neat rows, rolls of scratch tickets, twelve different brands of bottled water, beer, sandwich bread, a case of meats and cheeses nobody ever bought, a tray of stale Portuguese rolls, a basket of plastic-wrapped fruit, a whole wall of magazines that I avoided. I didn't want to read more than newspaper headlines. I steered clear of anything that might pique my intellect or make me envious or anxious. I kept my head down.

Reva would show up at my apartment with a bottle of wine from time to time and insist on keeping me company. Her mother was dying of cancer. That, among many other things, made me not want to see her.

"You forgot I was coming over?" Reva would ask, pushing her way past me into the living room and flipping on the lights. "We talked last night, remember?"

I liked to call Reva just as the Ambien was kicking in, or the Solfoton, or whatever. According to her, I only ever wanted to talk about Harrison Ford or Whoopi Goldberg, which she said was fine. "Last night you recounted the entire plot of *Frantic*. And you did the scene where they're driving in the car, with the cocaine. You went on and on."

"Emmanuelle Seigner is amazing in that movie."

"That's exactly what you said last night."

I was both relieved and irritated when Reva showed up, the way you'd feel if someone interrupted you in the middle of suicide. Not that what I was doing was suicide. In fact, it was the opposite of suicide. My hibernation was self-preservational. I thought that it was going to save my life.

"Now get in the shower," Reva would say, heading into the kitchen. "I'll take out the trash."

I loved Reva, but I didn't like her anymore. We'd been friends since college, long enough that all we had left in common was our history together, a complex circuit of resentment, memory, jealousy, denial, and a few dresses I'd let Reva borrow, which she'd promised to dry clean and return but never did. She worked as an executive assistant for an insurance brokerage firm in Midtown. She was an only child, a gym rat, had a blotchy red birthmark on her neck in the shape of Florida, a gum-chewing habit that gave her TMJ and breath that reeked of cinnamon and green apple candy. She liked to come over to my place, clear a space for herself on the armchair, comment on the state of the apartment, say I looked like I'd lost more weight, and complain about work, all while refilling her wine glass after every sip.

"People don't understand what it's like for me," she said. "They take it for granted that I'm always going to be cheerful. Meanwhile, these assholes think they can go around treating everyone below them like shit. And I'm supposed to giggle and look cute and send their faxes? Fuck them. Let them all go bald and burn in hell."

Reva was having an affair with her boss, Ken, a middle-aged man with a wife and child. She was open about her obsession with him, but she tried to hide that they were sexually involved. She once showed me a picture of him in a company brochure—tall, big shoulders, white button-down shirt, blue tie, face so nondescript, so boring, he may as well have been molded out of plastic. Reva had a thing for older men, as did I. Men our age, Reva said, were too corny, too affectionate, too needy. I could understand her disgust, but I'd never met a man like that. All the men I'd ever been with, young as well as old, had been detached and unfriendly.

"You're a cold fish, that's why," Reva explained. "Like attracts like."

As a friend, Reva was indeed corny and affectionate and needy, but she was also very secretive and occasionally very patronizing. She couldn't or simply *wouldn't* understand why I wanted to sleep all the time, and she was always rubbing my nose in her moral high ground and telling me to "face the music" about whatever bad habit I'd been stuck on at the time. The summer I started sleeping, Reva admonished me for "squandering my bikini body." "Smoking *kills*." "You should get out more." "Are you getting enough protein in your diet?" Et cetera.

"I'm not a baby, Reva."

"I'm just worried about you. Because I care. Because I *love* you," she'd say.

Since we'd met junior year, Reva could never soberly admit to any desire that was remotely uncouth. But she wasn't perfect. "She's no white lily," as my mother would have said. I'd known for years that Reva was bulimic. I knew she masturbated with an electric neck massager because she was too embarrassed to buy a proper vibrator from a sex shop. I knew she was deep in debt from college and years of maxed-out credit cards, and that she shoplifted testers from the beauty section of the health food store near her apartment on the Upper West Side. I'd seen the tester stickers on various items in the huge bag of makeup she carried around wherever she went. She was a slave to vanity and status, which was not unusual in a place like Manhattan, but I found her desperation especially irritating. It made it hard for me to respect her intelligence. She was so obsessed with brand names, conformity, "fitting in." She made regular trips down to Chinatown for the latest knockoff designer handbags. She'd given me a Dooney & Bourke wallet for Christmas once. She got us matching fake Coach key rings.

Ironically, her desire to be classy had always been the déclassé thorn in her side. "Studied grace is not grace," I once tried to explain. "Charm is not a hairstyle. You either have it or you don't. The more you try to be fashionable, the tackier you'll look." Nothing hurt Reva more than effortless beauty, like mine. When we'd watched *Before Sunrise* on video one day, she'd said, "Did you know Julie Delpy's a feminist? I wonder if that's why she's not skinnier. No way they'd cast her in this role if she were American. See how soft her arms are? Nobody here tolerates arm flab. Arm flab is a killer. It's like the SAT's. You don't even exist if you're below 1400."

"Does it make you happy that Julie Delpy has arm flab?" I'd asked her.

"No," she'd said after some consideration. "Happiness is not what I'd call it. More like *satisfaction*."

Jealousy was one thing Reva didn't seem to feel the need to hide from me. Ever since we'd formed a friendship, if I told her that something good happened, she'd whine "No fair" often enough that it became a kind of catchphrase that she would toss off casually, her voice flat. It was an automatic response to my good grade, a new shade of lipstick, the last popsicle, my expensive haircut. "No fair." I'd make my fingers like a cross and hold them out between us, as though to protect me from her envy and wrath. I once asked her whether

her jealousy had anything to do with her being Jewish, if she thought things came easier to me because I was a WASP.

"It's not because I'm Jewish," I remember her saying. This was right around graduation, when I'd made the dean's list despite having skipped more than half my classes senior year, and Reva had bombed the GRE. "It's because I'm fat." She really wasn't. She was very pretty, in fact.

"And I wish you'd take better care of yourself," she said one day visiting me in my half-awake state at my apartment. "I can't do it for you, you know. What do you like so much about Whoopi Goldberg? She's not even funny. You need to be watching movies that are going to cheer you up. Like *Austin Powers*. Or that one with Julia Roberts and Hugh Grant. You're like Winona Ryder from *Girl, Interrupted* all of a sudden. But you look more like Angelina Jolie. She's blond in that."

This was how she expressed her concern for my well-being. She also didn't like the fact that I was "on drugs."

"You really shouldn't mix alcohol with all your medications," she said, finishing the wine. I let Reva have all the wine. In college, she'd called hitting the bars "going to therapy." She could suck a whiskey sour down in one sip. She popped Advil between drinks. She said it kept her tolerance up. She would probably qualify as an alcoholic. But she was right about me. I *was* "on drugs." I took upwards of a dozen pills a day. But it was all very regulated, I thought. It was all totally aboveboard. I just wanted to sleep all the time. I had a plan.

"I'm not a junkie or something," I said defensively. "I'm taking some time off. This is my year of rest and relaxation."

"Lucky you," Reva said. "I wouldn't mind taking time off from work to loaf around, watch movies, and snooze all day, but I'm not complaining. I just don't have that luxury." Once she was drunk, she'd put her feet up on the coffee table, scooching my dirty clothes and unopened mail to the floor, and she'd go on and on about Ken and catch me up on the latest episode of their soap opera drama, *Office Romance*. She'd brag about all the fun things she was going to do over the weekend, complain that she'd gone off her most recent diet and had to do overtime at the gym to make up for it. And eventually, she'd cry about her mother. "I just can't talk to her like I used to. I feel so sad. I feel so abandoned. I feel very, very alone."

"We're all alone, Reva," I told her. It was true: I was, she was. This was the maximum comfort I could offer.

"I know I have to prepare for the worst with my mom. The prognosis isn't good. And I don't even think I'm getting the full story about her cancer. It just makes me feel so desperate. I wish there was someone to hold me, you know? Is that pathetic?"

"You're needy," I said. "Sounds frustrating."

"And then there's Ken. I just can't stand it. I'd rather kill myself than be all alone," she said.

"At least you have options."

If I was up for it, we'd order salads from the Thai place and watch movies on pay-per-view. I preferred my VHS tapes, but Reva always wanted to see whatever movie was "new" and "hot" and "supposed to be good." She took it as a source of pride that she had a superior knowledge of pop culture during this period. She knew all the latest celebrity gossip, followed the newest fashion trends. I didn't give a shit about that stuff. Reva, however, studied *Cosmo* and watched *Sex and the City*. She was competitive about beauty and "life wisdom." Her envy was very self-righteous. Compared to me, she was "underprivileged." And according to her terms, she was right: I looked like a model, had money I hadn't earned, wore real designer clothing, had majored in art history, so I was "cultured." Reva, on the other hand, came from Long Island, was an 8 out of 10 but called herself "a New York three," and had majored in economics. "The Asian nerd major," she named it.

Reva's apartment across town was a third-floor walk-up that smelled like sweaty gym clothes and French fries and Lysol and Tommy Girl perfume. Although she'd given me a spare set of keys to the place when she moved in, I'd been over only twice in five years. She preferred coming to my apartment. I think she enjoyed being recognized by my door-man, taking the fancy elevator with the gold buttons, watching me squander my luxuries. I don't know what it was about Reva. I couldn't get rid of her. She worshipped me, but she also hated me. She saw my struggle with misery as a cruel parody of her own misfortunes. I had chosen my solitude and purposelessness, and Reva had, despite her hard work, simply failed to get what she wanted—no husband, no children, no fabulous career. So when I started sleeping all the time, I think Reva took some satisfaction in watching me crumble into the ineffectual slob she hoped I was becoming. I wasn't interested in competing with her, but I resented her on princi-ple, and so we did argue. I imagine this is what having a sister is like, someone who loves you enough to point out all your flaws. Even on weekends, if she'd stayed over late, she'd re-fuse to sleep over. I wouldn't have wanted her to anyway, but she always made a fuss about it, as though she had responsi-bilities I would never understand.

I took a Polaroid of her one night and stuck it into the frame of the mirror in the living room. Reva thought it was a loving gesture, but the photo was really meant as a reminder of how little I enjoyed her company if I felt like calling her later while I was under the influence.

"I'll lend you my confidence-boosting CD set," she would say if I alluded to any concern or worry.

Reva was partial to self-help books and workshops that usually combined some new dieting technique with professional development and romantic relationship skills, under the guise of teaching young women "how to live up to their full potential." Every few weeks, she had a whole new paradigm for living, and I had to hear about it. "Get good at knowing when you're tired," she'd advised me once. "Too many women wear themselves thin these days." A lifestyle tip from *Get the Most Out of Your Day, Ladies* included the suggestion to preplan your outfits for the workweek on Sunday evenings.

"That way you won't be second-guessing yourself in the morning."

I really hated when she talked like that.

"And come out to Saints with me. It's ladies' night. Girls drink for free until eleven. You'll feel so much better about yourself." She was an expert at conflating canned advice with any excuse for drinking to oblivion.

"I'm not up for going out, Reva," I said.

She looked down at her hands, fiddled with her rings, scratched her neck, then stared down at the floor.

"I miss you," she said, her voice cracking a little. Maybe she thought those words would break through to my heart. I'd been taking Nembutals all day.

"We probably shouldn't be friends," I told her, stretching

out on the sofa. "I've been thinking about it, and I see no rea-son to continue."

Reva just sat there, kneading her hands against her thighs. After a minute or two of silence, she looked up at me and put a finger under her nose—something she did when she was about to start crying. It was like an Adolf Hitler impression. I pulled my sweater over my head and grit my teeth and tried not to laugh while she sputtered and whined and tried to compose herself.

"I'm your best friend," she said plaintively. "You can't shut me out. That would be very self-destructive."

I pulled the sweater down to take a drag of my cigarette. She batted the smoke out of her face and fake coughed. Then she turned to me. She was trying to embolden herself by mak-ing eye contact with the enemy. I could see the fear in her eyes, as though she were staring into a black hole she might fall into.

"At least I'm making an effort to change and go after what I want," she said. "Besides sleeping, what do *you* want out of life?"

I chose to ignore her sarcasm.

"I wanted to be an artist, but I had no talent," I told her.

"Do you really need talent?"

That might have been the smartest thing Reva ever said to me.

"*Yes*," I replied.

She got up and ticktocked across the floor in her heels and shut the door softly behind her. I took a few Xanax and ate a few animal crackers and stared at the wrinkled seat of the empty armchair. I got up and put in *Tin Cup,* and watched it halfheartedly as I dozed on the sofa.

Reva called half an hour later and left a voice mail saying she'd already forgiven me for hurting her feelings, that she was worried about my health, that she loved me and wouldn't abandon me, "no matter what." My jaw unclenched listening to the message, as though I'd been gritting my teeth for days. Maybe I had been. Then I pictured her sniffling through Gristedes, picking out the food she'd eat and vomit up. Her loyalty was absurd. This was what kept us going.

"You'll be fine," I told Reva when she said her mother was starting a third round of chemo.

"Don't be a spaz," I said when her mother's cancer spread to her brain.

I CAN'T POINT TO any one event that resulted in my decision to go into hibernation. Initially, I just wanted some downers to drown out my thoughts and judgments, since the constant barrage made it hard not to hate everyone and everything. I thought life would be more tolerable if my brain were slower to condemn the world around me. I started seeing Dr. Tuttle in January 2000. It started off very innocently: I was plagued with misery, anxiety, a wish to escape the prison of my mind and body. Dr. Tuttle confirmed that this was nothing unusual. She wasn't a good doctor. I had found her name in the phone book.

"You've caught me at a good moment," she said the first time I called. "I just finished rinsing the dishes. Where did you find my number?"

"In the Yellow Pages."

I liked to think that I'd picked Dr. Tuttle at random, that there was something fated about our relationship, divine in some way, but in truth, she'd been the only psychiatrist to answer the phone at eleven at night on a Tuesday. I'd left a dozen messages on answering machines by the time Dr. Tuttle picked up.

"The biggest threats to brains nowadays are all the microwave ovens," Dr. Tuttle explained on the phone that night. "Microwaves, radio waves. Now there are cell phone towers blasting us with who knows what kind of frequencies. But that's not my science. I deal in treating mental illness. Do you work for the police?" she asked me.

"No, I work for an art dealer, at a gallery in Chelsea."

"Are you FBI?"

"No."

"CIA?"

"No, why?"

"I just have to ask these questions. Are you DEA? FDA? NICB? NHCAA? Are you a private investigator hired by any private or governmental entity? Do you work for a medical insurance company? Are you a drug dealer? Drug addict? Are you a clinician? A med student? Getting pills for an abusive boyfriend or employer? NASA?"

"I think I have insomnia. That's my main issue."

"You're probably addicted to caffeine, too, am I right?"

"I don't know."

"You better keep drinking it. If you quit now, you'll just go crazy. Real insomniacs suffer hallucinations and lost time and usually have poor memory. It can make life very confusing. Does that sound like you?"

"Sometimes I feel dead," I told her, "and I hate everybody. Does that count?"

"Oh, that counts. That certainly counts. I'm sure I can help you. But I do ask new patients to come in for a fifteen-minute consultation to make sure we'll make a good fit. Gratis. And I recommend you get into the habit of writing notes to remind yourself of our appointments. I have a twenty-four-hour cancellation policy. You know Post-its? Get yourself some Post-its. I'll have some agreements for you to sign, some contracts. Now write this down."

Dr. Tuttle told me to come in the next day at nine A.M.

Her home office was in an apartment building on Thirteenth Street near Union Square. The waiting room was a dark, wood-paneled parlor full of fake Victorian furniture, cat toys, pots of potpourri, purple candles, wreaths of dead purple flowers, and stacks of old *National Geographic* magazines. The bathroom was crowded with fake plants and peacock feathers. On the sink, next to a huge bar of cracked lilac soap, was a wooden bowl of peanuts in an abalone shell. That baffled me. She hid all her personal toiletries in a large wicker basket in the cabinet under the sink. She used several antifungal powders, a prescription steroid cream, shampoo and soap and lotions that smelled like lavender and violet. Fennel toothpaste. Her mouthwash was prescription. When I tried it, it tasted like the ocean.

The first time I met Dr. Tuttle, she wore a foam neck brace because of a "taxi accident" and was holding an obese tabby, whom she introduced as "my eldest." She pointed out the tiny yellow envelopes in the waiting room. "When you come in, write your name on an envelope and fold your check inside. Payments go in here," she said, knocking on the wooden box on the desk in her office. It was the kind of box they have in churches for accepting donations for candles. The fainting couch in her office was covered in cat fur and piled on one end with little antique dolls with chipped porcelain faces. On her desk were half-eaten granola bars and stacked Tupperware containers of grapes and cut-up melon, a mammoth old computer, more *National Geographic* magazines.

"What brings you here?" she asked. "Depression?" She'd already pulled out her prescription pad.

My plan was to lie. I'd given it careful consideration. I told her I'd been having trouble sleeping for the past six months, and then complained of despair and nervousness in social situations. But as I was reciting my practiced speech, I realized it was somewhat true. I wasn't an insomniac, but I was miserable. Complaining to Dr. Tuttle was strangely liberating.

"I want downers, that much I know," I said frankly. "And I want something that'll put a damper on my need for company. I'm at the end of my rope," I said. "I'm an orphan, on top of it all. I probably have PTSD. My mother killed herself."

"How?" Dr. Tuttle asked.

"Slit her wrists," I lied.

"Good to know."

Her hair was red and frizzy. The foam brace she wore around her neck had what looked like coffee and food stains on it, and it squished the skin on her neck up toward her chin. Her face was like a bloodhound's, folded and drooping, her sunken eyes hidden under very small wire-framed glasses with Coke-bottle lenses. I never got a good look at Dr. Tuttle's eyes. I suspect that they were crazy eyes, black and shiny, like a crow's. The pen she used was long and purple and had a purple feather at the end of it.

"Both my parents died when I was in college," I went on. "Just a few years ago."

She seemed to study me for a moment, her expression blank and breathless. Then she turned back to her little prescription pad.

"I'm very good with insurance companies," she said matter-of-factly. "I know how to play into their little games. Are you sleeping at *all*?"

"Barely," I said.

"Any dreams?"

"Only nightmares."

"I figured. Sleep is key. Most people need upwards of fourteen hours or so. The modern age has forced us to live unnatural lives. Busy, busy, busy. Go, go, go. You probably work too much." She scribbled for a while on her pad. "*Mirth*," Dr. Tuttle said. "I like it better than *joy*. *Happiness* isn't a word I like to use in here. It's very arresting, happiness. You should know that I'm someone who appreciates the subtleties of human experience. Being well rested is a precondition, of course. Do you know what *mirth* means? M-I-R-T-H?"

"Yeah. Like *The House of Mirth*," I said.

"A sad story," said Dr. Tuttle.

"I haven't read it."

"Better you don't."

"I read *The Age of Innocence*."

"So you're educated."

"I went to Columbia."

"That's good for me to know, but not much use to you in your condition. Education is directly proportional to anxiety, as you've probably learned, having gone to Columbia. How's your food intake? Is it steady? Any dietary restrictions? When you walked in here, I thought of Farrah Fawcett and Faye Dunaway. Any relation? I'd say you're what, twenty pounds below an ideal Quetelet index?"

"I think my appetite would come back if I could sleep," I said. It was a lie. I was already sleeping upwards of twelve hours, from eight to eight. I was hoping to get pills to help me sleep straight through the weekends.

"Daily meditation has been shown to cure insomnia in rats. I'm not a religious person, but you could try visiting a church or synagogue to ask for advice on inner peace. The Quakers seem like reasonable people. But be wary of cults. They're often just traps to enslave young women. Are you sexually active?"

"Not really," I told her.

"Do you live near any nuclear plants? Any high-voltage equipment?"

"I live on the Upper East Side."

"Take the subway?"

At this point, I took the subway each day to work.

"A lot of psychic diseases get passed around in confined public spaces. I sense your mind is too porous. Do you have any hobbies?"

"I watch movies."

"That's a fun one."

"How'd they get the rats to meditate?" I asked her.

"You've seen rodents breed in captivity? The parents *eat* their babies. Now, we can't demonize them. They do it out of compassion. For the good of the species. Any allergies?"

"Strawberries."

With that, Dr. Tuttle put her pen down and stared off into space, deep in thought, it seemed.

"*Some* rats," she said after a while, "probably deserve to be demonized. Certain individual rats." She picked her pen back up with a flourish of the purple feather. "The moment we start making generalizations, we give up our right to self-govern. I hope you follow me. Rats are very loyal to the planet. Try these," she said, handing me a sheath of prescriptions. "Don't fill them all at once. We need to stagger them so as not to raise any red flags." She got up stiffly and opened a wooden cabinet full of samples, flicked sample packets of pills out onto the desk. "I'll give you a paper bag for discretion," she said. "Fill the lithium and Haldol prescriptions first. It's good to get your case going with a bang. That way later on, if we need to try out some wackier stuff, your insurance company won't be surprised."

I can't blame Dr. Tuttle for her terrible advice. I elected to be her patient, after all. She gave me everything I asked for, and I appreciated her for that. I'm sure there were others like her out there, but the ease with which I'd found her, and the immediate relief that her prescriptions provided, made me feel that I'd discovered a pharmaceutical shaman, a magus, a sorcerer, a sage. Sometimes I wondered if Dr. Tuttle were even real. If she were a figment of my imagination, I'd find it funny that I'd chosen her over someone who looked more like one of my heroes—Whoopi Goldberg, for example.

"Dial 9-1-1 if anything bad happens," Dr. Tuttle told me. "Use reason when you feel you can. There's no way to know how these medications will affect you."

At the beginning of this, I'd look up any new pills she gave me on the Internet to try to learn how much I was likely to sleep on any given day. But reading up on a drug sapped its magic. It made the sleep seem trite, just another mechanical function of the body, like sneezing or shitting or bending at the joint. The "side effects and warnings" on the Internet were discouraging, and anxieties over them amplified the volume of my thoughts, which was the exact opposite of what I hoped the pills would do. So I filled prescriptions for things like Neuroproxin, Maxiphenphen, Valdignore, and Silencior and threw them into the mix now and then, but mostly I took sleeping aids in large doses, and supplemented them with Seconols or Nembutals when I was irritable, Valiums or Libriums when I suspected that I was sad, and Placidyls or Noctecs or Miltowns when I suspected I was lonely.

Within a few weeks, I'd accumulated an impressive library of psychopharmaceuticals. Each label bore the sign of the sleepy eye, the skull and crossbones. "Do not take this if you become pregnant." "Take with food or milk." "Store in a dry place." "May cause drowsiness." "May cause dizziness." "Do not take aspirin." "Do not crush." "Do not chew." Any normal person would have worried about what the drugs would do to her health. I wasn't completely naive about the potential dangers. My father had been eaten alive by cancer. I'd seen my mother in the hospital full of tubes, brain dead. I'd lost a childhood friend to liver failure after she took acetaminophen on top of DayQuil in high school. Life was fragile and fleeting and one had to be cautious, sure, but I would risk death if it meant I could sleep all day and become a whole new person. And I figured I was smart enough to know in advance if the pills were going to kill me. I'd start having premonition nightmares before that happened, before my heart failed or my brain exploded or hemorrhaged or pushed me out my seventh-story window. I trusted that everything was going to work out fine as long as I could sleep all day.

I'D MOVED INTO MY apartment on East Eighty-fourth Street in 1996, a year after I graduated from Columbia. By summer 2000, I still hadn't had a single conversation with any of my neighbors—almost four years of complete silence in the elevator, each awkward ride a performance of hypnotized spaceout. My neighbors were mostly fortysomething married people without children. Everyone was well-groomed, professional. A lot of camel-hair coats and black leather briefcases. Burberry scarves and pearl earrings. There were a few loudmouthed single women my age I saw from time to time gabbing on their cell phones and walking their teacup poodles. They reminded me of Reva, but they had more money and less self-loathing, I would guess. This was Yorkville, the Upper East Side. People were uptight. When I shuffled through the lobby in my pajamas and slippers on my way to the bodega, I felt like I was committing a crime, but I didn't care. The only other slovenly people around were elderly Jews with rent-controlled apartments. But I was tall and thin and blond and pretty and young. Even at my worst, I knew I still looked good.

My building was eight stories high, concrete with burgundy awnings, an anonymous facade on a block otherwise lined with pristine town houses, each with its own placard warning people not to let their dogs piss on their stoops because it would damage the brownstone. "Let us honor those who came before us, as well as those who will follow," one sign read. Men took hired cars to work downtown, and women got Botox and boob jobs and vaginal "cinches" to keep their pussies tight for their husbands and personal trainers, or so Reva told me. I had thought the Upper East Side could shield me from the beauty pageants and cockfights of the art scene in which I'd "worked" in Chelsea. But living uptown had infected me with its own virus when I first moved there. I'd tried being one of those blond women speed walking up and down the Esplanade in spandex, Bluetooth in my ear like some self-important asshole, talking to whom—Reva?

On the weekends, I did what young women in New York like me were supposed to do, at first: I got colonics and facials and highlights, worked out at an overpriced gym, lay in the hammam there until I went blind, and went out at night in shoes that cut my feet and gave me sciatica. I met interesting men at the gallery from time to time. I slept around in spurts, going out more, then less. Nothing ever panned out in terms of "love." Reva often spoke about "settling down." That sounded like death to me.

"I'd rather be alone than anybody's live-in prostitute," I said to Reva.

Still, a romantic urge surfaced now and then with Trevor, a recurring ex-boyfriend, my first and only. I was only eighteen, a freshman, when I met him at a Halloween party in a loft near Battery Park. I went with a dozen girls from the sorority I was rushing. Like most Halloween costumes, mine was an excuse to go around town dressed like a whore. I went as Detective Rizzoli, Whoopi Goldberg's character in *Fatal Beauty*. In the first scene of the movie, she's undercover and disguised as a hooker, so to copy her, I'd teased out my hair, wore a tight dress, high heels, gold lamé jacket, and white cat-eye sunglasses. Trevor had on an Andy Warhol costume: blond bobbed wig, thick black glasses, tight striped shirt. My first impression of him was that he was free spirited, clever, funny. That proved to be completely inaccurate. We left the party together and walked around for hours, lied to each other about our happy lives, ate pizza at midnight, took the Staten Island Ferry back and forth and watched the sun rise. I gave him my phone number at the dorm. By the time he finally called me, two weeks later, I'd become obsessed with him. He kept me on a long, tight leash for months—expensive meals, the occasional opera or ballet. He took my virginity at a ski lodge in Vermont on Valentine's Day. It wasn't a pleasurable experience, but I trusted he knew more about sex than I did, so when he rolled off and said, "That was amazing," I believed him. He was thirty-three, worked for Fuji Bank at the World Trade Center, wore tailored suits, sent cars to pick me up at my dorm, then the sorority house sophomore year, wined and dined me, and asked for head with no shame in the back of cabs he charged to the company account. I took this as proof of his masculine value. My "sisters" all agreed; he was "suave." And I was impressed by how much he liked talking about his emotions, something I'd never seen a man do. "My mom's a pothead now, and that's why I have this deep sadness." He took frequent trips to Tokyo for work and to San Francisco to visit his twin sister. I suspected she discouraged him from dating me.

He broke up with me the first time freshman year because I was "too young and immature. I can't be the one to help you grow out of your abandonment issues," he explained. "It's too much of a responsibility. You deserve someone who can really support your emotional development." So I spent that summer at home upstate with my parents and had sex with a boy from high school, who was far more sensual and interested in how the clitoris "works," but not quite patient enough to really interact with mine successfully. It was helpful, though. I reclaimed a bit of my dignity by feeling nothing for that boy, using him. By Labor Day, when I moved into Delta Gamma, Trevor and I were back together.

Over the next eight years, Trevor would periodically deplete his self-esteem in relationships with older women, i.e., women his age, then return to me to reboot. I was always available. I dated guys from time to time, but there was never another real "boyfriend," if I could even call Trevor that. He wouldn't have agreed to carry that title. There were plenty of one-night stands in college while we were on the outs, but nothing worth repeating. After I graduated and was flung into the world of adulthood—already orphaned—I was bolder in my desperation, made frequent appeals to Trevor to take me back. I could hear his cock harden on the phone whenever I called to beg him to come over and hold me. "I'll see if I can squeeze it in," he'd say. Then he'd be there and I'd shiver in his arms like the child I still was, swoon with gratitude for his recognition, savor the weight of him in the bed next to me. It was as though he were some divine messenger, my soul mate, my savior, whatever. Trevor would be very pleased to spend a night at my apartment on East Eighty-fourth Street, earning back all the bravado he'd lost in his last affair. I hated seeing that come on in him. One time he said he was afraid of fucking me "too passionately" because he didn't want to break my heart. So he fucked me efficiently, selfishly, and when he was done, he'd get dressed and check his pager, comb his hair, kiss my forehead, and leave.

I asked Trevor once, "If you could have only blow jobs or only intercourse for the rest of your life, which one would you choose?"

"Blow jobs," he answered.

"That's kind of gay, isn't it?" I said. "To be more interested in mouths than pussies?"

He didn't speak to me for weeks.

But Trevor was six foot three. He was clean and fit and confident. I'd choose him a million times over the hipster nerds I'd see around town and at the gallery. In college, the art history department had been rife with that specific brand of young male. An "alternative" to the mainstream frat boys and premed straight and narrow guys, these scholarly, charmless, intellectual brats dominated the more creative departments. As an art history major, I couldn't escape them. "Dudes" reading Nietzsche on the subway, reading Proust, reading David Foster Wallace, jotting down their brilliant thoughts into a black Moleskine pocket notebook. Beer bellies and skinny legs, zip-up hoodies, navy blue peacoats or army green parkas, New Balance sneakers, knit hats, canvas tote bags, small hands, hairy knuckles, maybe a deer head tattooed across a flabby bicep. They rolled their own cigarettes, didn't brush their teeth enough, spent a hundred dollars a week on coffee. They would come into Ducat, the gallery I ended up working at, with their younger—usually Asian—girlfriends. "An Asian girlfriend means the guy has a small dick," Reva once said. I'd hear them talk shit about the art. They lamented the success of others. They thought that they wanted to be adored, to be influential, celebrated for their genius, that they deserved to be worshipped. But they could barely look at themselves in the mirror. They were all on Klonopin, was my guess. They lived mostly in Brooklyn, another reason I was glad to live on the Upper East Side. Nobody up there listened to the Moldy Peaches. Nobody up there gave a shit about "irony" or Dogme 95 or Klaus Kinski.

The worst was that those guys tried to pass off their insecurity as "sensitivity," and it worked. They would be the ones running museums and magazines, and they'd only hire me if they thought I might fuck them. But when I'd been at parties with them, or out at bars, they'd ignored me. They were so self-serious and distracted by their conversation with their look-alike companions that you'd think they were wrestling with a decision of such high stakes, the world might explode. They wouldn't be distracted by "pussy," they would have me believe. The truth was probably that they were just afraid of vaginas, afraid that they'd fail to understand one as pretty and pink as mine, and they were ashamed of their own sensual inadequacies, afraid of their own dicks, afraid of themselves. So they focused on "abstract ideas" and developed drinking problems to blot out the self-loathing they preferred to call "existential ennui." It was easy to imagine those guys masturbating to Chloë Sevigny, to Selma Blair, to Leelee Sobieski. To Winona Ryder.

Trevor probably masturbated to Britney Spears. Or to Janis Joplin. I never understood his duplicity. And Trevor had never wanted to "kneel at the altar." I could count the number of times he'd gone down on me on one hand. When he'd tried, he had no idea what to do, but seemed overcome with his own generosity and passion, as though delaying getting his dick sucked was so obscene, so reckless, had required so much courage, he'd just blown his own mind. His style of kissing was aggressive, rhythmic, as though he'd studied a manual. His jaw was narrow and angular, his chin a lame afterthought. His skin was evenly toned and well moisturized, smoother than mine even. He barely had to shave. He always smelled like a department store. If I'd met him now, I would have assumed that he was gay.

But at least Trevor had the sincere arrogance to back up his bravado. He didn't cower in the face of his own ambition, like those hipsters. And he knew how to manipulate me—I had to respect him for that at least, however much I hated him for it.

TREVOR AND I WEREN'T SPEAKING when I went into hibernation. I probably called him at some point under the black veil of Ambien early on, but I don't know if he ever answered. I could easily imagine him diving into a complicated, fortysomething-year-old's vagina, dismissing any thought of me the way you'd walk past boxes of mac 'n' cheese or marshmallow cereal on a shelf in the grocery store. I was kids' stuff. I was nonsense. I wasn't worth the calories. He said he preferred brunettes. "They give me space to be myself," he told me. "Blondes are distracting. Think of your beauty as an Achilles' heel. You're too much on the surface. I don't say that offensively. But it's the truth. It's hard to look past what you look like."

Since adolescence, I'd vacillated between wanting to look like the spoiled WASP that I was and the bum that I *felt* I was and should have been if I'd had any courage. I'd shopped at Bergdorf's and Barneys and high-end vintage boutiques in the East Village. The result was an amazing wardrobe, my main professional asset as a new college graduate. I easily landed the job as a gallery girl at Ducat, one of a dozen "fine art" galleries on West Twenty-first Street. I had no big plan to become a curator, no great scheme to work my way up a ladder. I was just trying to pass the time. I thought that if I did normal things—held down a job, for example—I could starve off the part of me that hated everything. If I had been a man, I may have turned to a life of crime. But I looked like an off-duty model. It was too easy to let things come easy and go nowhere. Trevor was right about my Achilles' heel. Being pretty only kept me trapped in a world that valued looks above all else.

Natasha, my boss at Ducat, was in her early thirties. She hired me on the spot when I came in for an interview the summer I finished school. I was twenty-two. I barely remember our conversation, but I know I wore a cream silk blouse, tight black jeans, flats—in case I was taller than Natasha, which I was by half an inch—and a huge green glass necklace that thudded against my chest so hard it actually gave me bruises when I ran down the subway stairs. I knew not to wear a dress or look too prim or feminine. That would only elicit patronizing contempt. Natasha wore the same kind of outfit every day—a YSL blazer and tight leather pants, no makeup. She was the kind of mysteriously ethnic woman who would blend in easily in almost any country. She could have been from Istanbul or Paris or Morocco or Moscow or New York or San Juan or even Phnom Penh in a certain light, depending on how she wore her hair. She spoke four languages fluently and had once been married to an Italian aristocrat, a baron or a count, or so I'd heard.

The art at Ducat was supposed to be subversive, irreverent, shocking, but was all just canned counterculture crap, "punk, but with money," nothing to inspire more than a trip around the corner to buy an unflattering outfit from Comme des Garçons. Natasha had cast me as the jaded underling, and for the most part, the little effort I put into the job was enough. I was fashion candy. Hip decor. I was the bitch who sat behind a desk and ignored you when you walked into the gallery, a pouty knockout wearing indecipherably cool avant-garde outfits. I was told to play dumb if anyone asked a question. Evade, evade. Never hand over a price list. Natasha paid me just $22,000 a year. Without my inheritance, I would have been forced to find a job that paid more money. And I would probably have had to live in Brooklyn, with room-mates. I was lucky to have my dead parents' money, I knew, but that was also depressing.

Natasha's star artist was Ping Xi, a pubescent-looking twenty-three-year-old from Diamond Bar, California. She thought he was a good investment because he was Asian American and had been kicked out of CalArts for firing a gun in his studio. He would add a certain cachet. "I want the gallery to get more *cerebral*," she explained. "The market is moving away from emotion. Now it's all about process and ideas and branding. Masculinity is hot right now." Ping Xi's work first appeared at Ducat as part of a group show called "Body of Substance," and it consisted of splatter paintings, à la Jackson Pollock, made from his own ejaculate. He claimed that he'd stuck a tiny pellet of powdered colored pigment into the tip of his penis and masturbated onto huge canvases. He titled the abstract paintings as though each had some deep, dark political meaning. *Blood-Dimmed Tide,* and *Wintertime in Ho Chi Minh City* and *Sunset over Sniper Alley. Decapitated*

Palestinian Child. Bombs Away, Nairobi. It was all nonsense, but people loved it.

Natasha was particularly proud of the "Body of Substance" show because all the artists were under twenty-five, and she'd discovered them herself. She felt this would prove her gift for spotting genius. The only piece I liked in the show was by Aiyla Marwazi, a nineteen-year-old who went to Pratt. It was a huge white carpet from Crate & Barrel stained with bloody footprints and a wide bloody streak. It was supposed to look as though a bleeding body had been dragged across it. Natasha told me that the blood on the carpet was human, but she didn't put that in the press release. "You can order anything online from China, apparently. Teeth. Bones. Body parts." The bloody rug was priced at $75,000.

Annie Pinker's *Cling Film* series consisted of clumps of small objects wrapped in Saran Wrap. There was one of tiny marzipan fruits and rabbit-foot key chains, one of dried flowers and condoms. Rolled-up used thong panty liners and rubber bullets. A Big Mac and fries and cheap plastic rosaries. The artist's baby teeth, or so she claimed, and Christmas-colored M&M's. Cheap transgressions going for $25,000 a pop. And then there were the large-scale photographs of mannequins draped in flesh-colored fabric, by Max Welch. He was a total moron. I suspected that he and Natasha were fucking. On a low pedestal in the corner, a small sculpture by the Brahams Brothers—a pair of toy monkeys made using human pubic hair. Each monkey had a little erection poking out of its fur. The penises were made of white titanium and had cameras in them positioned to take crotch shots of the viewer. The images were downloaded to a Web site. A specific password to log in to see the crotch shots cost a hundred dollars. The monkeys themselves cost a quarter million for the pair.

AT WORK, I took hour-long naps in the supply closet under the stairs during my lunch breaks. "Napping" is such a childish word, but that was what I was doing. The tonality of my night sleep was more variable, generally unpredictable, but every time I lay down in that supply closet I went straight into black emptiness, an infinite space of nothingness. I was neither scared nor elated in that space. I had no visions. I had no ideas. If I had a distinct thought, I would hear it, and the sound of it would echo and echo until it got absorbed by the darkness and disappeared. There was no response necessary. No inane conversation with myself. It was peaceful. A vent in the closet released a steady flow of fresh air that picked up the scent of laundry from the hotel next door. There was no work to do, nothing I had to counteract or compensate for because there was nothing at all, period. And yet I was aware of the nothingness. I was awake in the sleep, somehow. I felt good. Almost happy.

But coming out of that sleep was excruciating. My entire life flashed before my eyes in the worst way possible, my mind refilling itself with all my lame memories, every little thing that had brought me to where I was. I'd try to remember something else—a better version, a happy story, maybe, or just an equally lame but different life that would at least be refreshing in its digressions—but it never worked. I was always still me. Sometimes I woke up with my face wet with tears. The only times I cried, in fact, were when I was pulled out of that nothingness, when the alarm on my cell phone went off. Then I had to trudge up the stairs, get coffee from the little kitchen, and rub the boogers out of my eyes. It always took me a while to readjust to the harsh fluorescent lighting.

FOR A YEAR OR SO, everything seemed fine with Natasha. The most grief she gave me was about ordering the wrong pens.

"Why do we have all these cheap clicky pens? They're so loud when you click them. You can't hear this?" She stood there, clicking at me.

"Sorry, Natasha," I said. "I'll order quieter pens."

"Has FedEx come yet?"

I would rarely know how to answer that.

Once I'd started seeing Dr. Tuttle, I was getting in fourteen, fifteen hours of sleep a night during the workweek, plus that extra hour at lunchtime. Weekends I was only awake for a few hours a day. And when I was awake, I wasn't fully so, but in a kind of murk, a dim state between the real and the dream. I got sloppy and lazy at work, grayer, emptier, less there. This pleased me, but having to *do* things became very problematic. When people spoke, I had to repeat what they'd said in my mind before understanding it. I told Dr. Tuttle I was having trouble concentrating. She said it was probably due to "brain mist."

"Are you sleeping enough?" Dr. Tuttle asked every week I went to see her.

"Just barely," I always answered. "Those pills hardly put a dent in my anxiety."

"Eat a can of chickpeas," she said. "Otherwise known as garbanzos. And try *these*." She scribbled on her prescription pad. The array of medicines I was accumulating was awe inspiring. Dr. Tuttle explained that there was a way to maximize insurance coverage by prescribing drugs for their side effects, rather than going directly to those whose main purposes were to relieve my symptoms, which were in my case "debilitating fatigue due to emotional weakness, plus insomnia, resulting in soft psychosis and belligerence." That's what she told me she was going to write in her notes. She termed her prescribing method "ecoscripting," and said she was writing a paper on it that would be published soon. "In a journal in Hamburg." So she gave me pills that targeted migraine headaches, prevented seizures, cured restless leg syndrome, prevented hearing loss. These medicines were supposed to relax me so that I could get some "much-needed rest."

ONE DAY IN MARCH 2000, I returned to my desk at Ducat after a visit to the infinite abyss of the supply closet and found what would light the path toward my eventual dismissal. "Sleep at *night*," the note read. It was from Natasha. "This is a place of business." I can't blame Natasha for wanting to fire me. I'd been napping at work for almost a year by then. Over the final few months, I had stopped dressing up for work. I just sat at my desk in a hooded sweatshirt, three-day-old mascara caked and smeared around my eyes. I lost things. I confused things. I was bad at my job. I could plan to do something and then find myself doing the opposite. I made messes. The interns wrangled me back on task, reminding me of what I'd asked them to do. "What next?"

What next? I couldn't imagine.

Natasha started to take notice. My sleepiness was good for rudeness to visitors to the gallery, but not for signing for packages or noticing if someone had come in with a dog and tracked paw prints all over the floor, which happened a few times. There were a few spilled lattes. MFA students touching paintings, once even rearranging an installation of shattered CD jewel cases in a Jarrod Harvey installation to spell out the word "HACK." When I noticed it, I just shuffled the shards of plastic around, no one the wiser. But when a homeless woman set herself up in the back room one afternoon, Natasha found out. I'd had no idea how long the woman had been there. Maybe people thought she was part of the artwork. I ended up paying her fifty bucks out of petty cash to leave. Natasha couldn't hide her irritation.

"When people walk in, you make an impression on my behalf. You know Arthur Schilling was in here last week? I just got a call." She thought I was on drugs, I'm sure.

"Who?"

"Christ. Study the roster. Study everybody's photos," she said. "Where's the packing list for Earl?" Et cetera, et cetera . . .

That spring, the gallery was putting up Ping Xi's first solo show—"Bowwowwow"—and Natasha was up in arms about every little detail. She probably would have fired me sooner had she not been so busy.

I tried to feign interest and mask my horror whenever Natasha talked about Ping Xi's "dog pieces." He had taxidermied a variety of pure breeds: a poodle, a Pomeranian, a Scottish terrier. Black Lab, Dachshund. Even a little Siberian husky pup. He'd been working on them for a long time. He and Natasha had grown close since his cum paintings had sold so well.

During the installation, I overheard one of the interns whispering to the electrician.

"There's a rumor going around that the artist gets the dogs as puppies, raises them, then kills them when they're the size he wants. He locks them in an industrial freezer because that's the most humane way to euthanize them without compromising the look of the animal. When they thaw, he can get them into whatever position he wants."

"Why doesn't he just poison them, or break their necks?"

I had a feeling the rumor was true.

When the dogs were set up, the wires connected, all the electric cords plugged in, Natasha killed the lights and turned each dog on. Red lasers shot out of their eyes. I petted the black Lab while the workers swept up the dog hair that had fallen out. Its face was silky and cold.

"Please, no petting," Ping Xi said suddenly in the darkness.

Natasha took his arm, gushing to him that she was ready

for outrage from PETA, a protest or two, an Op-Ed in the *New York Times* that would be publicity gold. Ping Xi nodded blankly.

I called in sick the day of the opening. Natasha didn't seem to care. She had Angelika fill in at the front desk. She was an anorexic Goth, a senior at NYU. The show was a "brutal success," one critic called it. "Cruelly funny." Another said Ping Xi "marked the end of the sacred in art. Here is a spoiled brat taking the piss out of the establishment. Some are hailing him as the next Marcel Duchamp. But is he worth the stink?"

I don't know why I didn't just quit. I didn't need the money. I was relieved when, at last, in June, Natasha called from Switzerland to fire me. I had messed up a shipment of press materials for Art Basel, apparently.

"Out of curiosity, what are you *on*?" she wanted to know.

"I've just been really tired."

"Is it a medical issue?"

"No," I said. I could have lied. I could have told her that I had mono, or some sleep disorder. Cancer maybe. Everybody was getting cancer. But defending myself was useless. I had no good reason to fight to keep my job. "Are you letting me go?"

"I'd love it if you'd stay on until I get back and use the time to show Angelika the ropes, the filing system, whatever you've been doing on the computer, if anything." I hung up the phone, took a handful of Benadryl, and went down to the supply closet and fell sleep.

OH, SLEEP. nothing else could ever bring me such pleasure, such freedom, the power to feel and move and think and imagine, safe from the miseries of my waking consciousness. I was not a narcoleptic—I never fell asleep when I didn't want to. I was more of a somniac. A somnophile. I'd always loved sleeping. It was one thing my mother and I had enjoyed doing together when I was a child. She was not the type to sit and watch me draw or read me books or play games or go for walks in the park or bake brownies. We got along best when we were asleep.

When I was in the third grade, my mother, due to some unspoken conflict with my father, let me sleep with her in their bed because, as she said, it was easier to wake me up in the mornings if she didn't have to get up and go across the hall. I accumulated thirty-seven tardies and twenty-four absences that year. Thirty-seven times, my mother and I woke up together, bleary and exhausted at seven A.M., tried to get up, but fell back into bed and slept on while cartoons flashed from the small television on her bedside table. We'd wake up a few hours later—shades drawn, extra pillows lying shipwrecked on the rough beige rug—dress in a daze and lurch out into the car. I remember her holding one eye open with one hand, steering with the other. I've often wondered what *she* was on that year, and if she'd been slipping me any of it. Twenty-four times we slept through the alarm, got up sometime past noon, and abandoned the thought of school altogether. I'd eat cereal and read or watch television all day. My mother would smoke cigarettes, talk on the phone, hide from the housekeeper, take a bottle of wine with her into the master bathroom, and draw a bubble bath and read Danielle Steel or *Better Homes & Gardens*.

My father slept on the sofa in the den that year. I remember his thick glasses perched on the oak end table, their greasy lenses magnifying the dark grain of the wood. Without his glasses on, I barely recognized him. He was fairly nondescript—thinning brown hair, loosening jowls, a single wrinkle of worry etched deep into his brow. That wrinkle made him look perpetually perplexed, yet passive, like a man trapped behind his own eyes. He was kind of a nonentity, I thought, a stranger gently puppeting his way through his life at home with two strange females he could never hope to understand. Each night, he'd plop an Alka-Seltzer tablet in a glass of water. I stood by as it dissolved. I remember listening to the fizzing sound as he silently removed the cushions from the sofa and stacked them in the corner, his sad colorless pajamas dragging across the floor. Maybe that's when his cancer started, a few odd cells forming during a bad night's sleep in the living room.

My father was neither an ally nor a confidant, but it seemed backward to me that this hardworking man would be relegated to the sofa while my lazy mother got the king-size bed. I resented her for that, but she seemed immune to guilt and shame. I think she got away with so much because she was beautiful. She looked like Lee Miller if Lee Miller had been a bedroom drunk. I assume she blamed my father for ruining her life—she got pregnant and dropped out of college to marry him. She didn't have to, of course. I was born in August 1973, seven months after *Roe v. Wade*. Her family was the country club brand of alcoholic Southern Baptists— Mississippi loggers on one side, Louisiana oilmen on the other—or else, I assumed, she would have aborted me. My father was twelve years older than my mother. She'd been just nineteen years old and already four months pregnant when they got married. I'd figured that out as soon as I could do the math. Stretch marks, loose skin, scars across her belly she said looked like "a raccoon had disemboweled her," glaring at me as if I'd wrapped my umbilical cord around my neck on purpose. Maybe I did. "You were blue when they cut me open and pulled you out. After all the hell I went through, the consequences, your father, and the baby goes and dies? Like dropping a pie on the floor as soon as you pull it out of the oven."

The only intellectual exercise my mother got was doing crossword puzzles. She'd come out of the bedroom some nights to ask my father for hints. "Don't tell me the answer. Just tell me what the word *sounds* like," she'd say. As a professor, my father was good at guiding people to their own conclusions. He was dispassionate, sulky, even a little snide at times. I took after him. My mother did say once we were both "stone wolves." But she herself had a cold aura, too. I don't think she realized it. None of us had much warmth in our hearts. I was never allowed to have any pets. Sometimes I think a puppy might have changed everything. My parents died one after the other my junior year of college—first my dad from cancer, then my mother from pills and alcohol six weeks later.

All of this, the tragedy of my past, came reeling back with great force that night I woke up in the supply closet at Ducat for the last time.

It was ten at night and everyone had gone home. I trudged up the dark stairway to clean out my desk. There was no sadness or nostalgia, only disgust that I'd wasted so much time on unnecessary labor when I could have been sleeping and feeling nothing. I'd been stupid to believe that employment would add value to my life. I found a shopping bag in the break room and packed up my coffee mug, the spare change of clothes I kept in my desk drawer along with a few pairs of high heels, panty hose, a push-up bra, some makeup, a stash of cocaine I hadn't used in a year. I thought about stealing something from the gallery—the Larry Clark photo hanging in Natasha's office, or the paper cutter. I settled on a bottle of champagne—a lukewarm, and therefore appropriate, consolation.

I turned off all the lights, set the alarm, and walked out. It was a cool early-summer night. I lit a cigarette and stood facing the gallery. The lasers weren't on, but through the glass I could see the tall white poodle that looked out onto the sidewalk. It was baring its teeth, with one gold fang glinting in the light of the streetlamp. There was a red velvet bow tied around its little bouffant hairdo. Suddenly, a feeling rose up in me. I tried to squash it down, but it nestled into my bowels. "Pets just make messes. I don't want to have to go around picking dog hairs out of my teeth," I remembered my mother saying.

"Not even a goldfish?"

"Why? Just to watch it swim around and die?"

Maybe this memory triggered the hemorrhage of adrenaline that pushed me to go back inside the gallery. I pulled a few Kleenex from the box on my old desk, flipped the power switch to turn on the lasers, and stood between the stuffed black Lab and the sleeping dachshund. Then I pulled down my pants, squatted, and shat on the floor. I wiped myself and shuffled across the gallery with my pants around my ankles and stuffed the shitty Kleenex into the mouth of that bitchy poodle. That felt like vindication. That was my proper good-bye. I left and caught a cab home and drank the whole bottle of champagne that night and fell asleep on my sofa watching *Burglar*. Whoopi Goldberg was one reason to stay alive, at least.

THE NEXT DAY, I filed for unemployment, which Natasha must have resented. But she never called. I set up a weekly pickup with the Laundromat and automatic payments on all my utilities, bought a wide selection of used VHS tapes from the Jewish Women's Council Thrift Shop on Second Avenue, and soon I was hitting the pills hard and sleeping all day and all night with two- or three-hour breaks in between. This was good, I thought. I was finally doing something that really mattered. Sleep felt productive. Something was getting sorted out. I knew in my heart—this was, perhaps, the only thing my heart knew back then—that when I'd slept enough, I'd be okay. I'd be renewed, reborn. I would be a whole new person, every one of my cells regenerated enough times that the old cells were just distant, foggy memories. My past life would be but a dream, and I could start over without regrets, bolstered by the bliss and serenity that I would have accumulated in my year of rest and relaxation.

Two

I'D BEEN SEEING Dr. Tuttle once a week, but after I left Ducat, I didn't want to have to make the trek down to Union Square that often. So I told her that I was "freelancing in Chicago" and could only see her in person once a month. She said we could talk over the phone every week, or not, as long as I gave her postdated checks for my copayments in advance. "If your insurance asks, say you were here weekly in person. Just in case." She never caught on that I was having her call in my refills to my local Rite Aid in Manhattan. She never asked how my work in Chicago was going, or what I was doing there. Dr. Tuttle knew nothing about my hibernation project. I wanted her to think I was a nervous wreck, but fully operative, so she'd prescribe whatever she thought might knock me out the hardest.

I plunged into sleep full force once this arrangement had

been made. It was an exciting time in my life. I felt hopeful. I felt I was on my way to a great transformation.

I SPENT THAT FIRST WEEK in a soft twilight zone. I didn't leave the apartment at all, not even for coffee. I kept a jar of macadamia nuts by the bed, ate a few whenever I rose to the surface, sucked a bottle of Poland Spring, gravitated to the toilet maybe once a day. I didn't answer the phone—nobody but Reva ever called me anyway. She left me messages so long and breathless that they got cut off midsentence. Usually she called while she was on the StairMaster at her gym.

One night, she came over unannounced. The doorman told her he thought I'd gone out of town.

"I've been worried," Reva said, barging in with a bottle of sparkling rosé. "Are you sick? Have you been eating? Did you take time off of work?"

"I quit," I lied. "I want to devote more time to my own interests."

"What interests? I didn't know you had *interests*." She sounded utterly betrayed. She stumbled a little on her heels.

"Are you drunk?"

"You really quit your job?" she asked, kicking her shoes off and flopping down on the armchair.

"I'd rather eat shit than have to work for that cunt one more day," I told her.

"Didn't you say she was married to a prince or something?"

"Exactly," I answered. "But that was just a rumor anyway."

"So you're not sick?"

"I'm *resting*." I lay down on the sofa to demonstrate.

"That makes sense," Reva said, nodding compliantly, although I could tell she was suspicious. "Take some time off and think about your next move. Oprah says we women rush into decisions because we don't have faith that something better will ever come along. And that's how we get stuck in dissatisfying careers and marriages. *Amen!*"

"I'm not making a career move," I started to explain, but I went no further. "I'm taking some time off. I'm going to sleep for a year."

"And how are you going to do that?"

I pulled a vial of Ativan out from between the sofa cushions, unscrewed the cap, and fished out two pills. Out of the corner of my eye, I could see Reva squirming. I chewed the pills up—simply to horrify her—swallowed and gagged, then stuffed the vial back between the cushions and lay down and closed my eyes.

"Well, I'm glad you have a life plan. But to be honest," Reva began, "I'm concerned about your health. You've lost at least three pounds since you started taking all those medications." Reva was expert at guessing the weights of things and people. "What about the long term? Are you going to take pills for the rest of your life?"

"I'm not thinking that far ahead. And I might not live that long." I yawned.

"Don't say that," Reva said. "Look at me. Please."

I blinked my eyes open and turned to face the perfumed haze on the armchair. I squinted and focused. Reva was wearing a dress I recognized from a J. Crew catalogue the year before: a raw silk shift in a shade of pink I could only describe as "taffy." Orange-hued lipstick.

"Don't get defensive, but you're kind of off these days," she said. "You've been sort of distant. And you're just getting thinner and thinner." I think that bothered Reva more than anything. She must have felt that I was cheating in the game of skinniness, which she had always worked so hard to play. We were about the same height, but I wore a size 2 and Reva wore a 4. "A six when I'm PMSing." The discrepancy between our bodies was huge in Reva's world.

"I just don't think it's healthy to sleep all day," she said, popping a few sticks of gum in her mouth. "Maybe all you need is a shoulder to cry on. You'd be surprised how much better you'll feel after a good cry. Better than any pill can make you feel." When Reva gave advice, it sounded as though she were reading a bad made-for-TV movie script. "A walk around the block could do wonders for your mood," she said. "Aren't you hungry?"

"I'm not in the mood for food," I said. "And I don't feel like going anywhere."

"Sometimes you need to *act as if.*"

"Dr. Tuttle can probably give you something to get rid of your gum addiction," I told her flatly. "They have pills for everything now."

"I don't *want* to get rid of it," Reva replied. "And it's not an addiction. It's a habit. And I enjoy chewing gum. It's one of the few things in my life that makes me feel good about myself, because I do it for my own pleasure. Gum and the gym. Those are like my therapy."

"But you could have the medication instead," I argued. "And spare your jaw from all that chewing." I didn't really care about Reva's jaw.

"Uh-huh," she replied. She was looking straight at me, but was so entranced by her gum chewing, her mind seemed to drift off. When it returned, she got up and spat her gum out in the kitchen trash can, came back, lay down on the floor and started doing rhythmic crunches, crinkling the midsection of her dress. "We all have our own ways to cope with stress," she said, and rambled on about the benefits of habitual behaviors. "Self-soothing," is how she described it. "Like meditation." I yawned, hating her. "Sleeping all the time isn't really going to make you feel any better," she said. "Because you're not changing anything in your sleep. You're just avoiding your problems."

"What problems?"

"I don't know. You seem to think you have a lot of problems. And I just don't get it. You're a *smart girl*," Reva said. "You can do anything you put your mind to." She got up and fished in her bag for her lip gloss. I could see her eyeing the sweaty bottle of rosé. "Come out with me tonight, pretty please? My friend Jackie from Pilates is having a birthday party at a gay bar in the Village. I wasn't going to go, but if you come with me it could be fun. It's only seven thirty. And it's Friday night. Let's drink this and go out. The night is young!"

"I'm tired, Reva," I said, peeling the wrapper off the cap of a bottle of NyQuil.

"Oh, come on."

"You go without me."

"You want to stay here and sleep your life away? That's it?"

"If you knew what would make you happy, wouldn't you do it?" I asked her.

"See, you *do* want to be happy. Then why did you tell me

that being happy is dumb?" she asked. "You've said that to me more than once."

"Let me be dumb," I said, glugging the NyQuil. "You go be smart and tell me how great it is. I'll be here, hibernating."

Reva rolled her eyes.

"It's *natural*," I told her. "People used to hibernate all the time."

"People never *hibernated*. Where are you getting this?"

She could look really pathetic when she was outraged. She got up and stood there holding her stupid knockoff Kate Spade bag or whatever it was, her hair pulled back into a ponytail and crowned with a useless, plastic, tortoiseshell headband. She was always getting her hair blown out, her eyebrows waxed into thin arched parentheses, her fingernails painted various shades of pink and purple, as though all of this made her a wonderful person.

"It's not up for discussion, Reva. This is what I'm doing. If you can't accept it, then you don't have to."

"I accept it," she said, her voice dropping. "I just think it's a shame to miss out on a fun evening." She wrestled her white feet into her fake Louboutin stilettos. "You know, in Japan, companies have special rooms for businessmen to take naps in. I read about it in *GQ*. I'll check on you tomorrow. I *love* you," she said, grabbing the bottle of rosé on her way out.

. . .

I DREAMT A LOT at the beginning, especially when the summer started in full force and the air in my apartment got thick with the sickly chill of AC. Dr. Tuttle said my dreams might indicate how well certain medications were working. She suggested I keep a log of my dreams as a way of tracking the "waning intensity of suffering."

"I don't like the term 'dream journal,'" she told me at our in-person appointment in June. "I prefer 'night vision log.'"

So I made notes on Post-its. Each time I awoke, I scribbled down whatever I could remember. Later I copied the dreams over in crazier-looking handwriting on a yellow legal pad, adding terrifying details, to hand in to Dr. Tuttle in July. My hope was that she'd think I needed more sedation. In one dream, I went to a party on a cruise ship and watched a lone dolphin circling in the distance. But in the dream journal, I reported that I was actually on the *Titanic* and the dolphin was a shark that was also Moby Dick and also Dick Tracy and also a hard, inflamed penis, and the penis was giving a speech to a crowd of women and children and waving his gun around. "Then I saluted everyone like a Nazi and jumped overboard and everybody else got executed."

In another dream, I lost my balance standing in a speeding subway car, "and accidentally grabbed and ripped the hair off an old woman's head. Her scalp was teeming with larvae, and the larvae were all threatening to kill me."

I dreamt I drove a rusted Mercedes up onto the Esplanade by the East River, "skinny joggers and Hispanic housekeepers and toy poodles thudding under the tires, and my heart exploded with happiness when I saw all the blood."

I dreamt I jumped off the Brooklyn Bridge and found an underwater village abandoned because its inhabitants had heard life was better somewhere else. "A fire-breathing serpent disemboweled me and slurped up my entrails." I dreamt I stole somebody's diaphragm and put it in my mouth "before giving my doorman a blow job." I cut off my ear and e-mailed it to Natasha with a bill for a million dollars. I swallowed a live bee. "I ate a grenade." I bought a pair of red suede ankle boots and walked down Park Avenue. "The gutters were flooded with aborted fetuses."

"Tsk-tsk," Dr. Tuttle replied, when I showed her the "log." "Looks like you're still in the depths of despair. Let's up your Solfoton. But if you have nightmares about inanimate objects coming to life, or if you experience such things while you're awake, *discontinue*."

And then there were the dreams about my parents, which I never mentioned to Dr. Tuttle. I dreamt my dad had an illegitimate son he kept in the closet of his study. I discovered the boy, pale and undernourished, and together we conspired to burn down the house. I dreamt that I lathered up my mother's pubic hair with a bar of Ivory soap in the shower, then pulled a tangle of hair out of her vagina. It was like the kind of fur ball a cat coughs up, or a clog in a bathtub drain. In the dream, I understood that the tangle of hair was my father's cancer.

I dreamt that I dragged both my parents' dead bodies down into a ravine, then waited calmly in the moonlight, watching for vultures. In a few dreams, I'd answer the phone and hear a long silence, which I interpreted as my mother's speechless disdain. Or I heard crackling static, and cried out, "Mom? Dad?" into the receiver, desperate and devastated that I couldn't hear what they were saying. And other times, I was just reading transcripts of dialogues between the two of them, typed on aging onionskin paper that fell apart in my hands. Occasionally I'd spot my parents in places like the lobby of my apartment building or on the steps of the New York Public Library. My mother seemed disappointed and rushed, as though the dream had pulled her away from an important task. "What happened to your hair?" she asked me in the Starbucks on Lexington Avenue, then she trotted down the hall to the restroom.

My father was always sick in my dreams, sunken eyes, greasy smudges on the thick lenses of his glasses. Once, he was my anesthesiologist. I was getting breast implants. He put his hand out a little hesitantly for me to shake, as though he wasn't sure who I was or if we'd met before. I lay down on the steel gurney. Those dreams with him were the most upsetting. I'd wake up in a panic, take a few more Rozerem or whatever, and go back to sleep.

In my waking hours, I often thought about my parents' house—its nooks and corners, the way a room looked in the morning, in the afternoon, in the still of the night during summer, the soft yellow light of the streetlamp out front glinting off the polished wooden furniture in the den. The estate lawyer had recommended that I sell the house. The last time I'd been up there was the summer after my parents had died. Trevor and I were in the midst of one of our many failed romantic reunions, so we spent a weekend in the Adirondacks and took a detour to my hometown on the drive back down to the city. Trevor stayed in the rented convertible as I walked around the perimeter of the house, peering through the dusty windows at the empty spaces inside. It hardly looked any different from when I'd lived in it. "Don't sell until the market improves," Trevor yelled. I got emotional and embarrassed, ducked away and jumped in the mucky pond behind the garage, then emerged covered in rotting moss. Trevor got out of the car to hose me off in the garden, made me strip and put on his blazer before getting back into the car, then asked for a blow job in the parking lot of the Poughkeepsie Galleria before he went in to buy me a new outfit. I acquiesced. For him, this was erotic gold.

When Trevor dropped me off at school, I called the lawyer and told him that I couldn't let go of the house. "Not until I'm sure I'll never get married and have children," I said. It wasn't true. And I didn't care about the housing market or how much money I could get. I wanted to hold on to the house the way you'd hold on to a love letter. It was proof that I had not always been completely alone in this world. But I think I was also holding on to the loss, to the emptiness of the house itself, as though to affirm that it was better to be alone than to be stuck with people who were supposed to love you, yet couldn't.

There were moments when I was little, my mother could make me feel very special, stroking my hair, her perfume sweet and light, her pale, bony hands cool and jangling with gold bracelets, her frosted hair, her lipstick, breath woody with smoke and stringent from booze. But the next moment she'd be in a haze, distracted, suffering from some grave fear or worry and struggling to put up with even the thought of me. "I can't listen to you now," she'd say in these moments, and she'd move from room to room, away, looking for some piece of paper where she'd scrawled down a phone number. "If you threw it away, I swear," she'd warn. She was always calling someone—some new friend, I guess. I never knew where she met these women, these new friends—at the beauty parlor? At the liquor store?

I could have acted out if I'd wanted to. I could have dyed my hair purple, flunked out of high school, starved myself, pierced my nose, slutted around, what have you. I saw other teenagers doing that, but I didn't really have the energy to go to so much trouble. I did crave attention, but I refused to humiliate myself by asking for it. I'd be punished if I showed signs of suffering, I knew. So I was good. I did all the right things. I rebelled in silent ways, with my thoughts. My parents barely seemed to notice I existed. Once I heard them whispering in the hallway while I was using the bathroom.

"Did you see she has two blemishes on her chin?" my mother asked my father. "I can't stand to look at them. They're so *pink*."

"Take her to a dermatologist if you're that concerned," my father said.

A few days later, our housekeeper brought me a tube of Clearasil. It was the tinted kind.

At the private all girls' high school I went to, I'd had a flock of Reva-like adorers. I was emulated and gossiped about. I was blond and thin and pretty—that's what people noticed. That's what those girls cared about. I learned to float on cheap affections gleaned from other people's insecurities. I didn't stay out late. I just did my homework, kept my room clean, bided my time until I could move out and grow up and feel normal, I hoped. I didn't go out with boys until college, until Trevor.

When I was applying to schools, I overheard my mother talking to my father about me one more time.

"You should read her college essay," said my mother. "She'll never let me look at it. I'm worried she might try to do something creative. She'll end up at some awful state school."

"I've had some very bright graduate students who went to state schools," my father replied calmly. "And if she just wants to major in English or something like that, it doesn't really matter where she goes."

In the end I did show my college essay to my mother. I didn't tell her that Anton Kirschler, the artist I wrote about, was a character of my own invention. I wrote that his work was instructive for how to maintain "a humanistic approach to art facing the rise of technology." I described various made-up pieces: *Dog Urinating on Computer, Stock Market Hamburger Lunch.* I wrote that his work spoke to me personally because I was interested in how "art created the future." It was a mediocre essay. My mother seemed unperturbed by it, which shocked me, and handed it back with the suggestion that I look up a few words in the thesaurus because I'd repeated them too often. I didn't take her advice. I applied to Columbia early decision and got in.

On the eve of my move to New York, my parents sat me down to talk.

"Your mother and I understand that we have a certain responsibility to prepare you for life at a coed institution," said my father. "Have you ever heard of oxytocin?"

I shook my head.

"It's the thing that's going to make you crazy," my mother said, swirling the ice in her glass. "You'll lose all the good sense I've worked so hard to build up in you since the day you were born." She was kidding.

"Oxytocin is a hormone released during *copulation*," my father went on, staring at the blank wall behind me.

"*Orgasm*," my mother whispered.

"Biologically, oxytocin serves a purpose," my father said.

"That warm *fuzzy* feeling."

"It's what bonds a couple together. Without it, the human species would have gone extinct a long time ago. Women experience its effects more powerfully than men do. It's good to be aware of that."

"For when you're thrown out with yesterday's trash," my mother said. "Men are dogs. Even professors, so don't be fooled."

"Men don't attach as easily. They're more rational," my father corrected her. After a long pause, he said, "We just want you to be careful."

"He means use a rubber."

"And take *these*."

My father gave me a small, pink, shell-shaped compact of birth control pills.

"Gross," was all I could say.

"And your father has cancer," my mother said.

I said nothing.

"Prostate isn't like breast," my father said, turning away. "They do surgery, and you move on."

"The man always dies first," my mother whispered.

My dad's chair screeched on the floor as he pushed himself away from the table.

"I was only teasing," my mom said, batting the smoke of her own cigarette away from her face.

"About the cancer?"

"No."

That was the end of the conversation.

Later, while I packed up to move into the dorm, my mother came and stood in the doorway of my bedroom, holding her cigarette out behind her in the hall as if it would make any difference. The whole house always smelled like stale smoke. "You know I don't like it when you cry," she said.

"I wasn't crying," I said.

"And I hope you're not packing any shorts. Nobody wears shorts in Manhattan. And they'll shoot you in the street if you go around in those disgusting tennis shoes. You'll look ridiculous. Your father isn't paying this much for you to go look ridiculous in New York City."

I wanted her to think that I was crying over my father's cancer, but that wasn't quite it. "Well, Goddamnit, if you insist on getting weepy," my mother said, turning to leave. "You know, when you were a baby, I crushed Valium into your bottle? You had colic and cried for hours and hours, inconsolable and for no good reason. And change your shirt. I can see the sweat under your arms. I'm going to bed."

A realty company managed my parents' property after they were dead. The house got rented out to a history professor and his family. I never had to meet them. The company handled the maintenance and gardening and made any repairs necessary. When something broke or wore out, they sent me a letter with a photo and an estimate. When I got lonely or bored or nostalgic, I'd go through the photos and try to disgust myself with the banality of the place—a cracked step, a leak in the basement, a peeling ceiling, a broken cabinet. And I'd feel sorry for myself, not because I missed my parents, but because there was nothing they could have given me if they'd lived. They weren't my friends. They didn't comfort me or give me good advice. They weren't people I wanted to talk to. They barely even knew me. They were too busy to want to imagine my life in Manhattan. My father was busy dying—within a year of his diagnosis, the cancer had spread to his pancreas, then his stomach—and my mother busy being herself, which in the end seemed worse than having cancer.

She visited me just once in New York, my sophomore year. She took the train down and was an hour late to meet me at the Guggenheim. I could smell alcohol on her breath as we wandered around. She was skittish and quiet. "Oh, isn't that pretty?" she said about a Kandinsky, a Chagall. She left me abruptly when we got to the top of the ramp, saying she'd lost track of time. I followed her down and out of the museum, watched her try to hail a cab, seething and flabbergasted when each passing taxi was occupied. I don't know what her problem was. Maybe she'd seen a piece of art that unnerved her. She never explained it. But she called me later from her hotel and had me meet her for dinner that evening. It was as if nothing strange had happened at the museum. She was accountable for nothing when she was drunk. I was used to it.

I paid for my apartment on East Eighty-fourth Street in cash from my inheritance. From the windows in the living room, I could see some of Carl Schurz Park and a sliver of the East River. I could see the nannies with their strollers. Wealthy housewives milled up and down the Esplanade in visors and sunglasses. They reminded me of my mother—pointless and self-obsessed—only she had been less physically active. If I leaned out my bedroom window, I could see the uppermost tip of Roosevelt Island with its weird geometry of low brick buildings. I liked to think those buildings housed the criminally insane, though I knew that wasn't the case, at least anymore. Once I started sleeping full time, I didn't look out my windows very often. A glimpse was all I ever wanted. The sun rose in the east and set in the west. That hadn't changed, and it never would.

THE SPEED OF TIME VARIED, fast or slow, depending on the depth of my sleep. I became very sensitive to the taste of the water from the tap. Sometimes it was cloudy and tasted of soft minerals. Other times it was gassy and tasted like somebody's bad breath. My favorite days were the ones that barely registered. I'd catch myself not breathing, slumped on the sofa, staring at an eddy of dust tumbling across the hardwood floor in the draft, and I'd remember that I was alive for a second, then fade back out. Achieving that state took heavy dosages of Seroquel or lithium combined with Xanax, and Ambien or trazodone, and I didn't want to overuse those prescriptions. There was a fine mathematics for how to mete out sedation. The goal for most days was to get to a point where I could drift off easily, and come to without being startled. My thoughts were banal. My pulse was casual. Only the coffee made my heart work a bit harder. Caffeine was my exercise. It catalyzed my anxiety so that I could crash and sleep again.

The movies I cycled through the most were *The Fugitive, Frantic, Jumpin' Jack Flash,* and *Burglar.* I loved Harrison Ford and Whoopi Goldberg. Whoopi Goldberg was my main hero. I spent a lot of time staring at her on screen and picturing her vagina. Solid, honest, magenta. I owned VHS copies of all her movies, but many of them were too powerful to watch often. *The Color Purple* was too sad. *Ghost* filled me with too much longing, and Whoopi only had a small part in it. *Sister Act* was tricky because the songs got stuck in my head and made me want to laugh, run wild, dance, be impassioned, or whatnot. That would not be good for my sleep. I could only handle it once a week or so. I usually watched *Soapdish* and *The Player* back-to-back as though they were two volumes of a single film.

On my visits to Rite Aid to pick up my pills, I'd buy a pre-owned VHS tape, maybe a box of microwave popcorn, sometimes a two-liter bottle of Diet Sprite if I felt I had the strength to carry it home. Those cheap movies were usually terrible—*Showgirls, Enemy of the State, I'll Be Home for Christmas* starring Jonathan Taylor Thomas, whose face unnerved me—but I didn't mind watching them once or twice. The stupider the movie, the less my mind had to work. But I preferred the familiar—Harrison Ford and Whoopi Goldberg, doing what they always do.

· · · ·

WHEN I WENT TO SEE Dr. Tuttle in early August for my monthly in-person visit, she wore a white sleeveless night-gown with tattered lace across her bosom and huge honey-tinted sunglasses with blinders. She still had the neck brace on. "I had a procedure done on my eyes," she explained, "and the central air has sprung a leak. Excuse the humidity." Sweat bubbled across her chest and arms like blisters. Her hair frizzed up and out. The fat cats lay on the fainting sofa. "They're overheated," Dr. Tuttle said. "Better not disturb them." There was no place else to sit, so I stood against the bookshelf, bracing myself and taking shallow breaths. The smell of ammonia in the room was intense. It seemed to be coming from the cats.

"Did you bring your book of nightmares?" Dr. Tuttle asked, sitting down behind her desk.

"I forgot my journal today," I said. "The nightmares have been getting worse and worse, though," I lied. My dreams had actually mellowed.

"Tell me about one of them, just so I can update my file," Dr. Tuttle said, pulling out a folder. She seemed harried and hot, but she was not disorganized.

"Well . . ." I mined my mind for something disturbing. All I could recall were the plots of the terrible movies I'd recently seen. "I had this one nightmare where I moved to Las Vegas and met a seamstress and gave lap dances. Then I ran into an old friend who gave me a floppy disk full of government secrets and I became a suspect in a murder case and the NSA chased me, and instead of getting a Porsche for Christmas, a football team left me stranded in the desert."

Dr. Tuttle scribbled dutifully, then lifted her head, waiting for more.

"So I started eating sand to try to kill myself instead of dying of dehydration. It was awful."

"Very troubling," Dr. Tuttle murmured.

I wobbled against the bookshelf. It was difficult to stay upright—two months of sleep had made my muscles wither. And I could still feel the trazodone I'd taken that morning.

"Try to sleep on your side when possible. There was recently a study in Australia that said that when you sleep on your back, you're more likely to have nightmares about drowning. It's not conclusive, of course, since they're on the opposite side of the Earth. So actually, you might want to try sleeping on your stomach instead, and see what that does."

"Dr. Tuttle," I began, "I was wondering if you could prescribe something a little stronger for bedtime. When I'm tossing and turning at night, I get so frustrated. It's like I'm in hell."

"Hell? I can give you something for that," she said,

reaching for her prescription pad. "Mind over matter, people say. But what *is* matter, anyway? When you look at it under a microscope, it's just tiny bits of stuff. Atomic particles. Sub-atomic particles. Look deeper and deeper and eventually you'll find nothing. We're mostly empty space. We're mostly nothing. *Tra-la-la*. And we're all the *same* nothingness. You and me, just filling the space with nothingness. We could walk through walls if we put our minds to it, people say. What they don't mention is that walking through a wall would most likely kill you. Don't forget that."

"I'll keep it in mind."

Dr. Tuttle handed me the prescriptions.

"Here, have some samples," she said, pushing a basket of Promaxatine toward me. "Oh no, wait, these are for impotent obsessive compulsives. They'd keep you up at night." She pulled the basket back. "See you in a month."

I took a cab home, filled the new prescriptions and re-filled the old ones at Rite Aid, bought a pack of Skittles, and went home and ate the Skittles and a few leftover primidone and went back to sleep.

THE NEXT DAY, Reva came over to whine about her dying mother and prattle on about Ken. Her drinking seemed to be getting worse that summer. She pulled out a bottle of Jose

Cuervo and a can of Diet Mountain Dew from her new huge lime green alligator-skin knockoff Gucci tote.

"Want some tequila?"

I shook my head no.

Reva had an interesting method of mixing her drinks. After each sip of Diet Mountain Dew, she'd pour a little Jose Cuervo into the can to take up the space her sip had displaced, so that by the time she finished, she was drinking straight tequila. It was fascinating to me. I caught myself imagining the ratio of Diet Mountain Dew to Jose Cuervo in that can, what the formula would be to measure it sip by sip. I'd studied Zeno's Paradox in high school algebra but never fully understood it. Infinite divisibility, the theory of halving, whatever it was. That philosophical quandary was exactly the kind of thing Trevor would have loved to explain to me. He'd sit across from me at dinner, slurping his ice water, muttering fluently about fractions of cents and the fluctuating price of oil, for example, all while his eyes scanned the room behind me as though to affirm to me that I was stupid, I was boring. Someone far better might be getting up from a table to go powder her nose. The thought stung. I still couldn't accept that Trevor was a loser and a moron. I didn't want to believe that I could have degraded myself for someone who didn't deserve it. I was still stuck on that bit of vanity. But I was determined to sleep it away.

"You're still obsessed with Trevor, aren't you," Reva said, slurping from her can.

"I think I have a tumor," I replied, "in my brain."

"Forget Trevor," Reva said. "You'll meet someone better, if you ever leave your apartment." She sipped and poured and went on about how "it's all about your attitude," and that "positive thinking is more powerful than negative thinking, even in equal amounts." She'd recently read a book called *How to Attract the Man of Your Dreams Using Self-hypnosis,* and so she went on to explain to me the difference between "wish fulfillment" and "manifesting your own reality." I tried not to listen. "Your problem is that you're passive. You wait around for things to change, and they never will. That must be a painful way to live. Very disempowering," she said, and burped.

I had taken some Risperdal. I was feeling woozy.

"Have you ever heard the expression 'eat shit or die'?" I asked.

Reva unscrewed the tequila and poured more into her can. "It's 'eat shit *and* die,'" she said.

We didn't talk for a while. My mind drifted back to Trevor, the way he unbuttoned his shirts and pulled at his tie, the gray drapes in his bedroom, the flare of his nostrils in the mirror when he clipped his nose hairs, the smell of his aftershave. I was grateful when Reva broke the silence.

"Well, will you come out for drinks on Saturday at least? It's my birthday."

"I can't, Reva," I said. "I'm sorry."

"I'm telling people to meet up at Skinny Kitty at nineish."

"I'm sure you'll have a better time if I'm not there to bum you out."

"Don't be that way," Reva crooned drunkenly. "Soon we'll be old and ugly. Life is short, you know? Die young and leave a beautiful corpse. Who said that?"

"Someone who liked fucking corpses."

REVA WAS ONLY a week older than me. On August 20, 2000, I turned twenty-seven in my apartment in a medicated haze, smoking stale menthols on the toilet and reading an old *Architectural Digest*. At some point I fumbled in my makeup drawer for eyeliner to circle things on the pages that I found appealing—the blank corners of rooms, the sharp glass crystals hanging from a chandelier. I heard my cell phone ring but I didn't answer it. "Happy birthday," Reva said in her message. "I *love* you."

AS SUMMER DWINDLED, my sleep got thin and empty, like a room with white walls and tepid air-conditioning. If I dreamt at all, I dreamt that I was lying in bed. It felt superficial, even boring at times. I'd take a few extra Risperdal and Ambien when I got antsy, thinking about my past. I tried not to think of Trevor. I deleted Reva's messages without listening to them. I watched *Air Force One* twelve times on mute. I tried to put everything out of my mind. Valium helped. Ativan helped. Chewable melatonin and Benadryl and NyQuil and Lunesta and temazepam helped.

My visit to Dr. Tuttle in September was also banal. Besides the sweltering heat I suffered walking from my building into a cab, and from the cab into Dr. Tuttle's office, I felt almost nothing. I wasn't anxious or despondent or resentful or terrified.

"How are you feeling?"

I stood and pondered the question for five minutes while Dr. Tuttle went around her office turning on an arsenal of fans, all the same make and model, two installed on the radiator under the windows, one on her desk, and two in the corners of the room on the floor. She was impressively nimble. She no longer wore the neck brace.

"I'm fine, I think," I yelled blandly over the roaring hum.

"You look pale," Dr. Tuttle remarked.

"I've been keeping out of the sun," I told her.

"Good thing. Sun exposure promotes cellular collapse, but nobody wants to talk about that."

She herself was a piglety shade of pink. She wore a straw-colored sack of a dress that looked like coarse linen. Her hair was at a high frizz. A tight, chunky strand of pearls rolled up and down her throat as she spoke. The fans stirred up a roar of wind and made me dizzy. I gripped the bookshelf, knocking a swollen copy of *Apparent Death* to the floor.

"Sorry," I yelled over the din, and picked it up.

"An interesting book about possums. Animals have so much wisdom," Dr. Tuttle paused. "I hope you're not a vegetarian," she said, lowering her glasses.

"I'm not."

"That's a relief. Now tell me how you feel. Your affect is very flat today," Dr. Tuttle said. She was right. I could barely arouse the enthusiasm to stand up straight. "Have you been taking your Risperdal?"

"I skipped yesterday. I was so busy at work, I just forgot. The insomnia is really bad these days," I lied.

"You're exhausted. Plain and simple." She scribbled on her prescription pad. "According to that book you're holding, the death gene is passed from mother to child in the birth canal. Something about microdermabrasions and infectious vaginal rash. Does your mother exhibit any signs of hormonal abnormalities?"

"I don't think so."

"You might want to ask her. If you *are* a carrier, I can

suggest something for you. An herbal lotion. Only if you want it. I'd have to order it special from Peru."

"I was born caesarian, in case that's a factor."

"The noble method," she said. "Ask her anyway. Her answer might shed some light on your mental and biorhythmic incapacities."

"Well, she's dead," I reminded her.

Dr. Tuttle put her pen down and folded her hands into prayer. I thought she was going to sing a song, or do some incantation. I didn't expect her to offer me any pity or sympathy. But instead, she squinched up her face, sneezed violently, turned to wipe her face with a huge bath towel lying on the floor by her desk chair, and scribbled on her pad some more.

"And how did she die?" she asked. "Not pineal failure, I suppose."

"She mixed alcohol with sedatives," I said. I was too lethargic to lie. And if Dr. Tuttle had forgotten that I'd told her my mother had slit her wrists, telling her the truth wouldn't matter in the long run.

"People like your mother," Dr. Tuttle replied, shaking her head, "give psychotropic medication a bad reputation."

SEPTEMBER CAME AND WENT. The sunlight tilted through the blinds once in a while, and I'd peek out to see if

81

the leaves on the trees were dying yet. Life was repetitive, resonated at a low hum. I shuffled down to the Egyptians. I filled my prescriptions. Reva continued to appear from time to time, usually drunk and always on the brink of hysteria or outrage or complete meltdown one way or another.

In October, she barged in while I was watching *Working Girl*.

"This again?" she huffed and threw herself down in the armchair. "I'm fasting for Yom Kippur," she sighed boastfully. This was not unusual. She'd been on some truly insane diets in the past. A gallon of salt water a day. Only prune juice and baking soda. "I can have as much sugar-free Jell-O as I want before eleven A.M." Or "I'm fasting," she'd say. "I'm fasting on weekends." "I'm fasting every other weekday."

"Melanie Griffith looks bulimic in this movie," Reva said now, pointing lazily at the screen. "See her swollen jowls? Her face looks fat, but her legs are super skinny. Or maybe she's just fat with skinny legs. Her arms look soft, don't they? I could be wrong. I don't know. I'm kind of out of it. I'm *fasting*," she said again.

"That's not puking, it's boozing, Reva," I told her, slurping drool from the corner of my mouth. "Not every skinny person has an eating disorder." It was the most I'd said in weeks to anyone.

"Sorry," Reva said. "You're right. I'm just in a mood. I'm

fasting, you know?" She dug around in her purse and pulled out her dwindling fifth of tequila. "Want some?" she asked.

"No."

She cracked open a Diet Mountain Dew. We watched the movie in silence. In the middle, I fell back asleep.

OCTOBER WAS PLACID. The radiator hissed and sputtered, releasing a sharp vinegary smell that reminded me of my dead parents' basement, so I rarely turned on the heat. I didn't mind the cold. My visit to Dr. Tuttle that month was relatively unremarkable.

"How is everything at home?" she asked. "Good? Bad? Other?"

"Other," I said.

"Do you have a family history of nonbinary paradigms?"

When I explained for the third time that both my parents had died, that my mother had killed herself, Dr. Tuttle unscrewed the cap of her value-size bottle of Afrin, twirled around in her chair, tilted her head back so that she was looking at me upside down, and started sniffing. "I'm listening," she said. "It's allergies, and now I'm hooked on this nasal spray. Please continue. Your parents are dead, and . . . ?"

"And nothing. It's fine. But I'm still not sleeping well."

"What a conundrum." She twirled back around and put

her Afrin in her desk drawer. "Here, let me give you my latest samples." She got up to open her little cabinet and filled a brown paper lunch bag with packets of pills. "Trick or treat," she said, dropping in a mint from the bowl on her desk. "Dressing up for Halloween?"

"Maybe I'll be a ghost."

"Economical," she remarked.

I went home and went to sleep. Outside of the occasional irritation, I had no nightmares, no passions, no desires, no great pains.

And during this lull in the drama of sleep, I entered a stranger, less certain reality. Days slipped by obliquely, with little to remember, just the familiar dent in the sofa cushions, a froth of scum in the bathroom sink like some lunar landscape, craters bubbling on the porcelain when I washed my face or brushed my teeth. But that was all that went on. And I might have just dreamt up the scum. Nothing seemed really real. Sleeping, waking, it all collided into one gray, monotonous plane ride through the clouds. I didn't talk to myself in my head. There wasn't much to say. This was how I knew the sleep was having an effect: I was growing less and less attached to life. If I kept going, I thought, I'd disappear completely, then reappear in some new form. This was my hope. This was the dream.

Three

IN NOVEMBER, however, an unfortunate shift occurred.

The carefree tranquility of sleep gave way to a startling subliminal rebellion—I began to do things while I was unconscious. I'd fall asleep on the sofa and wake up on the bathroom floor. Furniture got rearranged. I started to misplace things. I made blackout trips to the bodega and woke up to find popsicle sticks on my pillow, orange and bright green stains on my sheets, half a huge sour pickle, empty bags of barbecue-flavored potato chips, tiny cartons of chocolate milk on the coffee table, the tops of them folded and torn and gummy with teeth marks. When I came to after one of these blackouts, I'd go down to get my coffees as usual, try a little chitchat on the Egyptians in order to gauge how weirdly I'd acted the last time I was in there. Did they know that I'd been sleepwalking? Had I said anything revealing? Had I flirted? The Egyptians were generally indifferent and returned the standard chitchat or flat out ignored me, so it was hard to tell. It concerned me that I was venturing out of the apartment while unconscious. It seemed antithetical to my hibernation project. If I committed a crime or got hit by a bus, the chance for a new and better life would be lost. If my unconscious excursions went only as far as the bodega around the corner, that was okay, I thought. I could live. The worst that could happen was I'd make a fool of myself in front of the Egyptians and would have to start going to the deli a few blocks farther down First Avenue. I prayed that my subconscious understood the value of convenience. Amen.

This was when my online purchasing of lingerie and de-signer jeans began in earnest. It seemed that while I was sleeping, some superficial part of me was taking aim at a life of beauty and sex appeal. I made appointments to get waxed. I booked time at a spa that offered infrared treatments and colonics and facials. One day, I cancelled my credit card in the hope that doing so might deter me from filling my nonex-istent datebook with the frills of someone I used to think I was supposed to be. A week later, a new credit card showed up in the mail. I cut it in half.

My stress levels rose. I couldn't trust myself. I felt as though I had to sleep with one eye open. I even considered installing a video camera to record myself while I was unconscious, but I knew that would only prove to be a document of my resistance to my project. It wouldn't stop me from doing anything since I'd be unable to watch it until I woke up for real. So I was in a state of panic. I doubled my Xanax dosage in an attempt to counteract my anxiety. I lost track of the days, and as a result, missed my visit to Dr. Tuttle in November. She called and left me a message.

"I'll have to charge you for the missed appointment. Let me remind you, you did sign the agreement to my office policy. There's a twenty-four-hour cutoff for cancellations. Most doctors in the area require you to cancel thirty-six or forty-eight hours before the scheduled appointment, so I think I'm being pretty generous. And it concerns me that you'd be so flip about your mental health. Call me to reschedule. The ball is in your basket." She sounded stern. I felt terrible. But when I called to apologize and make another appointment, she was back to normal.

"See you Thursday," she said. "Toodle-oo."

Halfway through the month, my Internet use began to rise even more. I woke up with my laptop screen filled with AOL chat-room conversations with strangers in places like Tampa and Spokane and Park City, Utah. In my waking hours, I rarely thought of sex, but in my medicated blackouts, I guess my lusts arose. I scrolled through the transcripts. They were surprisingly polite. "How are you?" "I'm fine, thanks, how are you? Horny much?" It went on from there. I was relieved I never gave anyone my real name. My AOL screen name was "Whoopigirlberg2000." "Call me Whoopi." "Call me Reva," I once wrote. The photos men sent of their genitals were all banal, semierect, nonthreatening. "Your turn," they'd write. Usually I changed the subject.

"What's your favorite movie?"

Then one day I woke up to discover that I had dug out my digital camera and sent a bunch of strangers snapshots of my asshole, my nipple, the inside of my mouth. I'd written messages saying that I'd like it if they came and "tied me up" and "held me hostage" and "slurped my pussy like a plate of spaghetti." And there were numbers in my cell phone log I didn't recognize. So I made up a rule that whenever I took my pills, which was roughly every eight hours, I'd put my computer in the closet and power down my phone, seal it with packing tape in a Tupperware container, and stick the container in the back of a high kitchen cabinet.

But then I woke up with the unopened Tupperware next to me on the pillow.

The next night, the phone was on the window ledge, next to a dozen half-smoked cigarettes stubbed out on an Alanis Morissette CD case.

"Why are you killing yourself?" Reva asked, seeing the

butts in the trash can when she came over uninvited a few days later. Reva's mother's cancer had started in her lungs.

"My smoking has nothing to do with you or your mother. My mother's dead, too, you know," I added.

By this point, Reva's mother was in hospice care, in and out of consciousness. I was tired of hearing about it. It brought back too many memories. Plus, I knew she'd expect me to go to her mother's funeral. I really didn't want to do that.

"My mom's not dead *yet*," Reva said.

I didn't tell Reva about my Internet proclivities. But I did ask her to change my AOL password to something I could never guess. "Just some random letters and numbers. I waste too much time online," I told her.

"Doing what?"

"I send e-mails late at night and regret it," was the lie I knew she would believe.

"To Trevor, right?" she asked, nodding her head knowingly.

Reva changed my password, and once my AOL account was inaccessible, my sleep stayed low stakes for a while. The worst I did while I was unconscious was write letters to Trevor on a yellow legal pad—long petitions about our romantic history and how I wanted things to change so that we could be together again. The letters were so ridiculous, I wondered if they were written in my sleep to keep me entertained while I was awake. By the end of the month, my blackout excursions down to the bodega had become less frequent, maybe due to the onset of winter.

Reva's visits became less frequent, too. And her attitude shifted from melodrama to polite posturing. Instead of venting, she gave well-articulated summaries of her week, including the latest current events. I appreciated her self-control, I told her. She said she was trying to be more sensitive to my needs. When she would once have given me advice or commented on the state of the apartment, she now bit her tongue. She complained less. She also started giving me hugs and air kisses whenever she said good-bye. She did this by bending over me on the sofa. I imagine she got in the habit because of her bedbound mother. It made me feel like I was on my death-bed, too. In fact, I appreciated the affection. By Thanksgiving I'd been hibernating for almost six months. Nobody but Reva had touched me.

I DIDN'T TELL Dr. Tuttle about my blackouts. I was afraid she'd cut me off out of fear of potential lawsuits. So when I went to see her in December, I just complained that the insomnia had crept up with a vengeance. I lied that I could stay down for no more than a few hours at a time. Bouts of sweat and nausea made me dizzy and restless, I told her. Imaginary noises shook me awake so violently "I thought my building had been bombed or struck by lightning."

"You must have a callus on your cortex," Dr. Tuttle said, clucking her tongue. "Not figuratively. Not literally, I mean. I'm saying, *parenthetically*," she held up her hands and cupped them side by side to demonstrate the punctuation. "You've built up a tolerance, but it doesn't mean the drugs are failing."

"You're probably right," I replied.

"Not probably."

"Parenthetically speaking, I mean, I probably need something stronger."

"Aha."

"Pillwise, I mean."

"You're not being sarcastic, I hope," Dr. Tuttle said.

"Of course not. I take my health completely seriously."

"Well, in that case."

"I've heard of an anesthetic they give to people for endoscopies. Something that keeps you awake during the procedure, but you can't remember anything afterward. Something like that would be good. I have a lot of *anxiety*. And I have an important business meeting coming up later this month." Really, I just wanted something especially powerful to blindfold me through the holidays.

"Give these a try," Dr. Tuttle said, sliding a sample bottle of pills across her desk. "Infermiterol. If those don't put you down for the count, I'll complain directly to the manufacturer in Germany. Take one and let me know how it goes."

"Thank you, doctor."

"Any plans for Christmas?" she asked, scribbling my refills. "Seeing the folks? Where are you from again? Albuquerque?"

"My parents are dead."

"I'm sorry to hear that. But I'm not surprised," Dr. Tuttle said, writing in her file. "Orphans usually suffer from low immunity, psychiatrically speaking. You may consider getting a pet to build up your relational skills. Parrots, I hear, are nonjudgmental."

"I'll think about that," I said, taking the sheaf of prescriptions she'd written, and the Infermiterol sample.

It was freezing cold outside that afternoon. As I crossed Broadway, a sliver of moon appeared in the pale sky, then disappeared behind the buildings. The air had a metallic tinge to it. The world felt still and eerie, vibrating. I was glad not to see many people on the street. Those I did see looked like lumbering monsters, human shapes deformed by puffy coats and hoods, mittens and hats, snow boots. I assessed my reflection in the windows of a darkened storefront as I walked up West Fifteenth Street. It did comfort me to see that I was still pretty, still blond and tall and thin. I still had good posture. One might have even confused me for a celebrity in slovenly incognito. Not that people cared. I hailed a cab at Union Square and gave the driver the cross streets of Rite Aid uptown. It was already getting dark out, but I kept my sunglasses on. I didn't want to have to look anybody in the eye. I didn't want to relate to anybody too keenly. Plus, the fluorescent lights at the drug store were blinding. If I could have purchased my medications from a vending machine, I would have paid double for them.

The pharmacist on duty that evening was a young Latina woman—perfect eyebrows, fake nails. She knew me on sight. "Give me ten minutes," she said.

Next to the vitamins, there was a contraption to measure your blood pressure and pulse. I sat in the seat of the machine, took my arm out of the sleeve of my coat and stuck it in for testing. A pleather pillow inflated around my bicep. I watched numbers on the digital screen go up and down. Pulse 48. Pressure 80/50. That seemed appropriate.

I went to the rack of DVDs to browse the latest selection of pre-owned movies. *The Nutty Professor, Jumanji, Casper, Space Jam, The Cable Guy.* It was all kids' stuff. Then an orange discount sticker on the bottom shelf caught my eye—*9½ Weeks.* I picked it up. Trevor had claimed that it was one of his favorite movies. I still hadn't seen it.

"Mickey Rourke's performance in this is unparalleled. Who knows? You might relate to it." I resembled Kim Basinger, he explained, and just like me, her character worked in an art gallery. "This movie inspires me to try new things," he said.

"Like what?" I asked, amused by the thought that he might have the courage to do more in bed than reposition himself to get "better leverage."

He took me into his kitchen, turned his back, and said, "Get on your knees." I did as I was told and knelt down on the cold marble tile. "Keep your eyes closed," he said. "And open your mouth." I almost laughed, but I played along. Trevor took his blow jobs very seriously.

"Have you seen *Sex, Lies, and Videotape*?" I asked him. "James Spader in that—"

"Be quiet," he said. "Open up."

He put an unpeeled banana in my mouth, warning me that if I took it out he'd know, and he'd punish me emotionally.

"Okay, *master*," I mumbled sarcastically.

"Keep it in there," he said, and walked out of the kitchen. I didn't think it was very funny, but I played along. Back then, I interpreted Trevor's sadism as a satire of actual sadism. His little games were so silly. So I just knelt there with the banana in my mouth, breathing through my nose. I could hear him on the phone making a reservation for two for dinner that night at Kurumazushi. After twenty minutes he came back in, took the banana out of my mouth. "My sister's in town so you have to leave," he said, and put his flaccid penis in my mouth. When he wasn't hard after a few minutes, he got angry. "What are you even doing here? I don't have time for this." He ushered me out. "The doorman will hail you a cab," he said to me, like I was some one-night stand, some cheap prostitute, like somebody he didn't know at all.

Anal sex came up with Trevor only once. It was my idea. I told him I wanted to prove that I wasn't uptight—a complaint he gave because at some point I'd hesitated to give him a blow job while he sat on the toilet. We tried once on a night we'd both had a lot to drink, but he lost his erection as he tried to wedge it in. Then all of a sudden he got up and went into the shower, saying nothing to me. Maybe I should have felt vindicated by his failure, but instead I just felt rejected. I followed him to the bathroom.

"Is it because I smell?" I asked him through the shower curtain. "What's wrong? What did I do?"

"I have no idea what you're talking about."

"You just left without saying anything."

"There was *shit* all over my dick, okay?" he said angrily. But that was impossible. He hadn't even penetrated me. I knew he was lying. But I still apologized.

"I'm sorry," I said. "Are you mad?"

"I can't have this conversation with you right now. I'm tired and I'm not in the mood to deal with your drama." He was nearly yelling. "I just want to get some sleep. Jesus!"

I called him the next day and asked if he was free that weekend, but he said he'd already found a woman who wasn't going to "pull pranks for attention." A few nights later, I got drunk and called up Rite Aid and ordered a case of sexual lubricant to be delivered to him at his office the next morning. He sent me a note at the gallery by messenger in response. "Don't ever do that again," it said.

We got back together a few weeks later.

"Ma'am?" the pharmacist called out, snapping me out of my reverie. I put the DVD back on the rack and went to the pharmacy counter to get my pills.

The pharmacist's nails made an annoying clicking sound as she tapped her computer screen. I thought she seemed smug; she sighed as she ran each stapled paper bag under the scanner, as though it exhausted her to deal with me and all my mental health issues. "Check that box to say you're waiving the consultation."

"But I haven't waived it. You're consulting me now, aren't you?"

"Did you have a question about your medications, ma'am?"

She was judging me. I could feel it. She was modulating her voice a certain way so as not to sound patronizing.

"Of course I want a consultation," I said. "I'm ill, and this is my medicine, and I want to know you've done your job correctly. Look at all these pills. They could be dangerous. Wouldn't *you* want a consultation, if you were as sick as I am?" I pushed my sunglasses back down over my eyes. She unfolded the papers stapled to the bags and pointed out the potential side effects of each drug and the potential interactions with other medications I was taking.

"Don't drink with this," she said. "If you take this one and it doesn't put you to sleep, you might throw up. You might get a migraine. If you start to feel hot, call an ambulance. You could have seizures or a stroke. If you get blisters all over your hands, stop taking it and go to the emergency room." She wasn't saying anything I hadn't heard before. She tapped the paper packages with her long fingernails. "My advice, don't drink a lot of water before bed. If you get up in the middle of the night to go to the bathroom, you could hurt yourself."

"I'm not going to hurt myself," I said.

"I'm just saying, be careful."

I thanked her, complimented her on her gold nail polish, pressed the buttons on the payment pad, and left. There was a reason I preferred the pharmacy at Rite Aid over CVS and Duane Reade. The people who worked at Rite Aid didn't take my moodiness to heart. I'd sometimes heard them cracking up behind the high shelves of pills, talking about their weekends, gossiping about their friends and coworkers, somebody's bad breath, somebody's stupid voice on the phone. I'd come in and bitch at them on a regular basis. I blamed them if a prescription was out of stock, cursed them when the line at the pickup window was more than two customers deep, complained that they hadn't called my insurance company soon enough, were all morons, all uneducated, cruel, unfeeling thugs. Nothing seemed to provoke them to come back at me with anything more than a grin and an eye roll. They never confronted me about my attitude. "Don't call me ma'am. It's condescending," I'd once said. Clearly the woman with the golden fingernails hadn't gotten that memo. They were all so jovial and relaxed with one another, fraternal even. Maybe I was envious of that. They had lives—that was evident.

I ripped into the paper bags on the walk home, threw away all the printed materials, and sunk the medicine bottles deep into the pockets of my coat. The pills rattled like maracas as I dragged myself back through the snow. I shivered violently in my ski jacket. My face, hit by the wind, felt like it was being slapped. My eyes watered. My hands burned from the cold. From outside the bodega, I saw the Egyptians putting up the Christmas decorations in the window. I went in, ducked under the fluttering red tinsel, got my two coffees, went home and swallowed a few Ambien and went to sleep on the sofa watching *Primal Fear*.

. . .

FOR THE NEXT FEW DAYS, thoughts of Trevor called me out of sleep like rats scrabbling inside the walls. It took all the self-control I had not to call him. It took Solfoton and a bottle of Robitussin one day, Nembutal and Zyprexa the next. Reva came and went, blathering about her latest dates and heart-aches over her mother. I watched a lot of *Indiana Jones*. But I was still anxious. Trevor Trevor Trevor. I might have felt bet-ter if he were dead, I thought, since behind every memory of him was the possibility of reconciling, and thus more heart-break and indignity. I felt weak. My nerves were frayed and fragile, like tattered silk. Sleep had not yet solved my cranki-ness, my impatience, my memory. It seemed like everything now was somehow linked to getting back what I'd lost. I could picture my selfhood, my past, my psyche like a dump truck filled with trash. Sleep was the hydraulic piston that lifted the bed of the truck up, ready to dump everything out some-where, but Trevor was stuck in the tailgate, blocking the flow of garbage. I was afraid things would be like that forever.

MY LAST RENDEZVOUS WITH Trevor had been on New Year's Eve, 2000. I invited him to come to the party with me in DUMBO. I'd sensed he was between girlfriends.

"I'll come for a while," he agreed. "But there are other parties I'm already committed to. I'll stay at yours for an hour and then I'll have to leave, so don't get sensitive about it."

"That's fair," I said, though my feelings were already hurt.

He had me meet him in the lobby of his building in Tribeca. He very rarely asked me to come up to his apartment. I think he thought that seeing the place would make me want to marry him. In truth, I thought his apartment made him seem pathetic—status seeking, conformist, shallow. It reminded me of the loft Tom Hanks rents in *Big*, huge windows along three walls, high ceilings—only instead of pinball machines and trampolines and toys, Trevor had filled the apartment with expensive furniture—a narrow gray velvet sofa from Sweden, a huge mahogany secretary, a crystal chandelier. I assumed some ex-girlfriend had picked it all out for him, or multiple ex-girlfriends. That would have explained the mismatched aesthetic. He worked as a portfolio manager in the Twin Towers, had freckles, loved Bruce Springsteen, and yet the wall above his bed was decorated with horrifying African masks. He collected antique swords. He liked cocaine and cheap beer and top-shelf whiskey, always owned the latest video game system. He had a waterbed. He played acoustic guitar, badly. He owned a gun he kept in a safe in his bedroom closet.

I buzzed him when I got to his building and he came

down wearing a tuxedo under a long black coat with tasteful navy satin accents. I knew then that inviting him to the party had been a mistake. He clearly had somewhere more important to be, and was going to go there to be with someone more important than me after my hour with him was up.

He pulled on his gloves, hailed a taxi. "Whose party is this again?"

A video artist represented by Ducat had invited me to her party because I'd handled an important rights situation when Natasha was overseas. All I'd really done, in fact, was send a fax.

"She's going to be projecting live births from a video feed some guy set up in a village hospital in Bolivia," I told Trevor in the cab. I knew it would horrify him.

"Bolivia time is an hour ahead of New York," he said. "If they really think they can coordinate births, those babies won't be born until eleven, and I'm not staying past ten thirty. Anyway, gross."

"Do you think it's exploitative?"

"No, I just don't really want to see a bunch of Bolivian women bleeding and moaning for hours."

He fiddled with his phone as I recited language from the gallery's description of the videographer's work. Trevor repeated words sarcastically.

"'Tectonic,'" he said. "'Quasi.' Jesus!"

Then he called someone and had a very brief, yes-no conversation, said, "See you soon."

"Do you even like me?" I asked him once he'd hung up.

"What kind of question is that?"

"I *love* you," I was angry enough to say.

"How is that relevant?"

"Are you kidding?"

Trevor told the driver to drop me off at the nearest subway station. That was the last time I'd seen him. I didn't go to the party. I just got on the train and went back home.

I LOOKED OUT the windows at the darkening sky. I tried to rub the dirt off the glass, but it was impossible. The dirt was stuck on the other side. The trees were all bare and black against the pale snow. The East River was still and black. The sky was black and heavy over Queens, a blanket of blinking yellow lights spreading out into infinity. There were stars in the sky, I knew, but I couldn't see them. The moon was more visible now, a white flame glowing high while red lights of planes sailing down to LaGuardia blipped by. In the distance, people were living lives, having fun, learning, making money, fighting and walking around and falling in and out of love. People were being born, growing up, dropping dead. Trevor was probably spending his Christmas vacation

with some woman in Hawaii or Bali or Tulum. He was probably fingering her at that very moment, telling her he loved her.
He might actually be happy. I shut the window and lowered
all the blinds.

"Merry Christmas," Reva said in a voice mail. "I'm here at
the hospital, but I'm coming back to town for the office party
tomorrow. Ken will be there, of course. . . ."

I deleted her message and went back to sleep.

CHRISTMAS DAY, around nightfall, I woke up on the
sofa in a restless fog. Unable to sleep or use my hands to work
the remote or open the bottle of temazepam, I went out to get
my fix of coffee. Downstairs, the doorman sat reading the paper on his little stool.

"Merry Christmas," he yawned, turning the page, barely
looking up at me.

The sidewalks were piled high with snow. A foot-wide
pathway had been shoveled from the entrance of my building
to the bodega. My slippers were brown suede with shearling
on the inside, and the salt on the ground stained them with
white crusts. I kept my head down, away from the biting air
and the joy of the holiday. I didn't want to be reminded of
Christmases past. No associations, no heartstrings snagged on
a tree in a window, no memories. Since it had turned cold, I'd

lived in flannel pajamas, the big down-filled ski jacket. Sometimes I even slept in that jacket because I kept the temperature inside the apartment so low.

The Egyptian on duty gave me my coffees for free that night because the ATM had run out of cash. Stacks of old, unsold newspapers were piled up against a broken window next to the fridge of milk and sodas. I read the headlines slowly, my eyes blurring and crossing as I stared. The new president was going to be hard on terrorists. A Harlem teenager had thrown her newborn baby down a sewage drain. A mine caved in somewhere in South America. A local councilman was caught having gay sex with an illegal immigrant. Someone who used to be fat was now extremely thin. Mariah Carey gave Christmas gifts to orphans in the Dominican Republic. A survivor of the *Titanic* died in a car crash. I had a vague notion that Reva was coming over that night. She probably wanted to pretend to want to cheer me up.

"I'll pay you back for a pack of Parliaments," I told the Egyptian. "Plus a Klondike bar. And these M&M's." I pointed to the peanut kind. He nodded okay. I looked down through the sliding glass cover of the freezer where all the ice cream and popsicles were kept. There was stuff frozen solid at the bottom that had been there for years, embedded in the white fuzz of ice. A glacial world. I stared at the mountains of ice crystals and spaced out for a minute imagining that I was down there, climbing the ice, surrounded by the whiteness of the smoky air, an Arctic landscape. There was a row of old Häagen-Dazs down there, from before they changed the packaging. There were boxes of Klondike bars down there. Maybe that's where I should go, I thought—Klondike. Yukon. I could move to Canada. I leaned down into the freezer and scraped at the frost and managed to pick out a Klondike for Reva. If she brought me a Christmas gift and I had nothing for her, it would fuel her judgment and "concern" for weeks. I thought I'd also give her some of the fuchsia underwear from Victoria's Secret I never wore. And a pair of jeans. The looser styles might fit her, I thought. I was feeling generous. The Egyptian slid the cigarettes and M&M's across the counter with a scrap he'd ripped from a brown paper bag.

"You still owe me six fifty from last week," he said, and wrote down the sum I now owed on top of that, along with my name, which I was stunned he knew. I could only assume I'd come down for a snack during a blackout. The Egyptian taped the scrap of paper on the wall next to his rolls of scratch tickets. I put the cigarettes and the Klondike bar and the M&M's in my coat pocket, took my coffees, and went back upstairs to my apartment.

I suppose a part of me wished that when I put my key in the door, it would magically open into a different apartment, a different life, a place so bright with joy and excitement that

I'd be temporarily blinded when I first saw it. I pictured what a documentary film crew would capture in my face as I glimpsed this whole new world before me, like in those home improvement shows Reva liked to watch when she came over. First, I'd cringe with surprise. But then, once my eyes adjusted to the light, they'd grow wide and glisten with awe. I'd drop the keys and the coffee and wander in, spinning around with my jaw hanging open, shocked at the transformation of my dim, gray apartment into a paradise of realized dreams. But what would it look like exactly? I had no idea. When I tried to imagine this new place, all I could come up with was a cheesy mural of a rainbow, a man in a white bunny costume, a set of dentures in a glass, a huge slice of watermelon on a yellow plate—an odd prediction, maybe, of when I'm ninety-five and losing my mind in an assisted-living facility where they treat the elderly residents like retarded children. I should be so lucky, I thought. I opened the door to my apartment, and, of course, nothing had changed.

I threw my first empty coffee cup in the toppling pile of garbage around the trash can in the kitchen, broke back the lid of the second cup, downed a few trazodone, smoked a cigarette out the window, then flopped down on my sofa. I ripped open the M&M's, ate them and a couple of Zyprexa, and watched *Regarding Henry,* dozing, the forgotten Klondike bar melting in my pocket.

Reva showed up halfway through the movie with a huge tin of caramel popcorn. I answered the door on my hands and knees.

"Can I leave this here?" she asked. "If I keep it at my house, I'm afraid I'll eat it all."

"Uh-huh," I grunted. Reva helped me up off the floor. I was relieved that she had no elaborately wrapped gift for me. Although Reva was Jewish, she celebrated every Christian holiday. I went to the bathroom, took my coat off, turned the pocket inside out and threw it in the tub. I let the water rinse away the melted Klondike bar. As the chocolate flowed down toward the drain, it looked like blood.

"What are you doing here?" I asked Reva when I came back into the living room.

She ignored the question. "It's snowing again," she said. "I took a cab." She sat on the sofa. I reheated my half-drunk second cup of coffee in the microwave. I went to the VCR, moved the little elephant statue that I'd positioned to cover the glare from the digital clock. I rubbed my eyes. It was ten thirty. Christmas was almost over, thank God. When I looked at Reva, I saw that under her long black wool cape she was wearing a sparkly red dress and black stockings with boughs of holly embroidered on them. Her mascara was smudged, her face was droopy and swollen and caked with foundation and bronzer. Her hair was slicked back into a bun, shiny with gel.

She had kicked off her heels and was now cracking her toe knuckles against the floor. Her shoes lay under the coffee table, tipped over on their sides like two dead crows. She wasn't giving me any jealous, scornful looks, wasn't asking if I'd eaten anything that day, wasn't tidying up or putting the videotapes on the coffee table back in their cases. She was quiet. I leaned against the wall and watched her take her phone out of her purse and turn it off, then open the tin of popcorn, eat some, and put the cover back on. Something had happened, that was clear. Maybe Reva had gone to Ken's Christmas party and watched him carouse with his wife, who she'd told me was petite and Japanese and cruel. Maybe he'd finally ended the affair. I didn't ask. I finished my coffee and picked up the tin of popcorn, took it to the kitchen and emptied it into the garbage, which Reva had taken out, apparently, while I was washing my coat.

"Thanks," she said, when I sat down beside her on the sofa. I grunted and turned on the TV. We split the rest of the M&M's and watched a show about the Bermuda Triangle and I ate some melatonin and Benadryl and drooled a little. At some point I heard my phone ring from wherever I'd last hidden it.

"Is it a vortex to a new dimension? Or a myth? Or is there a conspiracy to cover up the truth? And where do people go when they disappear? Perhaps we'll never know."

Reva went to the thermostat and turned it up and came back to the sofa. The Bermuda Triangle episode ended and a new one started up, this time about the Loch Ness Monster. I closed my eyes.

"My mom died," Reva said during a commercial break.

"Shit," I said.

What else could I have said?

I pulled the blanket across our laps.

"Thanks," Reva said again, crying softly this time.

The ghoulish voice of the TV show's male narrator and Reva's sniffles and sighs should have lulled me to sleep. But I could not sleep. I closed my eyes. When the next episode, about crop circles, started, Reva poked me. "Are you awake?" I pretended I wasn't. I heard her get up and put her shoes back on, ticktock to the bathroom, blow her nose. She left without saying good-bye. I was relieved to be alone again.

I got up and went to the bathroom and opened the medicine cabinet. The Infermiterol pills Dr. Tuttle had given me were small and pellet-shaped, with the letter *I* etched into each one, very white, very hard, and strangely heavy. They almost seemed to be made of polished stone. I figured if there were ever a time to hit the sleep hard, it was now. I didn't want to have to make it through Christmas with the lingering stink of Reva's sadness. I took only one Infermiterol, as directed. The sharp beveled edges scraped my throat on the way down.

. . .

I AWOKE DRENCHED IN SWEAT to discover a dozen un-opened boxes of Chinese takeout on the coffee table. The air stank of pork and garlic and old vegetable oil. A pile of un-sheathed chopsticks lay beside me on the sofa. The television played an infomercial for a food dehydrator on mute.

I looked for the remote control but could not find it. The thermostat was set in the nineties. I got up and turned it back down and noticed that the large Oriental rug—one of the few things I'd kept from my parents' house—had been rolled up and set along the wall beneath the living room windows. And the blinds were raised. That startled me. I heard my phone ring and followed the sound into the bedroom. My phone was in a glass bowl sealed over in Saran Wrap sitting in the center of the bare mattress.

"Huh?" I answered. My mouth tasted like hell.

It was Dr. Tuttle. I cleared my throat and tried to sound like a normal person.

"Good morning, Dr. Tuttle," I said.

"It's four in the afternoon," she said. "I'm sorry it took me so long to return your call. My cats had an emergency. Are you feeling better? The symptoms you described in your mes-sage, frankly, puzzle me."

I realized I was wearing a hot pink Juicy Couture sweat

suit. A tag from the Jewish Women's Council Thrift Shop dangled from the cuff. There were new used VHS tapes stacked on the bare floor in the hallway, all Sydney Pollack movies: *Three Days of the Condor, Absence of Malice, The Way We Were. Tootsie. Out of Africa.* I had no memory of ordering Chinese food or going to the thrift store. And I had no memory of what I'd said in any message. Dr. Tuttle said she'd been "baffled by the emotional intensity" in my voice.

"I'm concerned for you. I'm very, very, very concerned." She sounded like she always sounded, her voice a breathy, high-pitched hoot. "When you say you're questioning your own existence," she asked, "do you mean you're reading philosophy books? Or is this something you thought up on your own? Because if it's suicide, I can give you something for that."

"No, no, nothing like suicide. I was just philosophizing, yes," I said. "Just thinking too much, I guess."

"That's not a good sign. It could lead to psychosis. How are you sleeping?"

"Not enough," I said.

"I suspected as much. Try a hot shower and some chamomile tea. It should settle you down. And give the Infermiterol a try. Studies have shown it wipes out existential anxiety better than Prozac."

I didn't want to admit that I'd already tried it, and it had resulted in this strange mess of food and thrift store purchases, at the very least.

"Thank you, doctor," I said.

I hung up the phone and found a voice mail from Reva giving me the details for her mother's funeral and reception in Long Island later that week. She sounded soft, sad, and a little scripted.

"Things are moving forward. I guess time is like that—it just keeps going. I hope you can come to the funeral. My mom really liked you." I'd met her mother once when she'd visited Reva at school senior year, but I'd completely forgotten it. "We set the date for New Year's Eve. If you could come up early to the house, that would be good," she said. "The train leaves from Penn Station every hour." She gave me specific instructions for how to buy my train ticket, where to stand on the platform, which car to sit in, where to get off. "You'll finally meet my dad."

I almost deleted the message, but then I thought I'd better keep it, and let my mailbox fill back up, so nobody could leave me any more voice mails.

My coat was still sopping wet in the tub, so I put on a denim jacket, pulled a pilly knit hat on, stuck my feet into my slippers, my debit card into my pocket, and went down to the Egyptians to get my coffees, shivering violently along the salted path in the dirty snow. The Christmas decorations at the bodega had been taken down already. The date on the newspapers was December 28, 2000.

"You owe this much now," said one of the smaller Egyptians, pointing to a scrap of paper taped to the counter. He looked like a lapdog, cute and small and squirrelly. "Forty-six fifty. Last night, you bought seven ice creams."

"I did?" He could have been messing with me. I wouldn't have known the difference.

"Seven ice creams," he repeated, shaking his head and stretching to reach for a pack of menthols from the back wall for the customer behind me. I wasn't going to argue. The Egyptians weren't like the people at Rite Aid. So I got cash out of the ATM and paid what I owed.

At home, I found seven pints of old Häagen-Dazs on the kitchen counter. I must have exerted great effort in removing them from the depths of the bodega's freezer: Coffee Toffee Crunch, Vanilla Fudge, Raspberry Fudge, Rum Raisin, Strawberry, Bourbon Pecan Praline, and Watermelon gelato. It had all melted. I wondered if I'd been expecting guests. The Chinese food spread out on the coffee table indicated a celebration perhaps, but it seemed as though I'd fallen asleep or gotten frustrated with the chopsticks and left it all there to stink up my apartment while I dreamt. The apartment still smelled strongly of a deep fryer. I opened a window in the living room a few inches, then sat on the sofa and started in on my second coffee. One by one, I lifted each greasy container of Chinese food, guessed its contents, then unfolded the top to see if I'd guessed correctly. What I guessed was pork fried rice was actually slippery lo mein jiggling around slivers of carrot and onion and dotted with tiny shrimp that made me think of pubic lice. My guess of broccoli in garlic sauce was wrong. That container was full of glimmering yellow curried chicken. My guess of white rice was a farty, cabbage-filled egg roll. White rice was a vegetable medley. White rice was spare ribs. When I found the rice, it was brown. I tasted it with my fingers. Nutty and smushy and cold. As I chewed, I could hear my phone ring. I knew it would be Reva calling to make sure I understood about the funeral, wanting me to promise that I'd be there for her, that I'd show up on time, and to confirm that I was so terribly sorry about her mother's passing, that I cared, that I felt her pain, that I'd do anything to ease her suffering, so help me God.

I didn't answer. I spat the rice out and carried all the containers of Chinese food to the garbage. Then I opened each pint of melted ice cream and poured the contents down the drain. I imagined Reva would gasp if she saw all the food I was throwing out, as if eating it all and vomiting it back up wasn't just as wasteful.

I took the garbage out into the hallway and threw it down the trash chute. Having a trash chute was one of my favorite things about my building. It made me feel important, like I was participating in the world. My trash mixed with the trash of others. The things I touched touched things other people had touched. I was contributing. I was connecting.

I took a Xanax and an Infermiterol, pulled my soggy coat out of the tub, and ran a hot bath. Then I went to the bedroom to find clean pajamas so that I could put them on right away and fall asleep to *Jumpin' Jack Flash*. The furniture in my bedroom had been reorganized. My bed had been turned around so the head of it faced the wall. I pictured myself, in a drugged blackout, assessing my home environs, and using my mind—what part of it, I'm not sure—to make decisions for how to strategically improve the spatial ambiance. Dr. Tuttle had predicted this kind of behavior. "Some activity in sleep is fine just as long as you don't operate heavy machinery. You don't have children, do you? Stupid question." Sleepwalking, sleeptalking, sleep-online-chatting, sleepeating—that was to be expected, especially on Ambien. I'd already done a fair amount of sleepshopping on the computer and at the bodega. I'd sleepordered Chinese delivery. I'd sleepsmoked. I'd sleeptexted and sleeptelephoned. This was nothing new.

But my experience with the Infermiterol was different. I remember pulling out a pair of leggings and a thermal shirt from my dresser drawer. I remember listening to the rumble of the water filling the tub while I brushed my teeth. I remember spitting bloody suds into the crusty sink. I even remember testing the temperature of the bath water with my toe. But I don't remember getting into the water, bathing, washing my hair. I don't remember leaving the house, walking around, getting into a cab, going places, or doing anything else I may have done that night or the next day or the day after that.

As if I'd just blinked, I woke up on an LIRR train wearing jeans and my old running shoes and a long white fur coat, the theme from *Tootsie* running through my head.

Four

DR. TUTTLE HAD WARNED ME of "extended night-mares" and "clock-true mind trips," "paralysis of the imagina-tion," "perceived space-time anomalies," "dreams that feel like forays across the multiverse," and "trips to ulterior di-mensions," et cetera.

And she had said that a small percentage of people taking the kind of medications she prescribed for me reported hav-ing hallucinations during their waking hours. "They're mostly pleasant visions, ethereal spirits, celestial light patterns, an-gels, friendly ghosts. Sprites. Nymphs. Glitter. Hallucinating is completely harmless. And it happens mostly to Asians. What, may I ask, is your ethnic background?"

"English, French, Swedish, German."

"You'll be fine."

The LIRR wasn't exactly celestial, but I wondered if I might be lucid dreaming. I looked down at my hands. It was hard to move them. They smelled like cigarettes and perfume. I blew on them, petted the cool white fur of the coat, made fists and punched down at my thighs. I hummed. It all felt real enough.

I took stock of myself. I wasn't bleeding. I hadn't pissed myself. I wasn't wearing any socks. My teeth felt gummy, my mouth tasted like peanuts and cigarettes, though I found no cigarettes in my coat pockets. My debit card and keys were in the back pocket of my jeans. At my feet was a Big Brown Bag from Bloomingdale's. Inside the bag, a size two Theory black skirt suit and a Calvin Klein matching nude bra and panty set. A small velveteen jewelry box contained an ugly topaz pendant necklace set in fake gold. On the seat beside me was an enormous bouquet of white roses. A square envelope was tucked beneath it, my handwriting on the front: "For Reva." Beside the flowers, there was a *People* magazine, a half-empty water bottle, and the wrappers from two Snickers bars. I took a sip from the water bottle and discovered it was filled with gin.

Out the window, the sun throbbed pale and yellow on the horizon. Was the sun coming up, or was it setting? Which way was the train headed? I looked at my hands again, at the gray line of dirt under my chewed-up fingernails. When a man in uniform passed, I stopped him. I was too shy to ask the important questions—"What day is it? Where am I going? Is it night or morning?"—so I asked him what the next stop on the train would be instead.

"Bethpage coming up. Yours is the station after." He plucked my ticket from where it was stuck on the seat back in front of me. "You can sleep for a few more minutes," he winked.

I couldn't sleep now. I stared out the window. The sun was definitely rising. The train rumbled, then slowed. Across the platform at Bethpage, a small crowd of long-coated middle-aged people with coffee cups stood waiting for the train coming in the opposite direction. I figured I could get off there and catch that train back into Manhattan. Once the train came to a stop, I stood. The fur coat swept down to the floor. It was heavy fur and tied with a white leather belt around my waist. My bare feet were damp inside my sneakers. I wasn't wearing a bra, either. My nipples rubbed against the soft fuzz on the inside of my sweatshirt, which felt new and cheap, the kind of sweatshirt you can buy for five dollars at Walgreens or Rite Aid. A bell clanged. I had to hurry. But as I gathered up my things, I had a sudden and overwhelming urge to shit. I left my bag and the roses on the seat and hurried down the aisle to the toilet. I had to take the coat off and turn it inside out before hanging it up so that only the silky pink lining rested against the grimy wall of the toilet stall. I don't know what I'd eaten, but it certainly was not the usual animal crackers or salad from the diner. I felt the train start back up as I sat there. I pushed up the large sleeves of the sweatshirt to survey my arms, looking for a stamp or mark or bruise or Band-Aid. I found nothing.

I felt again in the pockets of my coat for my phone, found only a receipt for a bubble tea in Koreatown and a rubber band. I used it to tie back my hair. From what I could make out in the dull, scratched-up mirror, I didn't look so bad. I slapped my cheeks and dug the sleep out of my eyes. I still looked pretty. I noticed that my hair was shorter. I must have gotten it cut in the blackout. I could look at my bank card statement to figure out what I'd done on the Infermiterol, I thought, but I didn't really care, as long I was intact, I wasn't bleeding. I wasn't bruised or broken. I knew where I was. I had my credit card and keys. That was all that mattered. I wasn't ashamed. One Infermiterol had taken days of my life away. It was the perfect drug in that sense.

I splashed my face with water, gargled, rubbed the plaque off my teeth with a paper towel. When I got back to my seat, I took a swig of gin, swished it around in my mouth and spit it back into the bottle. The train slowed again. I picked up my things, cradling the unwieldy bouquet in my arms like a baby. The roses were pristine and scentless. I touched them to see if they were real. They were.

. . .

FARMINGDALE WAS AN UGLY, flat, gray landscape spiked with telephone poles. In the distance, I could see rows of long, two-story buildings covered in beige aluminum siding, bare trees shaking in the wind, a silo maybe, a dark plume of smoke from some unseen source rising up into the pale wide gray sky. People bundled in coats and scarves and hats shuffled across a small ice-covered plaza toward minivans and cheap sedans whose running engines filled the small parking lot with a fog of exhaust. An enormous white Lincoln Continental pulled up alongside the curb and flashed its headlights.

It was Reva. She lowered the power window of the passenger seat and waved to me. I considered ignoring her and turning back across the tracks to catch the next train back to the city. She honked. I walked out to the road and got into the car. The interior was all burgundy leather and fake wood. It smelled like cigars and cherry air freshener. Reva's lap was filled with crumpled tissues.

"New coat? Is it real?" she asked, sniffling.

"A Christmas present," I mumbled. I shoved the shopping bag down between my feet and lay the bouquet across my lap. "To myself."

"This is my uncle's car," Reva said. "I can't believe you made it. I almost didn't believe you on the phone last night."

"You didn't believe *what* on the phone?"

"I'm just happy you got here." She had the radio on classical music.

"The funeral is today," I said, affirming what I was loath to believe. I really didn't want to go, but I was stuck now. I turned the music down.

"I just thought you'd be late, or sleep through the day or something. No offense. But here you are!" She patted my knee. "Pretty flowers. My mom would have loved them."

I slumped back in my seat. "I don't feel very well, Reva."

"You *look* nice," she said, eying the coat again.

"I brought an outfit to change into," I said, kicking the shopping bag. "Something black."

"You can borrow whatever you want," said Reva. "Makeup, whatever." She turned and smiled falsely, petted my hand with hers. She looked awful. Her cheeks were swollen, her eyes red, her skin waxy. She'd looked like that when she used to throw up all the time. Senior year, she'd even popped blood vessels in her eyes, so for weeks she'd worn dark glasses around campus. She kept them off at home in our dorm. It was hard to look at her.

She started driving.

"Isn't the snow so beautiful? It's peaceful here, right?

Away from the city? It really puts things in perspective. You know . . . *life*?" Reva looked at me for a reaction, but I gave none. She was going to be annoying, I could tell. She'd expect me to say comforting things, to put an arm around her shoulders while she sobbed at the funeral. I was trapped. The day would be hell. I would suffer. I felt I might not survive. I needed a dark, quiet room, my videos, my bed, my pills. I hadn't been this far from home in many months. I was frightened.

"Can we stop for coffee?"

"There's coffee at the house," Reva said.

I truly hated her in that moment, watching her navigating the icy roads, craning her neck to see over the dash from the sunken seat of the car. Then she gave a litany of everything that she'd been up to—cleaning the house, calling relatives and friends, making arrangements with the funeral home.

"My dad decided to cremate," she said. "He couldn't even wait until after the funeral. It seems so cruel. And it's not even *Jewish*. He was just trying to save money." Her cheeks sagged as she frowned. Her eyes filled with tears. It always impressed me how predictable Reva was—she was like a character in a movie. Every emotional gesture was always right on cue. "My mom is in this cheap little wooden box now," she whined. "It's only this big." She took her hands off the wheel to show me the dimensions, voguing. "They wanted us to buy this huge brass urn. They try to take advantage of you every step of the way, I swear. It's so disgusting. But my dad is so *cheap*. I told him I'm going to dump her ashes out in the ocean and he said that was undignified. What? How is the ocean undignified? What's more dignified than the ocean? The mantel over the fireplace? A cabinet in the kitchen?" She choked a bit on her own indignation, then turned to me softly. "I thought maybe you could come with me and we could drive down to Massapequa and do it and have lunch some time. Like next weekend, if you have time. Or any day, really. Maybe when it gets warmer. At least when it's not snowing. What did you do with *your* mom?" she asked.

"Buried her next to my father," I said.

"See, we should have buried her. At least you still have your parents somewhere. Like, they haven't been burned to ashes. At least they're in the ground, their bones are still there, I mean, in one place. You still have that."

"Pull over," I told her. I'd spotted a McDonald's up ahead. "Let's go through the drive-through. Let me buy you breakfast."

"I'm on a diet," Reva said.

"Let me buy *me* breakfast then," I said.

She pulled into the parking lot, got in line.

"Do you visit them? Your parents' graves?" she asked. Reva mistook my sigh of frustration for an expulsion of buried sadness. She turned to me with a high whining, "Mmm!" frowning in sympathy, and leaned on the horn by accident. It honked like a wounded coyote. She gasped. The person in the car ahead of us gave her the finger. "Oh, God. Sorry!" she yelled, and honked again in apology. She looked at me. "There's food at home. There's coffee, everything."

"All I want is coffee from McDonald's. That's all I ask. I came all this way."

Reva put the car into park. We waited.

"I can't even tell you how disturbing it was at the crematorium. It's the last place you want to be when you're in mourning. They give you all this literature about how they burn the bodies, like I really need to know. And in one of the pamphlets, they describe how they cremate dead babies in these little individual 'metal pans.' That's what they call them—'metal pans.' I can't stop thinking about that. 'Pans.' It's so gross. Like they're making personal pan pizzas. Isn't that just awful? Doesn't that make you sick?"

The car ahead pulled forward. I motioned for Reva to drive up to the intercom.

"Two large coffees, extra sugar, extra cream," I said and pointed to Reva to repeat the order. She did, and ordered herself an Oreo McFlurry.

"You can sleep over if you want," Reva said, driving up to the first window. "It's New Year's Eve, you know."

"I have plans in the city."

Reva knew I was lying. I looked at her, daring her to challenge me, but she just smiled and passed my debit card to the woman in the window.

"I wish I had plans in the city," Reva said.

We pulled up to the next window and Reva handed me my coffees. The lids smelled like cheap perfume and burnt hamburger.

"I can call you a cab back to the station after the reception," Reva went on, her voice high and phony as she spooned her McFlurry into her mouth. "Ken is coming, I think," she said. "And a few other people from work. Do you want to stay for dinner at least?" Speaking with her mouth full was another thing I couldn't stand about Reva.

"I need a nap first," I said. "Then I'll see how I feel."

Reva was quiet for a while, cold white puffs of air rising up off her tongue as she licked the long plastic spoon. The heating was way up. I was sweating under the fur. She stuck the McFlurry cup between her knees and continued to drive and eat.

"You can take a nap in my room," she said. "It should be quiet down there. My relatives are over, but they won't think you're being rude or anything. We don't have to be at the funeral home until two."

We passed a high school, a library, a strip mall. Why anyone would want to live in a place like that was beyond me. Farmingdale State College, a Costco, five cemeteries in a row, a golf course, block after block of white picket fences with perfectly snowblown driveways and walkways. It made sense that Reva had come from a place as lame as this. It explained why she slaved away to fit in and make a home for herself in New York City. Her father, she'd told me, was an accountant. Her mother had been a secretary at a Jewish day school. Reva was, like me, an only child.

"This is it," she said as we pulled into the driveway of a tan-colored brick house. It was ranch-style and small, probably built in the fifties. Just by looking at it from the outside, I could tell that it had wall-to-wall carpeting, humid, sticky air, low ceilings. I imagined cabinets full of crap, flies flurrying around a wooden bowl of brown bananas, an old refrigerator covered in magnets pinning down expired coupons for toilet paper and dish soap, a pantry packed with cheap store-brand foods. It looked like the opposite of my parents' house upstate. Their house was an eerily spare Tudor Colonial, very austere, very brown. The furniture was all dark, heavy wood, which the housekeeper polished religiously with lemon-scented Pledge. Brown leather sofa, brown leather armchair. The floors were varnished and shiny. There were stained-glass windows in the living room and a few large waxy plants in the foyer. Otherwise it was colorless inside. Monochromatic drapes and carpets. There was very little to catch your eye—cleared countertops, everything blank and dim. My mother was not the type to use alphabet magnets on the fridge to hold up my kindergarten finger paintings or first attempts at writing out words. She kept the walls of the house mostly clear. It was as though anything visually interesting was too much aggravation on my mother's eyes. Maybe that's why she ran out of the Guggenheim that one time she came to visit me in the city. Only the master bedroom, my mother's room, had any clutter in it—glass bottles of perfume and ashtrays, unused exercise equipment, piles of pastel and beige-colored clothing. The bed was a king, low to the ground, and whenever I slept in it, I felt very far away from the world, like I was in a spaceship or on the moon. I missed that bed. The stiff blankness of my mother's eggshell sheets.

I sucked down the rest of coffee number one and put the empty cup in my Big Brown Bag from Bloomingdale's. Reva parked the car in the driveway next to a rusting burgundy minivan and an old yellow Volvo station wagon.

"Come meet my relatives," she said. "And then I'll show you where you can lie down for a bit." She led me up the shoveled pathway to the house. She was talking again. "Since her passing, I've just been so exhausted all the time. I haven't been sleeping well with all these strange dreams. Creepy. Not really nightmares. Just weird. Totally bizarre."

"Everybody thinks their dreams are weird, Reva," I said.

"I'm overwhelmed, I guess. It's been hard, but also sort of beautiful in this sad and peaceful way. You know what she said before she died? She said, 'Don't worry so much trying to be everybody's favorite. Just go have fun.' That really hit me, 'everybody's favorite.' Because it's true. I do feel the pressure to be like that. Do you think I'm like that? I guess I just never felt good enough. This is probably healthy for me, to have to face life now, you know, on my own. My dad and I aren't really close. I'll just introduce you to my relatives real quick," she said, opening the front door.

The interior of the house was as I'd predicted—cushy, lime green carpeting, yellow glass chandelier, gold patterned wallpaper, and low stucco ceilings. The heat was blasting, and the air carried a smell of food and coffee and bleach. Reva led me into a sitting room with windows looking out onto the snow-covered front yard. A huge television was on mute, and a row of bald men wearing glasses sat on a long paisley sofa covered in glossy clear plastic. As Reva stomped snow off her boots on the mat, three fat women in black dresses and curlers in their hair came out from the kitchen with trays of donuts and Danishes.

"This is my friend, the one I had to go pick up," she said to the women.

I nodded. I waved. I could feel one of the women eying

my fur coat, my sneakers. She had Reva's eyes—honey brown. Reva took a donut off the tray the woman carried.

"Is your friend hungry?" one woman asked.

"Pretty flowers," said another.

"So you're the friend we've heard so much about," said the third.

"*Are* you hungry?" Reva asked.

I shook my head no, but Reva steered me into the brightly lit kitchen. "There's so much food. See?" The counters and the table were covered with bowls of pretzels, chips, nuts, a plate of cheeses, crudité, dip, cookies. "We finished all the bagels," Reva said. Coffee was brewing in a samovar on the counter. Huge pots on the stove steamed. "Chicken, spaghetti, some kind of ratatouille thing," she said, lifting each of the lids. She was oddly unembarrassed. It seemed like she had dispensed with her usual uppity pretentions. She made no attempt to excuse herself for being homey, folksy, or whatever the word she would have used to describe living in a home like hers—"unglamorous." Maybe she had just completely shut down. She opened the refrigerator to show me shelves of round Tupperware containers of steamed vegetables that she'd made in advance, she said, so she'd have something to snack on all day. She hadn't been to the gym since Christmas. "But whatever. Now is not the time. Want some broccoli?"

She popped the top off one of the containers. The smell hit me and nearly made me gag.

"Is this the sitting thing? You sit for ten days?" I asked, handing her the bouquet of flowers.

"Shiva is seven days. But no. My family isn't religious or anything. They just like to sit around and eat a lot. My aunts and uncles drove in from New Jersey." Reva put the flowers in the sink, poured herself a cup of coffee, tapped in a speck of Sweet'N Low from a crumpled packet she pulled from her pocket, and stirred mindlessly, staring down at the floor. I chugged the rest of the McDonald's coffee and refilled it from the samovar. The fluorescent lights glared off the linoleum floor and hurt my eyes.

"I really need to lie down, Reva," I told her. "I don't feel well."

"Oh, right," she said. "Follow me." We walked back through the sitting room. "Dad, don't let anyone go downstairs. My friend needs some privacy."

One of the bald men waved his hand dismissively and bit into a Danish. The crust flaked apart and fell down the front of his brown sweater-vest. He looked to me like a child molester. All those men did. But anyone would, in the right light, I thought—even *I* did. Even Reva. As her father tried to contain the flakes of pastry on his chest, the women got up and came at him, flicking the crumbs from his sweater onto their plates while he protested. If it weren't for the specter of death hanging over everything, I would have felt like I was in a John Hughes movie. I tried to picture Anthony Michael Hall making an appearance, maybe as the neighbor's kid coming to pay his condolences with a pie or a casserole. Or maybe this was a dark comedy, and Whoopi Goldberg would play the undertaker. I would have loved that. Just the thought of Whoopi soothed me. She really was my hero.

Reva led me down a spiral staircase into the basement, where there was a kind of rec room—rough blue carpeting, wood paneling, small windows up by the ceiling, a cluster of half-decent watercolors hanging crookedly above a frowning, wrinkled, mauve vinyl couch.

"Who did those?" I asked.

"Mom did. Aren't they beautiful? My room's through here." Reva opened a door into a narrow, pink-tiled bathroom. The toilet tank was running. "It's always like that," she said, jiggling the handle to no effect. Another door led to her bedroom. It was dark and muggy inside. "It gets stuffy down here. No windows," she whispered. She turned the bedside lamp on. The walls were painted black. The sliding door of the closet was cracked and had been taken off its runner and set to lean against the wall. The closet contained only a black dress and a few sweaters on hangers. Apart from a small chest of drawers, also painted black and topped with a sagging cardboard box, the room had very little in it. Reva turned on the ceiling fan.

"This was your room?" I asked her.

She nodded and pulled back the slippery blue nylon sleeping bag covering the bed, which was just a twin-size box spring and mattress on the floor. Reva's sheets had flowers and butterflies on them. They were sad, old, pilly sheets.

"I moved down here and painted the room black in high school. To be *cool*," Reva said sarcastically.

"It's very cool," I said. I put my shopping bag down, finished the coffee.

"When should I wake you up? We should leave here around one thirty. So factor in whatever time you'll need to get ready."

"Do you have shoes I can borrow? And tights?"

"I don't keep much here," Reva said, opening and shutting her drawers. "You can borrow something of my mom's, though. You're an eight in shoes, right?"

"Eight and a half," I said, getting into the bed.

"There's probably something up there that will fit you. I'll just wake you up around one."

She closed the door. I sat on the bed and turned off the light. Reva was making noise in the bathroom.

"I'm leaving clean towels for you here by the sink," she

said through the door. I wondered if my presence was keeping her from vomiting. I wished I could tell her I wouldn't mind it if she threw up. I really wouldn't have. I would have understood. If puking could have brought me any solace, I would have tried it years ago. I waited until I heard her close the outside door of the bathroom and creak up the stairs before I went and looked through her medicine cabinet. There was an old bottle of bubblegum-flavored amoxicillin and a half-empty tube of Monistat anti-itch cream. I drank the amoxicillin. I peed into the running toilet. The underwear I had on was white cotton with an old brown bloodstain. It reminded me that I hadn't menstruated in months.

I got back under the sleeping bag and listened to Reva's relatives through the ceiling—footsteps, whining, all that neurotic energy and food getting passed around, jaws grinding, the heartache and opinions and Reva's pent-up anguish or fury or whatever it was that she was trying to stuff down.

I lay awake for a long time. It was like sitting in a cinema after the lights go down, waiting for the previews to begin. But nothing was happening. I regretted the coffee. I sensed Reva's misery in the room with me. It was the particular sadness of a young woman who has lost her mother—complex and angry and soft, yet oddly hopeful. I recognized it. But I didn't feel it inside of me. The sadness was just floating around in the air. It became denser in the graininess of shadows. The obvious truth was that Reva had loved her mother in a way that I hadn't loved mine. My mother hadn't been easy to love. I'm sure she was complicated and worthy of further analysis, and she was beautiful, but I didn't ever really know her. So the sadness in the room felt canned to me. It felt trite. Like the nostalgia for a mother I'd seen on television—someone who cooked and cleaned, kissed me on the forehead and put Band-Aids on my knees, read me books at night, held and rocked me when I cried. My own mother would have rolled her eyes at the thought of doing that. "I'm not your *nanny*," she had often said to me. But I never had a nanny. There were babysitters—girls from the college my father's secretary had found. We always had a housekeeper, Dolores. My mother called her "the maid." I could make a case for my mother's rejection of domesticity as some kind of feminist assertion of her right to leisure, but I actually think that she refused to cook and clean because she felt that doing so would cement her failure as a beauty queen.

Oh, my mother. At her most functional, she kept to a strict diet of black coffee and a few prunes for breakfast. For lunch she'd have Dolores fix her a sandwich. She'd eat just a few bites, and put the leftovers on a bone china plate on the counter—a lesson for me, I took it, in how not to overindulge. In the evenings, she'd drink piss-colored Chardonnay on ice. There were cases of it in the pantry. I'd watched her face bloat and unbloat from day to day according to how much she drank. I liked to imagine her crying in private, mourning her shortcomings as a mother, but I doubt that was why she cried. A delicate puff under the eyes. She used hemorrhoid cream to bring down the swelling. I figured this out after she was dead, when I cleaned out her makeup drawer. Preparation H and Sweet Champagne eye shadow and Ivory Silk foundation, which she wore even just around the house. Fetish Pink lipstick. She hated where we lived, said it was "barbaric" because it was so far from the city. "There's no culture here," she said. But if there had been an opera house or a symphony orchestra—that's what she meant by "culture"—she never would have gone. She thought she was sophisticated—she liked fine clothes, good liquor—but she knew nothing about art. She didn't read anything but romance novels. There were no freshly cut flowers around the house. She mostly watched TV and smoked in bed all day, as far as I could tell. That was her "culture." Around Christmas each year, she'd take me to the mall. She'd buy me a single chocolate at the Godiva store, then we'd walk around all the shops and my mother would call things "cheap" and "hick-style" and "a blouse for the Devil's whore." She kind of came alive at the perfume counter. "This one smells like a hooker's panties." Those outings to the mall were the few times we had any fun together.

My father was joyless, too, at home. He was dull and quiet.

When I was growing up, we'd pass each other in the hallway in the morning like strangers. He was serious, sterile, a scientist. He seemed much more at ease around his students than with me or my mother. He was from Boston, the son of a surgeon and a French teacher. The most personal thing he'd told me was that his parents had died in a boating accident the year after I was born. And he had a sister in Mexico. She moved there in the early eighties to "be a beatnik," my father said. "We look nothing alike."

Pondering all this down in Reva's black room under her sad, pilly sheets, I felt nothing. I could *think* of feelings, emotions, but I couldn't bring them up in me. I couldn't even locate where my emotions came from. My brain? It made no sense. Irritation was what I knew best—a heaviness on my chest, a vibration in my neck like my head was revving up before it would rocket off my body. But that seemed directly tied to my nervous system—a physiological response. Was sadness the same kind of thing? Was joy? Was longing? Was love?

In the time I had to kill there in the dark of Reva's childhood bedroom, I decided I would test myself to see what was left of my emotions, what kind of shape I was in after so much sleep. My hope was that I'd healed enough over half a year's hibernation, I'd become immune to painful memories. So I thought back to my father's death again. I had been very emotional when it happened. I figured any tears I still had left to cry might be about him.

"Your father wants to spend his last days in the house," my mother had said on the phone. "Don't ask me why." He had been dying in the hospital for weeks already, but now he wanted to die at home. I left school and took the train up to see him the very next day, not because I thought it would mean so much to him to have me there, but to prove to my mother that I was a better person than she was: I was willing to be inconvenienced by someone else's suffering. And I didn't expect that my father's suffering would bother me very much. I barely knew him. His illness had been secretive, as though it were part of his work, something that ought not concern me, and nothing I'd ever understand.

I missed a week of classes sitting at home, watching him wither. A huge bed had been installed in the den, along with various pieces of medical equipment that I tried to ignore. One of two nurses was always there, feeling my father's pulse, swabbing his mouth with a soggy little sponge on a stick, pumping him with painkillers. My mother stayed mostly in her bedroom, alone, coming out every now and then to fill a glass with ice. She'd tiptoe into the den to whisper something to the nurse, hardly saying a word to me, barely looking at my father. I sat on the armchair by his bed pretending to read a course packet on Picasso. I didn't want to embarrass my father by staring, but it was hard not to. His hands had grown bony and huge. His eyes had sunk into his skull and darkened. His skin had thinned. His arms were like bare tree branches. It was a strange scene. I studied Picasso's *The Old Guitarist. The Death of Casagemas.* My father fit right into Picasso's Blue Period. *Man on Morphine.* Occasionally he'd jerk and cough, but he had nothing to say to me. "He's too drugged up to talk," the nurse said to console me. I put on my headphones and played old tapes on my Walkman as I read. Prince. Bonnie Raitt. Whatever. The silence was maddening otherwise.

Then, on a Sunday morning, my father was suddenly lucid and told me matter-of-factly that he would die in the afternoon. I don't know if it was the directness and certitude of his statement that rattled me—he was always clinical, always rational, always dry—or that his death was no longer just an idea—it was happening, it was real—or if, during the week I'd spent by his side, we had bonded without my knowledge or consent and, all of a sudden, I loved him. So I lost it. I started crying. "*I'll* be all right," my father told me. I got down on my knees beside him and buried my face in his stale blue blanket. I wanted him to pet my head. I wanted him to soothe me. He stared up at the ceiling as I begged him not to leave me alone with my mother. I was passionate in my supplication.

"Promise me that you'll send me a sign," I pleaded, reaching for his huge, weird hand. He jerked it away. "A *big* sign, more than once, that you're still here, that there's life on the other side. Okay? Promise me you'll come through to me somehow. Give me a sign that I won't expect to see. Something so I'll know you're watching over me. Something huge. Okay? Please? Do you promise?"

"Go get my wife," he said to the nurse.

When my mother came in, he pressed the button on his morphine drip.

"Any last words?" my mother asked.

"I hope this was all worth it," he replied. For the rest of his life—around four hours—I sat on the chair and cried while my mother got drunk in the kitchen, ducking her head in every now and then to see if he was dead yet.

Finally, he was.

"That's it, right?" my mother asked.

The nurse took his pulse, then pulled the blanket over his head.

The memory should have rustled up some grief in me. It should have reignited the coals of woe. But it didn't. Remembering it all now in Reva's bed, I felt almost nothing. Just a slight irritation at the lumpiness of the mattress, the loud swish of the sleeping bag whenever I turned over. Upstairs, Reva's relatives had the television on high volume. The suspenseful sound effects from *Law & Order* echoed down through the floor.

I hadn't been to a funeral since my mother's, almost exactly seven years earlier. Hers had been quick and informal in the funeral home chapel. The guests barely filled the first few rows—just me and my father's sister, a few neighbors, the housekeeper. The names in her address book had been doctors—hers and my father's. My high school art teacher was there. "Don't let this take you all the way down, honey," he said. "You can always call me if you need a grown-up to lean on." I never called him.

My father's funeral, on the other hand, had been a real production. There were printed programs, long speeches. People flew in from across the country to pay their respects. The pews in the university chapel were uncushioned, and the bones in my butt rocked against the hard wood. I sat beside my mother in the front row, trying to ignore her sighs and throat clearings. Her frosty lipstick was put on so thick it started melting down her chin. When the president of the university announced that the science department would establish a research fellowship in my father's name, my mother let out a groan. I reached for her hand and held it. It was bold of me to make such a move, but I thought we might bond now that we had something so huge in common—a dead man whose last name we shared. Her hand was cold and bony, like my father's had been on his deathbed just days earlier. An obvious foreshadowing to me now, but I didn't think of that then. Less than a minute later, she let go of my hand to dig around in her purse for her little pillbox. I didn't know exactly what she was taking that day—an upper, I thought. She kept her coat on in the chapel during the ceremony, fidgeted with her stockings, her hair, glanced back viciously at the crowded pews behind us each time she heard somebody sigh or sniffle or whisper. The hours felt interminable, waiting for everyone to arrive, sitting through the formal proceedings. My mother agreed. "This is like waiting for a train to hell," she whispered at some point, not to me directly, but up at the chapel ceiling. "I'm exhausted." Highway to hell. Slow road to hell. Express bus. Taxicab. Rowboat. First-class ticket. Hell was the only destination she ever used in her metaphors.

When it was time for people to go up and say nice things about my father, she glared at the line forming up the central aisle.

"They think they're special now because they know someone who died." She rolled her red, quick-roving eyes. "It makes them feel important. *Egomaniacs*." Friends, colleagues, coworkers, loyal students spoke emotionally from the rostrum. The people wept. My mother squirmed. I could see our reflections in the gloss of the casket in front of us. We were both just pale, floating, jittery heads.

I couldn't sleep in Reva's bed. It was a lost cause.

I decided to take a shower. I got up and undressed and turned the water on with a squelch, watched the bathroom fill with steam. Since I'd started sleeping all the time, my body had gotten very thin. My muscles had turned soft. I still looked good in clothes, but naked I looked fragile, weird. Protruding ribs, wrinkles around my hips, loose skin around my abdomen. My collarbones jutted out. My knees looked huge. I was all sharp corners at that point. Elbows, clavicles, hip points, the knobby vertebrae of my neck. My body was like a wooden sculpture in need of sanding. Reva would have been horrified to see me naked like that. "You look like a skeleton. You look like Kate Moss. *No fair*," she would have said.

The one time Reva saw me completely naked had been at the Russian bathhouse on East Tenth Street. But that was a year and a half earlier, before I'd gone on my "sleep diet," Reva would go on to call it. She had wanted to "drop weight" before going to a pool party in the Hamptons for the Fourth of July.

"I know it's just water weight I'm sweating off," Reva said. "But it's a good quick fix."

We went on the one day of the week the baths were open to women only. Most of the girls wore bikinis. Reva wore a one-piece bathing suit and wrapped a towel around her hips every time she stood up. It seemed silly to me. I went nude.

"What are you so uptight about, Reva?" I asked her while we were resting by the ice-water pool. "There aren't any men around. Nobody's ogling you."

"It's not about the men," she said. "*Women* are so judgmental. They're always comparing."

"But why do you care? It's not a contest."

"Yes, it is. You just can't see it because you've always been the winner."

"That's ridiculous," I said. But I knew Reva was right. I was hot shit. People were always telling me I looked like Amber Valletta. Reva was pretty, too, of course. She looked like Jennifer Aniston and Courteney Cox put together. I didn't tell her that then. She would have been prettier if she knew how to relax. "Chill," I said. "It's not that big a deal. You think people are going to judge you for not looking like a supermodel?"

"That's usually the first judgment people make in this city."

"What do you care what people think about you? New Yorkers are assholes."

"I *care*, okay? I want to fit in. I want to have a nice life."

"God, Reva. That's pathetic."

Then she got up and disappeared inside the eucalyptus mist in the steam room. It was a mild skirmish, one of hundreds about how arrogant I was for not counting my blessings. Oh, Reva.

The shower stall in her basement bathroom was small, the door clouded, gray glass. There was no soap, only a bottle of Prell. I washed my hair and stayed under the water until it ran cold. When I got out, I could hear the news blaring through the ceiling. The towels Reva had left for me on the sink were pink and seafoam green and smelled faintly of mildew. I rubbed the fog off the mirror and looked at myself again. My hair splatted against my neck. Maybe I should cut it even shorter, I thought. Maybe I would enjoy that. Boy cut. *Gamine.* I'd look like Edie Sedgwick. "You'd look like Charlize Theron," Reva would have said. I wrapped the towel around myself and lay back down on the bed.

There were other things that might make me sad. I thought of *Beaches, Steel Magnolias,* the assassination of Martin Luther King, Jr., River Phoenix dying on the sidewalk in front of the Viper Room, *Sophie's Choice, Ghost, E.T., Boyz n the Hood,* AIDS, Anne Frank. *Bambi* was sad. *An American Tail* and *The Land Before Time* were sad. I thought of *The Color Purple,* when Nettie gets kicked out and has to leave Celie in that house, a slave to her abusive husband. "Nothing but death can keep me from her!" *That* was sad. That should have done it, but I couldn't cry. None of that penetrated deep enough to press whatever button controlled my "outpouring of sorrow."

But I kept trying.

I pictured the day of my father's funeral—brushing my hair in the mirror in my black dress, picking at my cuticles until they bled, how my vision got blurry with tears walking down the stairs and I almost tripped, the streaks of autumn leaves blearing by as I drove my mother to the university chapel in her Trans Am, the space between us filling with tangled ribbons of pale blue smoke from her Virginia Slim, her saying not to open a window because the wind would mess up her hair.

Still, no sorrow.

"I'm just so sorry," Peggy said over and over at my father's funeral. Peggy was the only friend my mother had left by the end—a Reva type, for sure. She lived around the corner from my parents' house in a lavender Dutch Colonial with a front yard full of wildflowers in the summer, sloppy snowmen and forts built by her two young sons in the winter, tattered Tibetan prayer flags hanging over the front door, lots of wind chimes, a cherry tree. My father had called it "the hippie house." I sensed that Peggy wasn't very intelligent, and that my mother didn't really like her. But Peggy offered my mother a lot of pity. And my mother loved pity.

I stayed home for a week after my father's funeral. I wanted to do what I thought I was supposed to do—to mourn. I'd seen it happening in movies—covered mirrors and stilled grandfather clocks, listless afternoons silent but for sniffling and the creaks of old floorboards as someone in an apron came out from the kitchen saying, "You should eat something." And I wanted a mother. I could admit that. I wanted her to hold me while I cried, bring me cups of warm milk and honey, give me comfy slippers, rent me videos and watch them with me, order deliveries of Chinese food and pizza. Of course I didn't tell her that this was what I wanted. She was usually passed out in her bed with the door locked.

A few times that week, people visited the house, and my mother would do her hair and makeup, spray air freshener, raise the blinds. She got phone calls from Peggy twice a day. "I'm fine, Peggy. No, don't come over. I'm going to take a bath and a nap. Sunday? Fine, but call first."

In the afternoons, I took the car out, driving aimlessly or to the mall or the supermarket. My mother left me lists of things to buy, with a note for the guy at the liquor store. "This girl is my daughter, and I permit her to purchase alcohol. Call if you'd like to verify her identity. The number is . . ." I bought her vodka. I bought her whiskey and mixers. I didn't think she was in any real danger. She'd been a heavy drinker for years. Maybe I did take some pleasure in aiding her self-destruction by buying her booze, but I didn't want my mother to die. It wasn't like that. I remember one afternoon, she came out of her room and walked past me where I lay on the floor sobbing. She went to the kitchen, wrote a check for the housekeeper, took a bottle of vodka from the freezer, told me to turn down the television, and went back to her room.

That was the worst of it. I was pretty upset. I couldn't have described with any accuracy how I was "doing." And nobody called to ask me. Everyone I knew at school hated me because I was so pretty. In hindsight, Reva was a pioneer: she was the only friend who ever really dared to try to know me. We didn't get to be friends until later that year. For the rest of my week of mourning, my moods trespassed out of the standard categories I'd come to recognize. One moment was silent and gray, Technicolor and garish and absurd the next. I felt like I was on drugs, though I had taken nothing. I didn't even drink that week until a man from the university, Professor Plushenko, one of my father's colleagues, came to the house, and my mother attempted to entertain him.

Professor Plushenko had come under the veil of condolence with a store-bought Bundt cake and a bottle of Polish brandy. He was there to convince my mother to give him my father's papers. I had the feeling he wanted something my father wouldn't have given to him willingly. I felt a responsibility to watch and make sure the guy didn't take advantage of my mother's fragile state. Apparently the man had known my parents for many years.

"You look just like your mother," he said that night,

leering at me. His skin was cardboard colored and matte, his lips weirdly red and gentle. He wore a striped gray suit and smelled of sweet cologne.

"My daughter is barely nineteen years old," my mother scoffed. She wasn't defending me against his lechery. She was bragging. By then, I was actually twenty.

Of course there was no dinner—my mother was incapable of providing that—but there were drinks. I was allowed to drink. After a few, the man sat down on the sofa between us. He spoke of my father's invaluable contribution to future generations of scientists, how blessed he felt to have worked so closely beside him. "His legacy is in his students, *and* in his papers. I want to be the one to make sure nothing falls through the cracks. It's precious material. It must be handled very thoughtfully."

My mother could barely speak then. She allowed a tear to run down her face, leaving a muddled gray stripe through her makeup. The man put one arm around her shoulders. "Oh, you poor thing. A tragic loss. He was a great man. I know how much he loved you." I guess my mother was too aggrieved, too drunk, or too medicated to see the man's other arm snake over from his knee to mine at some point during the conversation. I was drunk, too, and I kept still. When my mother got up to use the bathroom, we were left alone on the sofa, and there was a kiss on my forehead, a finger traced down the side of my neck and over my left nipple. I knew what he was doing. I did not resist. "You poor thing."

My nipple was still erect when my mother came back in, tripping over the edge of the carpet.

My father had left everything to my mother, including the contents of his study. After she died, I was the one who went in there and packed things up and lugged the boxes to the basement. That colleague of his never saw a single page. What I was bartering for in letting that guy kiss me was still not immediately clear. Maybe my mother's dignity. Or maybe I just wanted a little affection. Trevor and I had been on the outs for months at the time. I hadn't called to tell him my father had died. I was saving it to tell him later, so he'd feel terrible.

I called a taxi to take me to the train station the morning after that kiss. I didn't wake my mother to tell her I was going back to school. I didn't leave a note. A week went by. She didn't call. When she "had her accident," which is how they termed it at the hospital, Peggy was the one to find her.

"Oh, sweetheart," she said on the phone. "She's still alive, but the doctors say you should come as soon as you can. I'm so, so sorry."

My knees didn't buckle. I didn't fall to the ground. I was at the sorority house. I could hear girls cooking in the kitchen, chatting about their fat-free diets and how not to "bulk up" at the gym.

"Thanks for letting me know," I told Peggy. She was whimpering and snorting. I didn't tell anyone at the sorority house what was happening. I didn't want to deal with the indignity of it all.

It took me almost an entire day to get up there. I wrote a final paper for a class on Hogarth on the train. Part of me was hoping my mother would be dead by the time I arrived.

"She knows you're here," Peggy said in the hospital room. I knew that wasn't true. My mother was in a coma. She was already gone. Once in a while, her left eye would blink open— clear blue, frozen, blind, a terrifying, empty, soulless eye. I remember noticing in the hospital room that her roots were showing. She'd been vigilant about keeping her hair icy blond as long as I'd known her, but her natural color had grown in, a warmer shade—honey blonde, my color. I'd never seen her real hair before.

My mother's body stayed alive for exactly three days. Even with a tube down her throat, a machine taped to her face to keep her breathing, she was still pretty. She was still prim. "Her organs are shutting down," the doctor explained. System failure. She felt nothing, he assured me. She was brain dead. She wasn't thinking or dreaming or experiencing anything, not even her own death. They turned off the machine and I sat there, waiting, watching the screen blip, then stop. She wasn't resting. She was not in a state of peace. She was in no state, not being. The peace to be had, I thought, watching them pull the sheet over her head, was mine.

"Oh, sweetheart. I'm so, so sorry." Peggy sobbed and embraced me. "You poor thing. You poor dear little orphan."

Unlike my mother, I hated being pitied.

There was nothing new to be gleaned from these memories, of course. I couldn't revive my mother and punish her. She took herself out before we could ever have a real conversation. I wondered if she'd been jealous of my father, at how well attended his funeral had been. She left a note. I found it at the house the night I came home from the hospital. Peggy drove me. I was stoic. I was numb. The note was on my father's desk. My mother had used a page from a yellow legal pad to write it. Her penmanship started off as bold, capital letters, but by the end it petered out into tight, itchy cursive. The letter was totally unoriginal. She felt she wasn't equipped to handle life, she wrote, that she felt like an alien, a freak, that consciousness was intolerable and that she was scared of going crazy. "Good-bye," she wrote, then gave a list of people she'd known. I was sixth on the list of twenty-five. I recognized some of the names—long abandoned girlfriends, her doctors, her hairdresser. I kept the letter and never showed it to anybody. Occasionally, over the years, when I'd felt abandoned and scared and heard a voice in my mind say, "I want my mommy," I took the note out and read it as a reminder of what she'd actually been like and how little she cared about me. It helped. Rejection, I have found, can be the only antidote to delusion.

My mother had been like I turned out to be—an only child with dead parents, so there wasn't any family left to contend with. My dad's sister flew back up from Mexico over Christmas and took what she wanted from the house—a few books, the silver. She dressed in colorful serapes and fringed silk shawls, but she had my father's septic attitude toward life. She wasn't sad to have lost her brother, it seemed, but was angry at "toxic waste," she said. "People didn't get cancer a thousand years ago. It's because of the chemicals. They're everywhere—in the air, in the food, in the water we drink." I guess she helped me insofar as she nodded along when I told her I was relieved my mother was gone but wished my father had held on long enough at least to help me take care of the house, put things in order. I tried to keep it together while she was around.

After she left, I spent days in the house alone, poring over my childhood photo albums, sobbing over piles of my mother's unopened packages of pantyhose. I cried over my father's deathbed pajamas, the dog-eared biographies of Theodore Roosevelt and Josef Mengele on his bedside table, a green nickel in the pocket of his favorite pants, a belt he'd had to drill holes in to make smaller as he'd grown sicker and thinner in the months leading up to his death.

There was no big drama. Things were quiet.

I imagined what I'd say to my mother if she suddenly reappeared now in Reva's basement. I imagined her disgust at the cheapness of things, the mustiness of the air. I couldn't think of anything I wanted to ask her. I had no burning urge to proclaim any fury or sadness. "Hello," was as far as I got in our hypothetical dialogue.

I got up out of bed and fished through one of the cardboard boxes on Reva's bureau. In her senior yearbook, I found only one photo of her, the standard portrait. Hers stood out in the rows of boring faces. She had big frizzy hair, chubby cheeks, overplucked eyebrows that zoomed across her forehead like crooked arrows, dark lipstick, thick black eyeliner. Her gaze was slightly off center, vague, unhappy, possessed. She looked like she'd been much more interesting before she left for college—a Goth, a freak, a punk, a reject, a delinquent, an outcast, a fuckup. As long as I'd known her, she'd been a follower, a plebeian, straitlaced and conformist. But it seemed as though she'd had a rich, secretive interior life in high school, with desires beyond the usual drinking and foosball soirees suburban Long Island had to offer. So, I gathered, Reva moved to Manhattan to go to college and decided she'd try to fit in—get skinny, be pretty, talk like all the other skinny, pretty girls. It made sense that she'd want me as her best friend. Maybe her best friend in high school had been one of the weirdos, like her. Maybe she'd had some kind of disability—a gimp arm, Tourette's, Coke-bottle glasses, alopecia. I imagined the two of them together in that black basement bedroom listening to music: Joy Division. Siouxsie and the Banshees. It made me a little jealous to think of Reva being depressed and dependent on anyone but me.

After my mother's funeral, I went back to school. My sorority sisters didn't ask if I was okay, if I wanted to talk. They all avoided me. Only a few left notes under my door. "I'm so sorry you're going through this!" Of course, I was grateful to be spared the humiliation of a patronizing confrontation by a dozen young women who would probably have just shamed me for not "being more open." They weren't my friends. Reva and I were in French class together that year. We were conversation partners. She took notes for me while I was away, and when I came back, she wasn't afraid to ask questions. In class, she diverged from the curriculum to ask, in halting, bad French, how I was doing, what had happened, if I felt sad or angry, if I wanted to get together outside of class to speak in English. I agreed. She wanted to know every detail of the whole ordeal with my parents, hear the deep insights I had gleaned, how I felt, how I'd mourned. I gave her the basic gist.

Talking to Reva about misery was insufferable. "Look on the bright side," was what she wanted everyone to do. But at least she cared.

Senior year, I moved out of the sorority house and into a two-bedroom suite with Reva in an off-campus dorm. Living together solidified our bond. I was the vacant, repressed depressive, and she was the obsessive blabbermouth, always knocking on my door, asking random questions, looking for any excuse to talk. I spent a lot of time staring at the ceiling that year, trying to cancel out thoughts about death with thoughts about nothingness. Reva's frequent interruptions probably kept me from jumping out the window. Knock, knock. "Chat break?" She liked to look through my closet, turning over price tags, checking the sizes of all the clothes I'd bought with the money I'd inherited. Her obsession with the material world pulled me out of whatever existential wormhole I'd wandered into.

I never confronted Reva about the fact that I could hear her vomiting when she came back from the dining hall each night. All she ate at home were sugar-free mini yogurts and baby carrots, which she dressed with yellow mustard. The palms of her hands were orange from all the carrots she ate. Dozens of mini yogurt containers cluttered the recycling bin.

That spring, I went for long walks around the city with earplugs in. I felt better just listening to the echoing sounds of my breathing, the phlegm roiling in my throat when I swallowed, my eyes blinking, the weak ticking of my heart. Gray days spent staring down at sidewalks, skipping classes, shopping for things I'd never wear, paying through the nose for a gay guy to put a tube up my asshole and rub my stomach, tell me how much better I would feel once my colon was clean. Together we watched little flakes of shit flowing through the outgoing tube. His voice was soft but enthusiastic. "You're doing great, doll," he'd say. More often than I needed, I'd get face peels and pedicures, massages, waxings, haircuts. That was how I mourned, I guess. I paid strangers to make me feel good. I might as well have hired a prostitute, I thought. That's kind of what Dr. Tuttle was years later, I thought—a whore to feed me lullabies. If anything was going to make me cry, it was the thought of losing Dr. Tuttle. What if she lost her license? What if she dropped dead? What would I do without her? Then, finally, in Reva's basement bedroom, I felt a tinge of sadness. I could feel it in my throat, like a chicken bone caught in my windpipe. I loved Dr. Tuttle, I guessed. I got up and drank some water from the tap in the bathroom. I went back to bed.

A few minutes later, Reva was knocking on the door.

"I brought you some quiche," she said. "Can I come in?"

Reva now wore a big red fleece robe. She had done her hair and makeup already. I was still in the towel, under the covers. I took the quiche and ate it while Reva sat on the edge of the bed. She prattled on about her mother, that she never appreciated her mother's artistic talent. It was going to be a long afternoon.

"She could have been great, you know? But in her generation, women were expected to be mothers and stay at home. She gave her life up just for me. Her watercolors are amazing, though. Don't you think?"

"They're decent amateur watercolors, yeah," I said.

"How was the shower?"

"No soap," I said. "Did you find any shoes I can borrow?"

"You should go up there and look yourself," said Reva.

"I really don't want to."

"Just go up there and pick something. I don't know what you want."

I refused.

"You're going to make me go back up there?"

"You said you'd bring me some options."

"I can't look in her closet. It's too upsetting. Will you just go look?"

"No. I'm not comfortable doing that, Reva. I can just stay here if you want and miss the funeral, I guess."

I put down the quiche.

"Okay, fine, I'll go," Reva sighed. "What do you need?"

"Shoes, stockings, some kind of shirt."

"What kind of shirt?"

"Black, I guess."

"Okay. But if you don't like what I bring down, don't blame me."

"I'm not going to blame you, Reva. I don't care."

"Just don't blame me," she repeated.

She got up, leaving little bits of red fuzz on the bed where she'd been sitting. I got out of bed and looked inside the bag from Bloomingdale's. The suit was made of stiff rayon. The necklace was nothing I'd ever wear. The Infermiterol seemed to ruin my usual good taste in things, although the white fur coat was interesting to me. It had personality. How many foxes had to die, I wondered. And how did they kill them so that their blood didn't stain their fur? Maybe Ping Xi could have answered that question, I thought. How cold would it have to be to freeze a live white fox? I tore the tags off the bra and panties and put them on. My pubic hair puffed out the panties. It was a good joke—sexy underwear with a huge bush. I wished I had my Polaroid camera to capture the image. The lightheartedness in that wish struck me, and for a moment I felt joyful, and then I felt completely exhausted.

When Reva came back with her arms full of shoes and shirts and an unopened package of flesh-colored nylons from the eighties, I handed her the necklace.

"I got you something," I said, "to condole you."

Reva dropped everything on the bed and opened the box. Her eyes filled with tears—just like in a movie—and she embraced me. It was a good hug. Reva had always been good at hugs. I felt like a praying mantis in her arms. The fleece of her robe was soft and smelled like Downy. I tried to pull away but she held me tighter. When she finally let go, she was crying and smiling. She sniffed and laughed.

"It's beautiful. Thanks. That's really sweet. Sorry," she said, wiping her nose on her sleeve. She put the necklace on and pulled the collar of her robe away and studied her neck in the mirror. Her smile turned a little phony. "You know, I don't think you can use 'condole' that way. I think you can 'condole *with*' someone. But you can't 'condole' someone."

"No, Reva. *I'm* not condoling you. The necklace is."

"But that's not the right word, I think. You can *console* someone."

"No, you can't," I said. "Anyway, you know what I mean."

"It's beautiful," Reva said again, flatly this time, touching the necklace. She pointed to the mess of black stuff she'd brought down. "This is all I found. I hope it's okay."

She took her dress out from the closet and went into the bathroom to change. I put the pantyhose on, picked through the shoes, found a pair that fit. From the tangle of shirts I pulled out a black turtleneck. I put it on, and put the suit on. "Do you have a brush I can borrow?"

Reva opened the bathroom door and handed me an old hairbrush with a long wooden handle. There was a spot on the back that was all scratched up. When I held it under the light, I could make out teeth marks. I sniffed it but couldn't detect the smell of vomit, only Reva's coconut hand cream.

"I've never seen you in a suit before," Reva said stiffly when she came out of the bathroom. The dress she wore was tight with a high center slit. "You look really put together," she said to me. "Did you get a haircut?"

"Duh," I said, handing her back the brush.

We put our coats on and went upstairs. The living room was empty, thank God. I filled my McDonald's cup with coffee again as Reva stood at the fridge, shoving cold steamed broccoli in her mouth. It was snowing again.

"I'm warning you," Reva said, wiping her hands. "I'm going to cry a lot."

"It would be weird if you didn't," I said.

"I just look so ugly when I cry. And Ken said he'd be there," she told me for the second time. "I know we should have waited until after New Year's. Not like it would have made a difference to my mom. She's already cremated."

"You told me."

"I'll try not to cry too hard," she said. "Tearing up is OK. But my face just gets so *puffy*." She stuck her hand in a box of Kleenex and pulled out a stack. "You know, in a way, I'm glad we didn't have to get her embalmed. That's just creepy. She was just a sack of bones, anyway. She probably weighed half of what I weigh now. Well, maybe not half exactly. But she was super skinny. Skinnier than Kate Moss, even." She stuck the tissues in her coat pocket and turned off the lights.

We went out the kitchen door into the garage. There was a storage freezer in the corner, shelves of tools and flowerpots and ski boots, a few old bikes, stacks of blue plastic storage bins along one wall. "It's unlocked," Reva said, motioning to a small silver Toyota. "This was my mom's car. I started it last night. Hopefully I can start it again now. She hadn't been driving it, obviously." Inside, it smelled like menthol rub. There was a polar bear bobblehead on the dash, an issue of the *New Yorker* and a bottle of hand cream on the passenger seat. Reva started the car, sighed, clicked the garage door opener clipped to the visor, and started crying.

"See? I warned you," she said, taking out the wad of tissues. "I'm just going to cry while the car heats up. Just a sec," she said. She cried on, gently shaking under her puffy jacket.

"There, there," I said, sucking down the coffee. I was intensely bored of Reva already. This would be the end of our friendship, I felt. Sometime soon, my cruelty would go too far, and now that her mother was dead, Reva's head would start to clear of its superficial nonsense. She'd probably go back into therapy. She'd realize that we had no good reason to be friends, and that she would never get what she needed from me. She'd send me a long letter explaining her resentments, her mistakes, explaining how she had to let me go in order to move on with her life. I could already imagine her phrasing. "I've come to realize that our friendship is no longer serving me"—that was language her therapist would have taught her—"which is not a criticism of you." But of course it was about me: I was the friend in the friendship she was describing.

As we drove through Farmingdale, I wrote my reply to her would-be "Dear John" letter in my head. "I got your note," I would begin. "You have confirmed what I've known about you since college." I tried to think of the worst thing I could say about a person. What was the cruelest, most cutting, truest thing? Was it worth saying? Reva was harmless. She wasn't a bad person. She'd done nothing to hurt me. I was the one sitting there full of disgust, wearing her dead mother's shoes. "Good-bye."

FOR THE REST OF THE DAY, through the proceedings at Solomon Schultz Funeral Home, I stayed by Reva's side but watched her as though from a distance. I started to feel strange—not guilty per se, but somehow responsible for her suffering. I felt as though she were a stranger I had hit with my car, and I was waiting for her to die so she wouldn't be able to identify me. When she talked, it was like I was watching a movie. "That's Ken, over there. See his wife?" The camera panned over the rows, narrowed in on a pretty half-Asian woman with freckles, wearing a black beret. "I don't want him to see me like this. Why did I invite him? I don't know what I was thinking."

"Don't worry," is all I could think to say. "He's not going to fire you for being sad at a funeral."

Reva sniffed and nodded, dabbed at her eyes with her tissue. "That's my mom's friend from Cleveland," she said as an obese woman in a black muumuu hoisted herself onto the stage. She sang "On My Own" from *Les Misérables,* a cappella. It was painful to watch. Reva cried and cried. Tissues stained with mascara like crushed inkblot tests piled up on her lap. A dozen people went up to say nice things about Reva's mother. A few made jokes, a few broke down shamelessly. Everyone agreed that Reva's mother had been a good woman, that her death was sad, but that life was mysterious, death more so, and what's the use in speculating so let's remember the good times—at least she'd lived at all. She'd been brave, she'd been generous, she'd been a good mother and wife, a good cook and a good gardener. "My wife's only wish was that we move on quickly and be happy," Reva's father said. "Everyone has already said so much about her." He looked out at the crowd, shrugged, then seemed to get flummoxed, turned red, but instead of bursting into tears, he started coughing into the microphone. Reva covered her ears. Someone brought her father a glass of water and helped him back to his seat.

Then it was Reva's turn to speak. She checked her makeup in her compact mirror, powdered her nose, dabbed her eyes with more tissues, then went up and stood at the rostrum and read lines off index cards, shuffling them back and forth as she sniffled and cried. Everything she said sounded like she'd read it in a Hallmark card. Halfway through, she stopped and looked down at me as though for approval. I gave her a thumbs-up. "She was a woman of many talents," Reva said, "and she inspired me to follow my own path." She went on for a while, mentioned the watercolors, her mother's faith in God. Then she seemed to space out. "To be honest . . ." she began. "It's like, you know . . ." She smiled and apologized and covered her face with her hands and sat back down next to me.

"Did I look like a complete idiot?" she whispered.

I shook my head no and put an arm around her, as awkwardly as such a thing can be done, and sat there until the funeral was over, this strange young woman in the throes of despair, trembling into my armpit.

. . .

THE RECEPTION AFTERWARD was at Reva's house. The same middle-aged women were there, the same bald men, only multiplied. Nobody seemed to notice us when we walked in.

"I'm starving," Reva said and went straight to the kitchen. I trudged back down to the basement and fell into a kind of half sleep.

I thought about whatever subliminal impulse had put me on the train to Farmingdale. Seeing Reva in full-blown Reva mode both delighted and disgusted me. Her repression, her transparent denial, her futile attempts to tap into the pain with me in the car, it all satisfied me somehow. Reva scratched at an itch that, on my own, I couldn't reach. Watching her take what was deep and real and painful and ruin it by expressing it with such trite precision gave me reason to think Reva was an idiot, and therefore I could discount her pain, and with it, mine. Reva was like the pills I took. They turned everything, even hatred, even love, into fluff I could bat away. And that was exactly what I wanted—my emotions passing like headlights that shine softly through a window, sweep past me, illuminate something vaguely familiar, then fade and leave me in the dark again.

I woke up briefly to the sound of the faucet running and

Reva retching in the bathroom. It was a rhythmic, violent song—throat grunts punctuated with splats and splashes. When she had finished, she flushed three times, turned off the faucet and went back up the stairs. I lay awake until I thought an appropriate amount of time had passed. I didn't want Reva to think I'd been listening to her vomit. My blind eye was the one real comfort I felt I could give her.

Eventually I got out of bed, got my things together, and went back upstairs to call a taxi to come take me to the train station. Most of the guests had left. The original bald men stood in the sunroom off the kitchen. The snow was coming down hard by then. The women were collecting the plates and mugs from the coffee table in the living room. I found Reva sitting on the sofa, eating from a bag of frozen peas in front of the muted television.

"Can I use the phone?" I asked.

"I'll drive you back to the city," Reva said calmly.

"But, Reva, do you think that's safe?" one of the women asked.

"I'll drive slow," Reva said. She got up, left the bag of peas on the coffee table, and took my arm. "Let's go before my dad tries to stop me," she said. From the kitchen she grabbed my bouquet of white roses from where they'd gotten stuck between the dirty dishes in the sink. They were still wrapped. "Take a few of those," she said, pointing the roses at the bottles of wine on the counter. I took three. The women watched. I laid them in the Big Brown Bag on top of my jeans and sweatshirt and dirty sneakers.

"I'll be right back," Reva said, and went down the dark hallway.

"You're Reva's friend from college?" a woman asked. She spoke to me through the bright doorway to the kitchen as she unloaded the dishwasher. "Good that you have each other. You've got friends, you're all right, no matter what." Steam filled the air around her. She looked exactly how I'd pictured Reva's mother. Her hair was brown and short. She wore big fake pearl earrings. Her dress was dark brown with gold flecks, long and tight and stretchy. I could see the cellulite on her legs through the material. The steam from the dishwasher smelled like vomit. I took a step back. "Reva's mother was my best friend," she continued. "We talked every day on the phone. I don't talk to my own children that much. Sometimes friends are better than family, because you can say anything. Nobody gets mad. It's a different kind of love. I'll really miss her." She paused as she looked into a cabinet. "But she's still here in spirit. I feel it. She's standing right beside me, saying, 'Debra, the tall glasses go on the shelf with the wine glasses.' She's bossing me around, like always. I just know it. The spirit never dies, and that's the truth."

"That's nice," I said, yawning. "I'm sorry for your loss."

Reva appeared wearing a huge beaver coat—her mother's, no doubt—big snow boots, and her gym bag slung over her shoulder.

"Let's go," she said roughly. "I'm ready." We headed for the door to the garage. "Tell Dad I'll call him tomorrow," she said to the women in the living room. They started to protest, but Reva kept walking. I followed her out and into her mother's car again.

REVA AND I DIDN'T TALK MUCH on the ride back into the city. Before we got on the highway, I suggested we stop for coffee, but Reva didn't respond. She turned the radio up, put the heating on full blast. Her face was tight and serious, but calm. I was surprised by my curiosity to know what she was thinking, but I kept quiet. When we got onto the Long Island Expressway, the radio DJ told listeners to call in to share their New Year's resolutions.

"*In 2001, I want to embrace every opportunity. I want to say 'yes' to every invitation I receive.*"

"*Two thousand and one is the year I finally learn to tango.*"

"I'm not making any resolutions this year," Reva said. She turned down the volume on the radio and changed the station. "I can never keep my promises to myself. I'm like my own worst enemy. What about you?"

"I might try to stop smoking. But the medications make it difficult."

"Uh-huh," she said mindlessly. "And maybe I'll try to lose five pounds." I couldn't tell if she was trying to insult me with sarcasm, or if she was being sincere. I let it go.

The visibility was bad. The windshield wipers screeched, clearing away the wet splats of snow. In Queens, Reva turned up the radio again and began to sing along to the music. Santana. Marc Anthony. Enrique Iglesias. After a while, I began to wonder if she was drunk. Maybe we'd die in a car accident, I thought. I leaned my forehead against the cool glass of the window and looked out at the dark water of the East River. It wouldn't be that bad to die, I thought. Traffic slowed.

Reva turned the radio down.

"Can I sleep over at your place?" she asked stiffly. "I don't want to be needy, but I'm afraid of being alone right now. I don't feel like myself and I'm afraid something bad is going to happen."

"Okay," I said, though I assumed she'd change her mind a few minutes past midnight.

"We can watch a movie," she said. "Whatever you want. Hey, can you dig my gum out of my purse? I don't want to take my hands off the wheel."

Reva's fake Gucci bag sat between us on the console. I

fished around tampons and perfume and hand sanitizer and her makeup kit and rolled up issues of *Cosmo* and *Marie Claire* and a hairbrush and a toothbrush and toothpaste and her huge wallet and her cell phone and her datebook and her sunglasses and finally found a single piece of cinnamon Extra in the little side pocket otherwise full of old LIRR ticket receipts. The paper had turned pink and oily.

"Wanna split it?" she asked.

"Gross," I said. "No."

Reva put her hand out. I watched her watching the road. Maybe she wasn't drunk, I thought, just exhausted. I placed the piece of gum in her palm. Reva unwrapped it and stuck it in her mouth and flicked the wrapper over her shoulder and chewed and kept on driving. I stared down into the East River again, black and glittering with the yellow lights of the city. The traffic wasn't budging. I thought of my apartment. I hadn't been there in days—not awake, anyway. I imagined the mess I'd discover with Reva when we walked in. I hoped she wouldn't comment. I didn't think she would, given the day.

"I always think about earthquakes when I'm on this bridge," Reva said. "You know, like in San Francisco when that bridge collapsed?"

"This is New York City," I said. "We don't get earthquakes."

"I was watching the World Series when it happened," Reva said. "With my dad. I totally remember it. Do you remember it?"

"No," I lied. Of course I remembered it, but I'd thought nothing of it.

"You're watching a baseball game and then all of a sudden, boom. And you're like, thousands of people just died."

"It wasn't thousands."

"A lot, though."

"Maybe a few hundred, max."

"A lot of people got crushed on that freeway. And on that bridge," Reva insisted.

"It's fine, Reva," I said. I didn't want her to cry again.

"And the next day on the news they were interviewing a guy who was on the lower deck of the freeway and they were like, 'What will you take with you from this experience?' And he goes, 'When I got out of my car, there was a brain jiggling on the ground. A whole brain, jiggling like a Jell-O mold.'"

"People die all the time, Reva."

"But isn't that just horrific? A brain jiggling on the ground like Jell-O?"

"Sounds made up."

"And the newscaster was silent. Speechless. So the guy goes, '*You* wanted to know. You *asked*. So I'm telling you. That's what I saw.'"

"Please, Reva, just stop."

"Well, I'm not saying that would happen here."

"That didn't happen anywhere. Brains don't pop out of people's heads and jiggle."

"I guess there were aftershocks."

I turned up the volume on the radio and rolled my window down.

"You know what I mean, though? Things could be worse," Reva shouted.

"Things can always be worse," I shouted back. I rolled the window back up.

"I'm a very safe driver," Reva said.

We were quiet for the rest of the ride, the car filling with the smell of cinnamon gum. I already regretted that I'd agreed to let Reva sleep over. Finally, we crossed the bridge and drove up the FDR. The road was slushy. Traffic was very slow. By the time we got to my block, it was half past ten. We got lucky with parking, fitting into a spot right in front of the bodega.

"I just want to pick up a couple things," I told Reva. She didn't protest. Inside, the Egyptians were playing cards behind the counter. There was a display of cheap champagne set up on a stack of boxes by the cases of beer and soda. I watched Reva eye the display, then open the freezer and lean in, struggling to excavate something stuck in the ice. I got my two coffees.

Reva paid.

"Is she your sister?" the Egyptian asked Reva, nodding in my direction as I sucked down my first coffee. It was extra burnt, and the cream I'd used had soured so that squishy strands of curd got caught on my teeth. I didn't care.

"No, she's my *friend*," Reva replied with some hostility. "You think we look alike?"

"You could be sisters," said the Egyptian.

"Thank you," Reva said dryly.

When we got to my building on East Eighty-fourth, the doorman put down his newspaper to say "Happy New Year."

In the elevator, Reva said, "Those guys at the corner store, do they look at you funny?"

"Don't be racist."

Reva held my coffees while I unlocked the door. Inside my apartment, the television was on mute, flashing large bare breasts.

"I've got to pee," said Reva, dropping her gym bag. "I thought you hated porn."

I sniffed the air for traces of anything uncouth, but smelled nothing. I found a stray Silenor on the kitchen counter and swallowed it.

"Your phone is in a Tupperware container floating in the tub," Reva yelled from the bathroom.

"I know," I lied.

We sat down on the sofa, me with my second coffee and

my sample bottle of Infermiterol, Reva with her fat-free strawberry frozen yogurt. We watched the rest of the porn movie in complete silence. After a day spent meditating on death, watching people have sex felt good. "Procreation," I thought. "The circle of life." During the blow job scene, I got up and peed. During the pussy-eating scene, Reva got up and puked, I thought. Then she found a corkscrew in the kitchen, opened a bottle of the funeral wine, came back to the sofa and sat down. We passed the bottle back and forth and watched ejaculate dribble over the girl's face. Gobs of it got stuck in her fake eyelashes.

I thought of Trevor and all his drips and splats on my belly and back. When we'd had sex at his place, he'd finish and instantly rush out and back in with a roll of paper towels, hold the little trash can out for me as I wiped myself off. "These sheets . . ." Trevor never once came inside of me, not even when I was on the pill. His favorite thing was to fuck my mouth while I lay on my back pretending to be asleep, as if I wouldn't notice his penis slamming into the back of my throat.

The credits rolled. Another porn movie started. Reva found the remote and hit unmute.

I opened the sample bottle of Infermiterol and took one, washing it down with the wine.

I remember listening to the stiff dialogue of the opening—the girl played a physical therapist, the guy played a football player with a pain in his groin. Reva cried for a while. When the fucking started, she lowered the volume and told me about her New Year's the year before. "I just wasn't in the mood to go to a couples party, you know? Everybody kissing at midnight? Ken was being a dick but I met him at like three in the morning at the Howard Johnson in Times Square." I was glad to hear she was drunk now. It took some of the tension out of the room. On-screen, there was a knock on the door. The fucking didn't stop. I was weaving in and out of sleep by then. Reva kept talking.

"And so then Ken was like . . . That was the first time . . . I told my mom . . . She said to pretend it never happened . . . Am I nuts?"

"Whoa," I said, pointing at the TV screen. A black girl had entered the scene in a cheerleader's uniform. "Do you think that's his jealous girlfriend?"

"What's going on in here?" the cheerleader asked, throwing down her pom-poms.

"You know you're my only single friend?" Reva asked in response. "I wish I had a big sister," she said. "Someone who could set me up with somebody. Maybe I'll ask my dad for money to pay a matchmaker."

"No man is worth paying for," I told her.

"I'll think about it," Reva said.

I was in the fog by then, eyes open just a crack. Through

them, I watched the black girl spread the lips of her vagina with long, sharp, pink fingernails. The inside of her glistened. I thought of Whoopi Goldberg. I remember that. I remember Reva setting the empty wine bottle down on the coffee table. And I remember her saying "Happy New Year" and kissing my cheek. I felt myself float up and away, higher and higher into the ether until my body was just an anecdote, a symbol, a portrait hanging in another world.

"I love you, Reva," I heard myself say from so far away. "I'm really sorry about your mom."

Then I was gone.

Five

I WOKE UP ALONE on the sofa a few days later. The air smelled like stale smoke and perfume. The TV was on at low volume. My tongue was thick and gritty, like I had dirt in my mouth. I listened to the world weather report: floods in India, an earthquake in Guatemala, another blizzard approaching the northeastern United States, fires burning down million-dollar homes in Southern California, "but sunny skies in our nation's capital today as Yasser Arafat visits the White House for talks with President Clinton aimed at reviving the stalled peace process in the Middle East. More on that story in a minute."

I opened my eyes. The room was dim, the shades were down. As I pushed myself upright, lifting my head slowly off the arm of the sofa, the blood drained out of my brain like sand in an hourglass. My vision pixelated, moiréed, then blurred and womped back into focus. I looked down at my feet. I had on Reva's dead mother's shoes, seascapes of salt rounding across the leather toes. Nude fishnet stockings. I undid the belt of my white fur coat and found that all I was wearing underneath was a flesh-colored bustier bodysuit. I looked down at my crotch. My pubic hair had been waxed off recently. A good waxing—my skin was neither red nor bumpy nor itchy. My fingernails, I saw, were French-manicured. I could smell my own sweat. It smelled like gin. It smelled like vinegar. A stamp across my knuckles showed I'd been to a club called Dawn's Early. I'd never heard of it. I sat back and closed my eyes and tried to remember the previous night. It was all black, empty space. "Let's take a look at the snowfall forecast for the New York metro area." I opened my eyes. The meteorologist on TV looked like a black Rick Moranis. He pointed to a swirling white cartoon cloud. "Happy New Year, Reva," I remember I'd said. That was all I could recall.

The coffee table was spread over with empty ice-cube trays and a full gallon jug of distilled water and an empty half-gallon jug of Gordon's gin and a ripped-out page from a book called *The Art of Happiness*. Reva had given it to me for my birthday a few years earlier, saying I'd "get a lot out of the Dalai Lama. He's really insightful." I'd never read the book. On the torn-out page, a single line had been underlined in blue ballpoint pen: "It didn't happen overnight," it read. I deduced that I'd been crushing Xanax with the handle of a butcher knife and snorting it with a rolled-up flyer for an open mic night at a club on Hester Street called Portnoy's Porthole. I'd never heard of it. A few dozen Polaroids splattered between my videotapes and empty cases proved that my blackout activities had not gone undocumented, although I didn't see my camera anywhere.

The photos were of pretty party people—young strangers making sultry, self-serious faces. Girls in dark lipstick, boys with red pupils, some caught unawares by the loud white flash of my camera, others posing fashionably or simply raising an eyebrow or faking wide smiles. Some photos appeared to have been taken on a downtown street at night, others in a dark, low-ceilinged interior with Day-Glo fake graffiti on the walls. I didn't recognize anybody in the photos. In one, a group of six clubgoers huddled together, each holding up a middle finger. In another, a skinny redhead flashed her breasts, revealing lavender pasties. A chubby black boy in a fedora and tuxedo T-shirt blew smoke rings. Male twins dressed as heroin-thin Elvises in slouchy gold lamé suits high-fived in front of a Basquiat rip-off. There was a girl holding a rat on a leash hooked to the bicycle chain she wore around her neck. A close-up shot showed someone's pale pink tongue, split to look like a snake's and pierced on both forks with big diamond studs. There was a series of snapshots taken in what I guessed was the line for the toilet. The whole place looked like some arty rave.

"Expect road closures, hurricane force gales, coastal flooding," the weatherman was saying. I dug the remote out from between the sofa cushions and turned the TV off.

One photo had fallen under the coffee table. I picked it up and flipped it over. A small Asian man stood still and apart from the crowd at the bar. He wore blue coveralls splattered in paint. I looked closely. He had a round face and ruddy acne scars. His eyes were closed. He seemed familiar. Then I recognized him. It was Ping Xi. There was a streak of pink glitter across his cheeks. I put the photo down.

IT HAD BEEN MONTHS since I'd even thought of Ping Xi. Whenever Ducat had popped into my mind, I'd tried to winnow my focus down to the simple memory of the long walk to the Eighty-sixth Street subway station, the express train to Union Square, the L train across town, the walk up Eighth Avenue and left on Twenty-third Street, the hobble over the old cobblestones in my high heels. Remembering the geography of Manhattan seemed worth hanging on to. But I would have preferred to forget the names and details of the people I'd met in Chelsea. The art world had turned out to be like the stock market, a reflection of political trends and the persuasions of capitalism, fueled by greed and gossip and cocaine. I might as well have worked on Wall Street. Speculation and opinions drove not only the market but the products, sadly, the values of which were hinged not to the ineffable quality of art as a sacred human ritual—a value impossible to measure, anyway—but to what a bunch of rich assholes thought would "elevate" their portfolios and inspire jealousy and, delusional as they all were, respect. I was perfectly happy to wipe out all that garbage from my mind.

I'd never been to the kind of party in the Polaroid photos, but I'd seen it from afar: young and beautiful and fascinating people hailing cabs and flicking cigarettes, cocaine, mascara, the diamond grit of a night out on the town, random sex a simple gesture in a bathroom stall, wading once onto the dance floor then back out again, screaming drink orders at the bar, everyone pushing toward the ecstasy of the dream of tomorrow, where they'd have more fun, feel more beautiful, be surrounded by more interesting people. I'd always preferred a septic hotel bar, maybe because that's where Trevor liked to take me. He and I agreed that people looked stupid when they were "having a good time."

The interns at the gallery had told me about their weekends out at Tunnel and Life and Sound Factory and Spa and Lotus and Centro-Fly and Luke + Leroy. So I had some sense of what went on in the city at night. And as Natasha's assistant, I'd been responsible for keeping a list of some of the most socially valuable people at an art party—specifically the young impresarios and their attendants. She invited them to openings and told me to study their bios. Maggie Kahpour's father had owned the largest private collection of Picasso doodles in the world, and when he died, she donated them to an abbey in the south of France. The monks named a cheese after her. Gwen Elbaz-Burke was the grandniece of Ken Burke, the performance artist who was eaten by the shark he kept in his swimming pool, and the daughter of Zara Ali Elbaz, a Syrian princess who was exiled for making a pornographic art film with her German boyfriend, a descendant of Heinrich Himmler. Stacey Bloom had started a magazine called *Kun(s)t* about "women in the arts," mostly profiles of rich art-party girls who were starting their own fashion lines or opening galleries or nightclubs or starring in indie movies. Her father was the president of Citibank. Zaza Nakazawa was a nineteen-year-old heiress who had written a book about being in a sexual relationship with her aunt, the painter Elaine Meeks. Eugenie Pratt was the half sister of the documentary filmmaker and architect Emilio Wolford who famously made her eat a raw lamb's heart on camera when she was twelve. There was Claudia Martini-Richards. Jane Swarovski-Kahn. Pepper Jacobin-Sills. Kylie Jensen. Nell "Nikita" Patrick. Patsy

Weinberger. Maybe these were the girls in the photos. I wouldn't have recognized them outside the gallery. Imogene Behrman. Odette Quincy Adams. Kitty Cavalli. I remembered their names. Dawn's Early must have been some new after-hours club for the next generation of rich kids and art hags if Ping Xi was hanging out there, presumably among his devotees. I vaguely remembered Natasha saying he'd gone to boarding school with a set of gay royal twins from Prussia. But how had I found him? Or had he found me?

I collected the photos and stuffed them under the sofa cushion, then got up to peek into my bedroom to make sure nobody was there. All my bedding was in a heap on the floor, the mattress bare. I stepped closer to make sure there was no human-sized bloodstain, nobody wrapped up in the sheets, no corpse tucked under the bed. I opened the closet and found nobody bound and gagged. Just the little plastic Baggies of Victoria's Secret lingerie spilled out. Nothing was amiss. I was alone.

Back in the living room, my phone was dead on the windowsill next to a single sneaker I'd used as an ashtray. I snagged down a slat in the blinds to look out the window. The snow was already beginning to fall. That was good, I thought—I'd stay home through the blizzard and get some hard sleeping done. I'd return to my old rhythm, my daily rituals. I needed the stability of my familiar routine. And I wouldn't take any more Infermiterol, at least for a while. It was working against my goal of doing nothing. I plugged my phone in to charge and threw the sneaker away in the kitchen. The trash was filled with the brittle peels of clementines and cloudy plastic packaging from single-serving slices of cheese, which I couldn't remember buying or eating. The fridge contained only the small, light wood crate the clementines came in, and a second gallon jug of distilled water.

I took off the white fur and the bustier and the fishnets and went to the bathroom to run the hot water in the shower. My toenails were painted lilac, my previously flaky calloused soles now smooth and soft. I used the toilet and watched a vein throb in my thigh. What had I done? Spent a spa day then gone out clubbing? It seemed preposterous. Had Reva convinced me to go "enjoy myself" or something just as idiotic? I peed, and when I wiped myself, it was slick. I had recently been aroused, it seemed. Who had aroused me? I remembered nothing. A wave of nausea made me lurch over and regurgitate an acrid globule of phlegm, which I spat into the sink. From the sandy feel of my mouth, I was expecting to see granules of dirt or the grit of a crushed pill speckling my saliva. Instead, it was pink glitter.

I opened the medicine cabinet and took two Valiums and two Ativans, guzzled water from the tap. When I righted myself, someone appeared in the mirror as if through a porthole window, and it startled me. My own startled face startled me. Mascara had streaked down my cheeks like a masquerade mask. Remnants of bright pink lipstick stained the outer edges and corners of my lips. I brushed my teeth and tried my best to scrub the makeup off. I looked in the mirror again. Wrinkles in my forehead and lines around my mouth looked like they'd been drawn in pencil. My cheeks were slack. My skin was pale. Something flashed in the gloss of my eyeballs. I got close up to the mirror and looked very carefully. There I was, a tiny dark reflection of myself deep down in my right pupil. Someone said once that pupils were just empty space, black holes, twin caves of infinite nothingness. "When something disappears, that's usually where it disappears—into the black holes in our eyes." I couldn't remember who had said it. I watched my reflection disappear in the steam.

IN THE SHOWER, a memory returned from middle school: a cop who visited our seventh grade class to warn us about the dangers of drug use. He hung up a chart depicting every illicit drug in Western civilization and pointed at the little sample pictures one by one—a pile of white powder, cloudy yellow crystals, blue pills, pink pills, yellow pills, black tar. Under each was the drug's name and nicknames. Heroin: smack, dope, horse, skag, junk, H, hero, white stuff, boy, chiva, black pearl, brown sugar. "This feels like this. That feels like that." The cop had some kind of disorder that made it hard for him to moderate the volume of his own voice. "Cocaine! Metham-phetamine! Psilocybin! PCP!" he shouted, then suddenly low-ered his voice to point at Rohypnol. "Forget-me pills, lunch money, Mexican Valium, mind eraser, rib, roach, roofies, trip-and-falls, wolfies . . ." He was almost inaudible. And then he was screaming again. "This is why you don't accept drinks from strangers! Girls! Never leave a friend alone at a party! The upside is that the victim forgets!" He stopped to catch his breath. He was a sweaty blonde with a V-shaped build like Superman. "But it isn't addictive," he said casually, then turned back to the chart.

So my memory seemed to be intact insofar as I could re-call with pristine clarity this moment from my adolescence, but I had no recall of what had happened under the influence of Infermiterol. Were there other holes in my memory? I hoped there might be. I tested myself: Who signed the Magna Carta? How tall is the Statue of Liberty? When was the Naz-arene Movement? Who shot Andy Warhol? The questions alone proved that my mind was still pretty sound. I knew my social security number. Bill Clinton was president, but not for much longer. In fact, my mind felt sharper, the pathways of my thoughts more direct than before. I could remember things I hadn't thought of in years: I could remember the time senior year of college when my heel broke on the way to Feminist Theories and Art Practices, 1960s–1990s, and I walked in late, limping and disgruntled, and the professor pointed at me and said, "We were just discussing feminist performance art as a political deconstruction of the art world as a commercial industry," and told me to stand at the front of the classroom, which I did, my left foot arched like a Barbie's, and the class analyzed it as a performance piece.

"I can't get past the context of the art history classroom," a Barnard girl said.

"There are so many conflicting layers of meaning here, it's wonderful," said the bearded TA.

And then, simply to humiliate me, the professor, a woman with long waxy hair and crude silver jewelry, asked me how much I'd paid for my shoes. They were black suede stiletto boots, and they'd cost almost five hundred dollars, one of many purchases I'd made to mitigate the pain of having lost my parents, or whatever it was I was feeling. I could remember all of this, each sniveling, pouty face in that classroom. One idiot said I was "broken by the male gaze." I remembered the tick of the clock as they stared. "I guess that's enough," said the professor, finally. I was permitted to take my seat. Out the window of the classroom, flat, wide yellow leaves fell from a single tree onto gray concrete. I dropped the class, had to explain to my adviser that I wanted to focus more on Neoclassicism, and switched to "Jacques-Louis David: Art, Virtue, and Revolution." *The Death of Marat* was one of my favorite paintings. A man stabbed to death in the bathtub.

I got out of the shower, took an Ambien and two Benadryl, wrapped a mildewed towel around my shoulders, and went back out into the living room to check my phone, which had charged sufficiently for me to turn it on. When I looked through my call history, the numbers I had dialed were Trevor's and an unidentified 646 number, which I had to assume was Ping Xi's. I deleted the number and took a Risperdal, pulled a gray cable-knit sweater and pair of leggings out of a pile of dirty laundry in the hallway, put the fur coat back on, stuck my feet into slippers, and looked for my keys. I found them still stuck in the lock on the door.

IT WAS MIDAFTERNOON, I gathered, from the clouds drifting overhead like crumpled bedsheets. In the lobby, I ignored the doorman's cautious salutation about the storm and shuffled out and down the disappearing path snaking between the banks of snow piled high on the sidewalk and over the curb. Everything was hushed, but the air was angry and wet. Any more snow and the whole city would be covered. I passed a twitching, sweater-clad Pomeranian and its nanny on the corner, watched it lift its leg and piss on a flat, glassy plane of ice on the pavement, heard the singe of the hot stuff melting through, steam spreading in a contained bubble for a moment, then dissipating.

The Egyptians extended no special greeting when I walked into the bodega. They just nodded as usual and went back to their cell phones. That was a good sign, I thought. Whatever I'd done on the Infermiterol, whomever I'd cavorted with or how hard I'd "partied," I hadn't behaved so badly at the bodega at least to solicit any special attention. I hadn't shit where I ate, as the saying goes. I got cash out of the ATM, poured my two coffees and stirred in the cream and sugar, then picked out a slice of prepackaged banana bread, a cup of organic yogurt, and a rock hard pear. Three Brearley girls in tracksuits formed a line at the counter. I glanced at the newspapers while I waited to pay. Nothing earth shattering was going on, it seemed. Strom Thurmond gave Hillary Clinton a hug. A pack of wolves was spotted in Washington Heights. Nigerians smuggled into Libya might one day be washing dishes at your favorite downtown bistro. Giuliani said cursing at a cop should be a crime. It was January 3, 2001.

In the elevator back up to my apartment, I thought up combinations of pills that I hoped would put me out—Ambien plus Placidyl plus Theraflu. Solfoton plus Ambien plus Dimetapp. I wanted a cocktail that would arrest my imagination and put me into a deep, boring, inert sleep. I needed to dispose of those photographs. Nembutal plus Ativan plus Benadryl. At home, I took a good helping of the latter, washing the pills down with the second coffee. Then I ate a handful of melatonin and the yogurt, and watched *The Player* and *Soapdish,* but I couldn't sleep. I was distracted by the Polaroids under the couch cushions. I put in *Presumed Innocent,* hit rewind, pulled the Polaroids out, and took them and sent them down the garbage chute. That was better, I thought, and went back in and sat down.

Night was falling. I felt tired, heavy, but not exactly sleepy. So I took another Nembutal, watched *Presumed Innocent,* then took a few Lunestas and drank the second bottle of funeral wine, but somehow the alcohol undid the sleeping pills, and I felt even more awake than before. Then I had to vomit, and did so. I had drunk too much. I lay back down on the sofa. Then I was hungry, so I ate the banana bread and watched *Frantic* three times in a row, taking a few Ativan every thirty minutes or so. But I still couldn't sleep. I watched *Schindler's List,* which I hoped would depress me, but it only irritated me, and then the sun came up, so I took some Lamictal and watched *The Last of the Mohicans* and *Patriot Games,* but that had no effect either, so I took a few Placidyl and put *The Player* back in. When it was over, I checked the digital clock on the VCR. It was noon.

I ordered Pad See Ew from the Thai place, ate half of it,

watched the 1995 remake of *Sabrina* starring Harrison Ford, took another shower, downed the last of my Ambien, and found the porn channel again. I turned the volume down low, shifted my body away from the screen so that the grunts and moans could lull me. Still, I didn't sleep. Life could go on forever like this, I thought. Life would, if I didn't take action. I fingered myself on the sofa under the blanket, came twice, then turned the TV off. I got up and raised the blinds and sat in a daze for a while and watched the sun go down—was it possible?—then I rewound *Sabrina* and watched it again and ate the rest of the Pad See Ew. I watched *Driving Miss Daisy* and *Sling Blade*. I took a Nembutal and drank half a bottle of Robitussin. I watched *The World According to Garp* and *Stargate* and *A Nightmare on Elm Street 3: Dream Warriors* and *Moonstruck* and *Flashdance,* then *Dirty Dancing* and *Ghost,* then *Pretty Woman.*

Not even a yawn. I wasn't remotely sleepy. I could tell my sense of balance was off—I nearly fell over when I tried to stand up, but I pushed through it and tidied up for a while, sliding the videocassettes into their cases and putting them back on the shelf. I thought some activity might tire me out. I took a Zyprexa and some more Ativan. I ate a handful of melatonin, chewing like a cow on cud. Nothing was working.

So I called Trevor.

"It's five in the morning," he said. He sounded irritated

and foggy, but he'd answered. My number must have shown up on his caller ID, and he'd answered.

"I've been sexually assaulted," I lied. I hadn't said anything aloud in days by then. My voice had a sexy rasp. I felt like I might vomit again. "Can you come over? I need you to come look to see if there are any tears in my vagina. You're the only one I trust," I said. "Please?"

"Who is it?" I heard a woman's voice murmuring in the distance.

"Nobody," Trevor said to her. Then, "Wrong number," he said to me and hung up.

I took three Solfoton and six Benadryl, put *Frantic* in to rewind, cracked the window in the living room to circulate the air, found the blizzard was howling outside, and then I remembered that I'd bought cigarettes, so I smoked one out the window, pressed "play" on the VCR, and lay back down on the sofa. I felt my head get heavy. Harrison Ford was my dream man. My heart slowed, but still, I couldn't sleep. I drank from the jug of gin. It seemed to settle my stomach.

At eight A.M., I called Trevor again. This time he didn't answer.

"Just checking in," I said in my message. "It's been a while. Curious how you've been and what you've been up to. Let's catch up soon."

I called again fifteen minutes later.

"Look, I don't know how to say this. I'm HIV positive. I probably got it from one of the black guys at the gym."

At eight thirty, I called and said, "I've been thinking I might get a boob job, just take them clean off. What do you think? Could I pull off the flat-chested look?"

At eight forty-five, I called and said, "I need some financial advice. Actually, I'm serious. I'm in a bind."

At nine o'clock, I called again. He answered.

"What do you want?" he asked.

"I was hoping to hear you say you miss me."

"I miss you," he said. "Is that it?"

I hung up.

I'D INHERITED the complete VHS set of *Star Trek: The Next Generation* from my father. Ordering those cassettes was probably the one time in my father's life that he'd dialed a 1-800 number. Watching *Star Trek* as an adolescent was when I first came to regard Whoopi Goldberg with the reverence she deserves. Whoopi seemed like an absurd interloper on the U.S.S. *Enterprise.* Whenever she appeared on-screen, I sensed she was laughing at the whole production. Her presence made the show completely absurd. That was true of all her movies, too. Whoopi in her nun's habit. Whoopi dressed like a church-going Georgian in the 1930s with her Sunday hat and Bible.

Whoopi in *Moonlight and Valentino* alongside the pasty Elizabeth Perkins. Wherever she went, everything around her became a parody of itself, gauche and ridiculous. That was a comfort to see. Thank God for Whoopi. Nothing was sacred. Whoopi was proof.

After a few episodes, I got up and took a few Nembutals and a Placidyl and guzzled another half a bottle of children's Robitussin and sat down to watch Whoopi—in a cornflower blue velour tunic and an upside-down cone-shaped hat like a futuristic bishop—have a heart-to-heart talk with Marina Sirtis. It was all nonsense. But I couldn't sleep. I kept watching. I went through three seasons. I took Solfoton. I took Ambien. I even made myself a cup of chamomile tea, the nauseating sweet smell wafting up from my chipped coffee cup like a hot diaper. This was supposed to be relaxing? I took a bath and put on a brand new set of slippery satin pajamas I found in the closet. Still I wasn't sleepy. Nothing was working. I thought I'd watch *Braveheart* again so I put it into the VCR and pressed "rewind."

And then the VCR broke.

I heard the wheels spin, then whine, then screech, then stop. I hit "eject" and nothing happened. I poked at all the buttons. I unplugged and replugged the machine. I picked it up and shook it. I banged on it with the butt of my hand, then a shoe. Nothing was working. Outside, it was dark. My phone said it was January 6, 11:52 P.M.

So now I was stuck with TV. I surfed the channels. A commercial for cat food. A commercial for home saunas. A commercial for low-fat butter. Fabric softener. Potato chips in individually portioned packages. Chocolate yogurt. Go to Greece, the birthplace of civilization. Drinks that give you energy. Face cream that makes you younger. Fish for your kitties. Coca-Cola means "I love you." Sleep in the most comfortable bed in the world. Ice cream is not just for children, ladies: your husbands like it, too! If your house smells like shit, light this candle that smells like freshly baked brownies.

My mother used to say that if I couldn't sleep I should count something that matters, anything but sheep. Count stars. Count Mercedes-Benzes. Count U.S. presidents. Count the years you have left to live. I might jump out the window, I thought, if I couldn't sleep. I pulled the blanket up to my chest. I counted state capitals. I counted different kinds of flowers. I counted shades of blue. Cerulean. Cadet. Electric. Teal. Tiffany. Egyptian. Persian. Oxford. I didn't sleep. I wouldn't sleep. I couldn't. I counted as many kinds of birds as I could think of. I counted TV shows from the eighties. I counted movies set in New York City. I counted famous people who committed suicide: Diane Arbus, the Hemingways,

Marilyn Monroe, Sylvia Plath, van Gogh, Virginia Woolf. Poor Kurt Cobain. I counted the times I'd cried since my parents died. I counted the seconds passing. Time could go on forever like this, I thought again. Time would. Infinity loomed consistently and all at once, forever, with or without me. Amen.

I pulled the blanket off me. On TV, a young couple spelunking in a cave in New Zealand lowered themselves down into a huge black crevasse, shimmied through a narrow crack in the stone, passed under a field of what looked like huge boogers dripping from the ceiling, and then entered a room illuminated by glowing blue worms. I tried to imagine something stupid Reva would have said to try to soothe me, but nothing came to mind. I was so tired. I truly believed I might never sleep again. So my throat clenched. I cried. I did it. My breath sputtered like from a scraped knee on the playground. It was so stupid. I counted down from a thousand and flicked the tears off my cheeks with my fingers. My muscles ticked like a car that's been driven a long distance and is left parked in the shade.

I changed the channel. It was a British nature show. A small white fox burrowed down into the snow on a blinding sunny day. "While many mammals hibernate during the winter, the arctic fox does not. With special fur and fat covering her stocky body, low temperatures are not going to slow down this little fox! Its tremendous tolerance for cold climes is thanks to an extraordinary metabolism. It only starts to increase at negative fifty degrees Centigrade. That means she doesn't even shiver before temps drop to negative seventy degrees and below. Wow."

I counted furs: mink, chinchilla, sable, rabbit, muskrat, raccoon, ermine, skunk, possum. Reva had taken her mother's beaver fur coat. It had a boxy cut and made me think of a gunslinging outlaw hiding out in a snow-filled forest, then taking off west along the train tracks by moonlight, his beaver fur keeping him warm against the biting wind. The image impressed me. It was unusual. I was being creative. Maybe I was dreaming, I thought. I pictured the man in the beaver fur rolling up the ankles of his worn-out trousers to cross an ice-cold brook, his feet so white, like fish in the water. There, I thought. A dream is starting. My eyes were closed. I felt myself begin to drift.

And then, as though she'd timed it, as though she'd heard my thoughts, Reva was banging on my door. I opened my eyes. Slivers of white, snowy light striped the bare floor. It felt like the crack of dawn.

"Hello? It's me, Reva."

Had I slept at all?

"Let me in."

I got up slowly and made my way down the hall.

"I'm *sleeping*," I hissed through the door. I squinted into the peephole: Reva looked bedraggled and deranged.

"Can I come in?" she asked. "I really need to talk."

"Can I just call you later? What time is it?"

"One fifteen. I tried calling," she said. "Here, the door-man sent up your mail. I need to talk. It's serious."

Maybe Reva had been involved somehow in my Infermiterol escapade downtown. Maybe she had some privileged information about what I'd done. Did I care? I did, a little. I unlocked the door and let her in. She wore, as I'd imagined, her mother's huge beaver coat.

"Nice sweater," she said, slicking past me into the apartment, a whiff of cold and mothballs. "Gray is in for spring."

"It's still January, right?" I asked, still paralyzed in the hallway. I waited for Reva to confirm but she just dumped the armful of mail on the dining table, then took off her coat and draped it over the back of the sofa next to my fox fur. Two pelts. I thought of Ping Xi's dead dogs again. A memory arose from one of my last days at Ducat: a rich gay Brazilian petting the stuffed poodle and telling Natasha he wanted "a coat just like this, with a hood." My head hurt.

"I'm thirsty," I said, but it came out like I was just clearing my throat.

"Huh?"

The floor shifted slightly beneath my feet. I felt my way into the living room, my hand skimming the cool wall. Reva had made herself comfortable in the armchair already. I steadied myself, hands free, before staggering toward the sofa.

"Well, it's over," Reva said, "It's officially over."

"What is?"

"With Ken!" Her bottom lip trembled. She crooked her finger under her nose, held her breath, then got up and came toward me, cornering me against the end of the sofa. I couldn't move. I felt slightly ill watching her face turn red from lack of oxygen, holding in her sobs, then realized that I was holding my breath, too. I gasped, and Reva, mistaking this for an exclamation of compassionate woe, put her arms around me. She smelled like shampoo and perfume. She smelled like tequila. She smelled vaguely of French fries. She held me and shook and cried and snotted for a good minute.

"You're so skinny," she said, between her sniffles. "No fair."

"I need to sit down," I told her. "Get off." She let me go.

"Sorry," she said and went into the bathroom to blow her nose. I lay down and turned to face the back of the sofa, snuggled against the fox and beaver furs. Maybe I could sleep now, I thought. I closed my eyes. I pictured the fox and the beaver, cozied up together in a little cave near a waterfall, the beaver's buckteeth, its raspy snore, the perfect animal avatar for Reva.

And me, the little white fox splayed out on its back, a bubble-gum pink tongue lolling out of its pristine, furry snout, impervious to the cold. I heard the toilet flush.

"You're out of toilet paper," Reva said, rupturing the vision. I'd been wiping myself with napkins from the bodega for weeks—she must have realized that before. "I could really use a drink," she huffed. Her heels clacked on the tile in the kitchen. "I'm sorry to come over like this. I'm such a mess right now."

"What is it, Reva?" I groaned. "Spit it out. I'm not feeling well."

I heard her open and close a few cabinets. Then she came back with a mug and sat down in the armchair and poured herself a cupful of gin. She wasn't crying anymore. She sighed once morosely, and then once again violently, and drank.

"Ken got me transferred. And he says he doesn't want to see me anymore. So that's it. After all this time. I've had such a day, I can't even tell you." But there she was, telling me. Five whole minutes spent on what it was like to come back from lunch and find a note on her desk. "Like you can break up with someone over memo. Like he doesn't care about me at all. Like I'm some kind of secretary. Like this is a matter of business. Which it is not!"

"Then what was it, Reva?"

"A matter of the heart!"

"Oh."

"So I go in and he's like, 'Leave the door open,' and my heart is pounding because, you know? A memo? So I just close the door and I'm like, 'What is this? How can you do this?' And he's like, 'It's over. I can't see you anymore.' Like in a movie!"

"What did the memo say?"

"That I'm getting a promotion, and they're transferring me to the Towers. On my first day back to work after my mom died. Ken was *at* the funeral. He *saw* the state I was in. And now suddenly it's over? Just like that?"

"You're getting a promotion?"

"Marsh is starting a new crisis consulting firm. Terrorist risks, blah blah. But did you hear what I said? He doesn't want to *see* me anymore, not even at the office."

"What a dick," I said robotically.

"I know. He's a coward. I mean, we were in *love*. Totally in love!"

"You were?"

"How do you just decide to turn that off?"

I kept my eyes closed. Reva went on without any breaks, repeating the story six or seven times, each version highlighting a new aspect of the experience and analyzing it accordingly. I tried to disengage from her words and just listen to the drone of her voice. I had to admit that it was a comfort to have

Reva there. She was just as good as a VCR, I thought. The ca-
dence of her speech was as familiar and predictable as the
audio from any movie I'd watched a hundred times. That's
why I'd held on to her this long, I thought as I lay there, not
listening. Since I'd known her, the drone of what-ifs, the
seemingly endless descriptions of her delusional romantic
projections had become a kind of lullaby. Reva was a magnet
for my angst. She sucked it right out of me. I was a Zen Bud-
dhist monk when she was around. I was above fear, above
desire, above worldly concerns in general. I could live in the
now in her company. I had no past or present. No thoughts. I
was too evolved for all her jibber-jabber. And too cool. Reva
could get angry, impassioned, depressed, ecstatic. I wouldn't.
I refused to. I would feel nothing, be a blank slate. Trevor had
told me once he thought I was frigid, and that was fine with
me. Fine. Let me be a cold bitch. Let me be the ice queen.
Someone once said that when you die of hypothermia, you get
cold and sleepy, things slow down, and then you just drift
away. You don't feel a thing. That sounded nice. That was the
best way to die—awake and dreaming, feeling nothing. I
could take the train to Coney Island, I thought, walk along
the beach in the freezing wind, and swim out into the ocean.
Then I'd just float on my back looking up at the stars, go
numb, get sleepy, drift, drift. Isn't it only fair that I should get
to choose how I'll die? I wouldn't die like my father did,

passive and quiet while the cancer ate him alive. At least my mother did things her own way. I'd never thought to admire her before for that. At least she had guts. At least she took matters into her own hands.

I opened my eyes. There was a spiderweb in the corner of the ceiling, fluttering like a scrap of moth-eaten silk in the draft. I tuned in to Reva for a moment. Her words cleansed the palette of my mind. Thank God for her, I thought, my whiny, moronic analgesic.

"So then I was like, 'I'm tired of you jerking me around.' And he starts talking about how he's my boss. All macho, right? And actually evading the real issue which is the thing I told you about, which I can't even think about right now." I had no memory of her telling me anything. The sound of more gin. "I mean, I'm not keeping it. Obviously. Especially not now! But no. Ken can't be bothered about that. Being evasive is totally his *thing*."

I turned around and peeked at her.

"If he thinks he can get rid of me so easily . . . ," she said, wagging her finger. "If he thinks he's gonna get away with this . . ."

"What, Reva? What are you going to do to him? Are you going to kill him? You're going to burn his house down?"

"If he thinks I'm just going to eat his shit and slink away . . ."

She couldn't finish her sentence. She had no threats to make. She was too afraid of her own rage to ever imagine it through to any violent end. She would never exact revenge. So I suggested, "Tell his wife he's been fucking you. Or sue him for sexual harassment."

Reva wrinkled her nose and sucked her teeth, her rage suddenly transformed into calculated pragmatism. "I don't want people to know, though. That puts me in such an awkward position. And I *am* getting a raise, so that's good. Plus, I've always wanted to work in the World Trade Center. So it's not like I can complain exactly. I just want Ken to feel bad."

"Men don't feel bad the way you want them to," I told her. "They just get grouchy and depressed when they can't have what they want. That's why you got fired. You're depressing. Consider it a compliment, if you want."

"Transferred, not fired." Reva set her mug down on the coffee table and lifted her hands up in front of her face. "Look, I'm shaking."

"I don't see it," I said.

"There's a tremor. I can feel it."

"Do you want a Xanax?" I asked sarcastically.

To my surprise, Reva said yes. I told her to bring me the bottle from the medicine cabinet. She clacked back and forth to the bathroom and handed me the bottle.

"There must be twenty prescriptions in there," she said. "Are you on all of them?"

I gave Reva one Xanax. I took two.

"I'm just going to lie here with my eyes closed, Reva. You can stay if you want, but I might fall asleep. I'm really tired."

"Yeah, OK," she said. "But can I keep talking, though?"

"Sure."

"Can I have a cigarette?"

I waved my hand. I'd never seen Reva so shamelessly unbridled. Even when she drank a lot, she was extremely uptight. I heard her spark the lighter. She coughed for a while.

"Maybe it's for the best," she said. She sounded calmer now. "Maybe I can move on and meet somebody new. Maybe I'll go online again. Or maybe there'll be someone at the downtown office. I kind of like the Twin Towers. It's peaceful up there. And I think if I start things off on the right foot, with a whole new group of people, they won't treat me like a slave. Nobody ever listened to me at Ken's office. We'd have these strategy meetings, and instead of letting me speak, they'd make me take notes like I'm some nineteen-year-old intern. And Ken treated me like shit at work because he didn't want people to know we're involved. *Were* involved. Isn't it kind of weird that he brought his wife to my mother's funeral? Who does that? What was that about?"

"He's an idiot, Reva," I mumbled into my pillow.

"Whatever. Everything's going to be different now," Reva said, putting out her cigarette in the mug. "I had a feeling this was going to happen. I told him I loved him, you know? Of course that would be the straw that broke the camel's back. What a pussy."

"Maybe you'll run into Trevor."

"Where?"

"At the World Trade Center."

"I don't even know what he looks like."

"He looks like any other corporate asshole."

"Do you still love him?"

"Gross, Reva."

"Do you think he still loves you?"

"I don't know."

"Do you wish he did?"

The answer was yes, but only so that he would feel the pain of me rejecting him.

"And did I tell you my dad's been having an affair?" Reva said. "Some client of his named *Barbara*. A divorcée with no kids. He's taking her to Boca. Apparently he went in on a timeshare there. He'd been planning it for months. Now I know why he was being so cheap. Cremation? And Florida? Mom dies and suddenly he likes warm weather? I don't understand him. I wish he had died and not her."

"Just wait," I said.

"Can I have another Xanax?" Reva asked.

"I can't spare another, Reva. Sorry."

She was quiet for a while. The air got tense.

"The only thing I can think to do to make Ken pay for the way he's jerked me around is to keep it. But I won't. Anyway, thanks for listening." She leaned over me on the sofa, kissed my cheek, said, "I *love* you," and left.

So I gathered that Reva was pregnant. I lay on the sofa contemplating that for a while. There was a tiny, living creature in her womb. The product of an accident. A side effect of delusion and sloppiness. I felt sorry for it, all alone, floating in the fluid of Reva's womb, which I imagined to be full of diet soda, constantly jostled around in her hysterical aerobic workouts and pinched and prodded as she tensed her torso furiously in her Pilates classes. Maybe she *should* keep the baby, I thought. Maybe a baby would wake her up.

I got up and took a Solfoton and a Xanax. Now more than ever, a movie would have helped me relax. I turned the TV on—ABC7 news—and off. I didn't want to hear about a shooting in the Bronx, a gas explosion on the Lower East Side, police cracking down on high school kids jumping the turnstiles in the subway, ice sculptures defaced at Columbus Circle. I got up and took another Nembutal.

I called Trevor again.

"It's me," is all he let me say before he started talking. It was the same speech he'd given me a dozen times: he's involved now and can't see me anymore.

"Not even as just friends," he said. "Claudia doesn't believe in platonic relationships between the sexes, and I'm starting to see that she's right. And she's going through a divorce, so it's a sensitive time. And I really like this woman. She's incredible. Her son is *autistic.*"

"I was just calling to ask if I could borrow some money," I told him. "My VCR just broke. And I'm horny."

I knew I sounded crazy. I could picture Trevor leaning back in his chair, loosening his tie, cock twitching in his lap despite his better judgment. I heard him sigh. "You need money? That's why you're calling?"

"I'm sick and can't leave my apartment. Can you buy me a new VCR and bring it over? I really need it. I'm on all this medication. I can barely make it to the corner. I can hardly get out of bed." I knew Trevor. He couldn't resist me when I was weak. That was the fascinating irony about him. Most men were turned off by neediness, but in Trevor, lust and pity went hand in hand.

"Look, I can't deal with you now. I've got to go," he said and hung up.

That was fair. He could keep his flabby old vagina lady and her retarded kid. I knew how this new affair would play out for him. He'd win her over with a few months of honorable declarations—"I want to be there for you. Please, lean on me. I *love* you!"—but when something actually difficult happened—her ex-husband sued her for custody, for example—Trevor would start to have doubts. "You're asking me to sacrifice my own needs for yours—don't you see how selfish that is?" They'd argue. He'd bolt. He might even call me to apologize for "being cold on the phone the last time we talked. I was under a lot of pressure at the time. I hope we can move past it. Your friendship means a lot to me. I'd hate to lose you." If he didn't come over now, I thought, it was just a matter of days. I got up and took a few trazodones and lay back down.

I called Trevor again. This time when he answered, I didn't let him say a word.

"If you're not over here fucking me in the next forty-five minutes then you can call an ambulance because I'll be here bleeding to death and I'm not gonna slit my wrists in the tub like a normal person. If you're not here in forty-five minutes, I'm gonna slit my throat right here on the sofa. And in the meantime, I'm going to call my lawyer and tell him I'm leaving everything in the apartment to you, especially the sofa. So you can lean on Claudia or whoever when it comes time to deal with all that. She might know a good upholsterer."

I hung up. I felt better. I called down to the doorman.

"My friend Trevor is on his way. Let him up when he gets here." I unlocked the door to my apartment, turned off my phone and sealed it in Tupperware with packing tape and slid it into the depths of the highest shelf in the cabinet over the sink. I took a few more Ambien, ate the pear, watched a commercial for ExxonMobil and tried not to think of Trevor.

While I waited, I ticked open a slat in the blinds and saw that it was the dead of night, black and cold and icy, and I thought of all the cruel people out there sleeping soundly, like newborn babes in blankets held to the bosoms of their loving mothers, and thought of my mother's bony clavicles, the white lace of her bras and white lace of her silk camisoles and slip dresses that she wore under everything, and the white of her terry-cloth robe hanging on the back of her bathroom door, thick and luxurious like the ones at nice hotels, and the gray satin dressing gown whose belt slipped out of its loops because it was slippery silk satin, and it rippled like the water in a river in a Japanese painting, my mother's taut, pale legs flashing like the white bellies of sun-flashed koi, their fanlike tails stirring the silt and clouding the pond water like a puff of smoke in a magic show, and my mother's powdered foundation, how when she dipped her fat, rounded brush in it, then lifted it to her wan, sallow face shiny with moisturizer, it also made a puff of smoke, and I remembered watching her "put her face on," as she called it, and wondering if one day I'd be like her, a beautiful fish in a man-made pool, circling and circling, surviving the tedium only because my memory can contain only what is imprinted on the last few minutes of my life, constantly forgetting my thoughts.

For a moment, a life like that didn't sound bad at all, so I got up off the sofa and took an Infermiterol, brushed my teeth, went into my room, took off all my clothes, got into bed, pulled the duvet up over my head, and woke up sometime later—a few days, I guessed—gagging and coughing, Trevor's testicles swinging in my face. "Jesus Christ," he was mumbling. I was still adrift, dizzy. I closed my eyes and kept them closed, heard the crackling of his hand jerking his spit-covered penis, then felt him ejaculate on my breasts. A drop slid down a ridge between my ribs. I turned away, felt him sit on the edge of the bed, listened to his breathing.

"I should go," he said after a minute. "I've been here too long again. Claudia will start to worry."

I tried to lift my hand to give him the finger, but I couldn't. I tried to speak but I groaned instead.

"VCRs are going to be obsolete in a year or two, you know," he said. Then I heard him in the bathroom, the clink of the seat hitting the tank, a spattering of piss, a flush, then a long rush of water at the sink. He was probably washing off his dick. He came back in and got dressed, then lay down behind me on the bed, spooned me for about twenty seconds.

His hands were cold on my breasts, his breath hot on my neck. "This was the last time," he said, as though he'd been put out, as though he'd done me some huge favor. Then he lurched up off the bed, making my body bounce like a buoy on an empty sea. I heard the door slam.

I got up, pulled on some clothes, took a few Advil, and dragged the duvet from the bedroom to the sofa. There on the coffee table was a DVD player, still in its box. The sight of it disgusted me, the receipt tucked under the lid. Paid in cash. Trevor would have known I didn't own any DVDs.

I put on the Home Shopping Network. In a haze, I ordered a rice cooker from the Wolfgang Puck Bistro Collection, a cubic zirconia tennis bracelet, two push-up bras with silicone inserts, and seven hand-painted porcelain figurines of sleeping babies. I'd give them to Reva, I reasoned, to *condole* her. Finally, exhausted, I drifted off just a centimeter from my mind, and spent the night on the sofa in fitful half sleep, my bones digging hard into the sagging cushions, my throat itchy and sore, my heart racing and slowing at intervals, my eyes flicking open now and then to make sure I was really alone in the room.

Six

IN THE MORNING, I called Dr. Tuttle.

"I'm having an insomnia flare-up," I said, which was finally true.

"I can hear it in your voice," she said.

"I'm low on Ambien."

"Well, *that's* no good. Excuse me while I put the phone down for a moment." I heard the whoosh of a toilet, some gutteral grunting that I assumed was the sound Dr. Tuttle made when she hoisted up her pantyhose, then a tinkle of water in the sink. She got back on the phone and coughed. "I don't care what the FDA has to say: a nightmare is just an invitation to rewire your neurocircuits. It's really a matter of listening to your instincts. People would be so much more at ease if they acted on impulse rather than reason. That's why drugs are so effective in curing mental illness—because they impair our judgment. Don't try to think too much. I hear myself saying that a lot these days. Have you been taking your Seroquel?"

"Every day," I lied. Seroquel did nothing for me.

"Ambien withdrawal can be dangerous. As a professional, I must discourage you from operating any heavy machinery—tractors or school buses, whatnot. Did you try the Infermiterol?"

"Not yet," I lied again.

Telling Dr. Tuttle the truth—that the Infermiterol had made me do things out of my nature for days at a time without my knowledge, that the stuff had ruined me for all other medication—would raise too many red flags, I thought. "Blacking out can be a symptom of shame-based disease," I imagined she would say. "Maybe you've been infected by regret. Or Lyme? Syphilis? Diabetes? I'll need you to see a quote-unquote medical doctor for thorough testing." That would ruin everything. I needed Dr. Tuttle's unwavering trust. There was no shortage of psychiatrists in New York City, but finding one as irresponsible and weird as Dr. Tuttle would be a challenge I didn't think I could handle.

"Nothing seems to be working," I told her on the phone. "I'm even losing faith in the Solfoton."

"Don't say *that*," Dr. Tuttle muttered, gasping casually. I hoped she'd prescribe something stronger for me, stronger than even Infermiterol. Phenobarbital. DMT. Anything. But in order to procure such a prescription, I had to make it seem like it was Dr. Tuttle's idea.

"What do you suggest?"

"I've heard from several esteemed colleagues in Brazil that regular Infermiterol use can activate a profound tectonic displacement. Followed up with some filigree work using low doses of aspirin and astral projecting, it's proven to be quite effective in curing solipsistic terror. If that doesn't work, we will reevaluate. We may need to rethink our approach to your treatment in general," she said. "There are alternatives to medication, though they tend to have more disruptive side effects."

"Like what?"

"Have you ever been in love?"

"In what sense?"

"We'll cross that road when we come to it. As far as drugs go, the next level up in home-use heavy-sedating anesthetic is a drug called Prognosticrone. I've seen it do wonders, but one of its known side effects is foaming at the mouth. Still, we can't discount the possibility that maybe—now this is rare, in fact, unprecedented in my professional experience—you've been misdiagnosed. You might be suffering from something, how shall I put this . . . *psychosomatic*. Running that risk, I believe we should be conservative."

"I'll try the Infermiterol," I said curtly.

"Good. And eat a high-dairy meal each day. Did you know that cows can choose to sleep standing up or lying down? Given the option, I know what *I'd* pick. Have you ever made yogurt on the stove? Don't answer that. We'll save the cooking lesson for our next meeting. Now write this down because I have a feeling you're too psychotic to remember: Saturday, January twentieth, at two o'clock. And try the Infermiterol. Bye-bye."

"Wait," I said. "The Ambien."

"I'll call it in right away."

I hung up and looked at my phone. It was only Sunday, January 7.

I went to the bathroom and took stock of the medicine cabinet, counting out all my pills on the grimy tile floor. In all, I had two Ambien but thirty more on the way, twelve Rozerem, sixteen trazodone, around ten each of Ativan, Xanax, and Valium, Nembutal, and Solfoton, plus single digit amounts of a dozen random medications that Dr. Tuttle had prescribed only once "because refilling something this peculiar might trigger speculation by the insurance wizards." In the past, this supply of medication would have been enough for a month of moderate sleeping, nothing too deep if I was conservative with the Ambien. But I knew in my heart that they were all useless now—a collection of foreign currency, a gun with no bullets. The Infermiterol had made all other drugs moot. Maybe it was radiating detoxifying energy into everything on the shelves, I thought, and although I knew that was nonsense, I put all the pills back in the medicine cabinet, but left the Infermiterol bottle out on the dining table, its blue plastic top flashing like a neon light as I looked through the mail. I took a few Nembutal and shot back the dregs of a bottle of Dimetapp.

I found a notice from the unemployment office: I'd forgotten to call them. The measly payments were running out anyway, so it wasn't a huge loss. I threw the notice in the trash. There was a postcard from my dentist reminding me to come in for my yearly cleaning. Trash. There was the bill from Dr. Tuttle for my missed appointment—a handwritten postcard on the back of an index card. "November 12th no show fee: $300." She'd probably forgotten all about it by now. I put it aside. I threw away a coupon to a new Middle Eastern restaurant on Second Avenue. I threw away spring catalogues from Victoria's Secret, from J. Crew, from Barneys. An old water shut-off notice from the super. More junk. I opened up last month's debit card statement and skimmed through all the charges. I found nothing out of the ordinary—mostly ATM withdrawals at the bodega. Only a few hundred dollars at Bloomingdale's. Maybe I had stolen the white fox fur coat, I thought.

And there was a Christmas card from Reva: "During this

hard time, you've been there for me. I don't know what I'd do without a friend like you to weather life's ups and downs. . . ." It was as poorly composed as the aborted eulogy she'd given for her mother. I threw it away.

I hesitated to open a letter from the estate lawyer, worried that it would be a bill that I'd have to pay, which would require that I find my checkbook and go out into the world to buy a stamp. But I took a deep breath and saw stars and opened the letter anyway. It was a brief handwritten note.

"I've tried to reach you by phone several times but it seems your mailbox is full. I hope you had a happy holiday. The professor is moving out. I think you should put the house on the market rather than look for a new tenant. Financially speaking, you're better off selling and putting the money into stocks. Otherwise it's just going to sit there empty."

A waste of space, he was saying.

But when I closed my eyes and pictured the house in that moment, it wasn't empty. The pastel depths of my mother's swollen closet lured me back. I went inside and peeked out between her hanging silk blouses at the rough beige carpeting of her bedroom, the cream ceramic lamp on her nightstand. My mother. And then I traveled up the hall, through the French doors, into my father's study: a dried plum pit on a tea saucer, his huge gray computer blinking neon green, a stack of papers he'd marked in red, mechanical pencils, yellow legal pads that flared open like daffodils. Journals and magazines and newspapers and manila folders, gummy pink erasers that struck me suddenly as somehow genital. Squat glass bottles of Canada Dry a quarter full. A chipped crystal dish of oxidizing paper clips, loose change, a crumpled lozenge wrapper, a button he had meant to sew back onto a shirt but never did. My father.

How many of my parents' hairs and eyelashes and skin cells and fingernail clippings had survived between the floorboards since the professor moved in? If I sold the house, the new owners might cover the hardwood with linoleum, or tear it out. They might paint the walls bright colors, build a deck in the back and seed the lawn with wildflowers. The place could look like "the hippie house" next door by spring, I thought. My parents would have hated that.

I put the letter from the lawyer aside and lay down on the sofa. I should have felt something—a pang of sadness, a twinge of nostalgia. I did feel a peculiar sensation, like oceanic despair that—if I were in a movie—would be depicted superficially as me shaking my head slowly and shedding a tear. Zoom in on my sad, pretty, orphan face. Smash cut to a montage of my life's most meaningful moments: my first steps; Dad pushing me on a swing at sunset; Mom bathing me in the tub; grainy, swirling home video footage of my sixth birthday in the backyard garden, me blindfolded and twirling to pin the tail on the donkey. But the nostalgia didn't hit. These weren't my memories. I felt just a tingling feeling in my hands, an eerie tingle, like when you nearly drop something precious off a balcony, but don't. My heart bumped up a little. I could drop it, I told myself—the house, this feeling. I had nothing left to lose. So I called the estate lawyer.

"What would make more money?" I asked him. "Selling the house, or burning it down?" There was a breathless pause on the phone. "Hello?"

"Selling it, definitely," the lawyer said.

"There are some things in the attic and the basement," I began to say. "Do I have to—"

"You can pick that up when we pass the papers. In due time. The professor moves out mid-February, and then we'll see. I'll let you know what transpires."

I hung up and put my coat on and went down to Rite Aid.

It was cold and windy out, snow brushing up off parked cars like rainbow glitter in the noon light. I could smell the coffee burning as I passed the bodega and was tempted to get some for the walk to the pharmacy, but I knew better. Caffeine wouldn't help me now. I was already shaky and nervous. I had high hopes for the Ambien. Four Ambien with a Dimetapp chaser could put me out for at least four hours, I thought. "Think positive," Reva liked to tell me.

At Rite Aid, I browsed the videos: *The Bodyguard, The*

Mighty Ducks, The Karate Kid Part III, Bullets over Broadway,
and *Emma,* then remembered, heartbreakingly, again—the
truth was cruel—that my VCR was still broken.

The woman working the pharmacy counter was old and
birdlike. I'd never seen her before. Her name tag said her
name was Tammy. The worst name on Earth. She spoke to me
with a clinical professionalism that made me hate her.

"Date of birth? Have you been here before?"

"Do you guys sell VCRs?"

"I don't think so, ma'am."

I could have made the trek to Best Buy on Eighty-sixth
Street. I could have taken a cab there and back. I was just too
lazy, I told myself. But really, by this point, I think I had re-
signed myself to fate. No stupid movie would save me. I could
already hear the jet planes thunder overhead, a rumble in the
atmosphere of my mind that would rend things open, then
obscure the damage with smoke and tears. I didn't know what
it would look like. That was fine. I paid for some Dimetapp,
the Ambien, a tiny tin of Altoids, and strutted home through
the cold—vibrating but relieved, the pills and mints now rat-
tling like snakes, I thought, with each step I took. Soon I'd be
home again. Soon, God willing, I'd be asleep.

A dog walker passed by with a team of yipping teacups
and lapdogs on whiplike leashes. The dogs skittered across
the wet blacktop as silently as cockroaches, each so small it

amazed me that they hadn't been squashed underfoot. Easy to love. Easy to kill. I thought again of Ping Xi's stuffed dogs, the preposterous myth of his industrial dog-killing freezer. A tight sheet of wind slapped me in the face. I pulled the collar of my fur coat up around my throat, and I pictured myself as a white fox curling up in the corner of Ping Xi's freezer, the room whirling with smoky air, swinging sides of cow creaking through the hum of cold, my mind slowing down until single syllables of thought abstracted from their meanings and I heard them stretched out as long-held notes, like foghorns or sirens for a blackout curfew or an air raid. "This has been a test." I felt my teeth chatter, but my face was numb. Soon. The freezer sounded really good.

"Some flowers just came for you," the doorman said as I walked back into my building. He pointed at a huge bouquet of red roses sitting on the mantel over the nonworking fireplace in the lobby.

"For me?"

Were the roses from Trevor? Had he changed his mind about his fat old girlfriend? Was this good? Was this the beginning of the new life? Renewed romance? Did I want that? My heart reared up like a frightened horse, an idiot. I went over to look at the flowers. The mirror hanging on the wall above the mantel showed a frozen corpse, still pretty.

And then I noticed that the glass vase was skull-shaped. Trevor wouldn't have sent me that. No.

"Did you see who dropped these off?" I asked the doorman.

"A delivery guy."

"Was he Asian?" I asked.

"Old black guy. A foot messenger."

Tucked between the flowers was a small note written in girly ballpoint: "To my muse. Call me and we'll get started."

I flipped it over: Ping Xi's business card with his name, number, e-mail address, and the corniest quotation I'd ever read: "Every act of creation is an act of destruction.—Pablo Picasso"

I took the vase off the mantel and got into the elevator, the smell of the roses like the stink off a dead cat in the gutter. Up on my floor, I opened the garbage chute in the hallway and stuffed the roses down, but I kept the card. However much Ping Xi disgusted me—I didn't respect him or his art, I didn't want to know him, I didn't want him to know me—he had flattered me, and reminded me that my stupidity and vanity were still well intact. A good lesson. "Oh, Trevor!"

At home, I stuck Ping Xi's business card into the frame of the mirror in the living room, next to the Polaroid of Reva. I popped four Ambien and sucked down some Dimetapp. "You are getting very sleepy," I said in my head. I dug in the linen closet for fresh sheets, made my bed, and got in. I shut my eyes and imagined darkness, I imagined fields of grain, I imagined the shifting patterns of sand between dunes in the desert, I imagined the slow sway of a willow by the pond in Central Park, I imagined looking out a hotel window in Paris, at the flat gray sky, warped green copper and slate roofs, and tendrils of black steel on balconies and wet sidewalks down below. I was in *Frantic* with the smell of diesel and people with trench coats flying like capes from their shoulders, hands on hats, bells ringing in the distance, a two-tone French siren, the fierce, unforgiving vroom of a motorcycle, tiny brown birds whipping by. Maybe Harrison Ford would show up. Maybe I'd be Emmanuelle Seigner and rub cocaine on my gums in a speeding car and dance at a nightclub like a boneless serpent, hypnotizing everyone with my body. "Sleep. Now!" I imagined a long hospital hallway, a nurse in blue scrubs and thick thighs rushing soberly toward me. "I'm so, so sorry," she was going to say. I turned away. I imagined Whoopi Goldberg in *Star Trek* wearing a purple robe standing at the huge panel through which outer space stretched into infinite mystery. She looked at me and said, "Isn't it pretty?" That smile. "Oh, Whoopi, it's beautiful." I took a step toward the glass. The sheets ruffled against my foot. I wasn't entirely awake, but I couldn't cross the line into sleep.

"Go. Go on. The abyss is right there. Just a few more steps."
But I was too tired to break through the glass. "Whoopi, can
you help?" No answer. I attuned my ears to the sounds in the
room, to cars driving slowly down my block, a door slamming, a set of high heels clomping up the sidewalk. Maybe
that's Reva, I thought. Reva. "Reva?" The thought jolted me
awake.

Suddenly I felt very strange, as though my head had come
off and was floating three inches above the stump of my neck.
I got out of bed and went to the windows and ticked open a
slat in the blinds and looked out. I fixed my eyes east toward
the bleak horizon over the river, perfectly visible through the
trees in Carl Schurz Park, which were black and skeletal. The
branches undulated tauntingly against the pale afternoon,
then stopped, froze, and trembled. Why were they shaking
like that? What was wrong with them? They looked like a
videotape in fast-forward. My VCR. My head floated a few
inches to the left.

I took three Nembutals and the last of the Ativan, then
flopped down on the sofa. The weird feeling in my head
seemed to descend into my torso. Instead of guts, I just had
air inside of me. I couldn't remember the last time I'd moved
my bowels. What if the only way to sleep is death? I thought.
Should I consult a priest? Oh, the absurdity. I started to wal-
low. I wished I'd never taken that damned Infermiterol. I

wanted the old half life back, when my VCR still worked and Reva would come over with her petty gripes and I could lose myself in her shallow universe for a few hours and then disappear into slumber. I wondered if those days were over now that Reva had been promoted and Ken was out of the picture. Would she suddenly grow into maturity and discard me as a relic from a failed past, the way I'd hoped to do to her when my year of sleep was over? Was Reva actually waking up? Did she now realize I was a terrible friend? Could she really dispose of me so easily? No. No. She was a drone. She was too far gone. If the VCR had been working, I would have watched *Working Girl* on high volume, munching melatonin and animal crackers, if I'd had any left. Why did I stop buying animal crackers? Had I forgotten that I was once a human child? Was that a good thing?

I turned on the TV.

I watched *Law & Order*. I watched *Buffy the Vampire Slayer*. I watched *Friends, The Simpsons, Seinfeld, The West Wing, Will & Grace*.

Hours clicked by in half-hour segments. For days, I watched, it seemed, and I didn't sleep. Occasionally I mistook vertigo and nausea for sleepiness, but when I closed my eyes, my heart raced. I watched *The King of Queens*. I watched *Oprah. Donahue. The Ricki Lake Show. Sally Jessy Raphael*. I wondered if I might be dead, and I felt no sorrow, only worry over the afterlife, if it was going to be just like this, just as boring. If I'm dead, I thought, let this be the end. The silliness.

At some point I got up to guzzle water from the tap in the kitchen. When I stood upright afterward, I started to go blind. The fluorescent lights were on overhead. The edges of my vision turned black. Like a cloud, the darkness came and rested in front of my eyes. I could move my eyes up and down, but the black cloud stayed fixed. Then it grew, widening. I buckled down to the kitchen floor and splayed out on the cold tile. I was going to sleep now, I hoped. I tried to surrender. But I would not sleep. My body refused. My heart shuddered. My breath caught. Maybe now is the moment, I thought: I could drop dead right now. Or now. Now. But my heart kept up its dull bang bang, thudding against my chest like Reva banging on my door. I gasped. I breathed. I'm here, I thought. I'm awake. I thought I heard something, a scratching sound at the door. Then an echo. Then an echo of that echo. I sat up. A rush of cold air hit my neck. "Kshhhh," the air said. It was the sound of blood rushing to my brain. My vision cleared. I went back to the sofa.

I watched Jenny Jones and Maury Povich and *Nightline*.

WHEN THE TWENTIETH CAME, I went downtown to see Dr. Tuttle. I felt drunk and crazy getting dressed and lacing up a pair of rubber-soled boots from the closet, which I hadn't remembered buying. I felt drunk in the elevator, I felt drunk walking across York, I felt drunk in the cab. I toddled up the steps to Dr. Tuttle's brownstone and leaned on the buzzer for a good minute until she came to the door. The snow-covered street blinded me. I shut my eyes. I *was* dying. I would tell Dr. Tuttle that. I was the walking dead.

"You look troubled," she said matter-of-factly through the glass. I looked at her standing in the foyer. She wore red long underwear under a fleece cape. Her hair came down over her forehead and covered the top halves of the lenses in her glasses. She had her neck brace on again.

"I've done some reorganizing," she said, opening the door. "You'll see."

I hadn't been to her office in over a month. A full meno-rah of candles had melted in a baking dish on top of the radi-ator in the waiting room. A fake Christmas tree had been wedged into the corner, the top third lopped off and placed next to it in a milk crate. The main part of the tree was deco-rated with purple strands of tinsel and what looked like costume jewelry—fake pearl necklaces, gold and silver ban-gles, children's rhinestone tiaras, baubley clip-on earrings.

Her office smelled like iodine and sage. Where the unsit-table fainting sofa had been there was now a large, Band-Aid–colored massage table.

"I've just been certified as a shaman, or sha-*woman*, if you please," Dr. Tuttle said. "You can hop up on the table if you prefer not to stand. You look worse for wear. Is that the expression?" I leaned carefully against the bookshelf.

"What do you use the massage table for?" I heard myself ask.

"Mystical recalibrations, mostly. I use copper dowels to locate *lugubriations* in the subtle body field. It's an ancient form of healing—locating and then surgically removing cancerous energies."

"I see."

"And by surgery I mean metaphysical operations. Like magnet sucking. I can show you the magnet machine if you're interested. Small enough to fit in a handbag. Costs a pretty penny, although it's very useful. Very. Not so much for insomniacs, but for compulsive gamblers and Peeping Toms—adrenaline junkies, in other words. New York City is full of those types, so I foresee myself getting busier this year. But don't worry. I'm not abandoning my psychiatric clients. There are only a few of you, anyway. Hence my new certification. Costly, but worth it. Sit on it," she insisted, so I did, grappling with the edge of the cool pleather of the massage table to hoist myself up. My legs swung like a kid's at the doctor's. "You really do look troubled. How are you sleeping these days?"

"Like I said, I've been having some serious issues," I began.

"Don't tell me, I know what you're going to say," Dr. Tuttle said. She picked a length of copper wire off her desk and put the tip to her cheek, poking in the soft flesh. Her skin looked suppler than I'd remembered it, and it struck me that Dr. Tuttle was probably younger than I had thought she was. She might only have been in her early forties. "It's the Infermiterol. It didn't work. Am I right?"

"Not really . . ."

"I know exactly what went wrong," she said, and put the wire down. "The sample I gave you was the children's dosage. That would only muddy up the waters, so to speak. The brain must cross a certain threshold before it can function abnormally. It's like filling a bathtub. It means nothing to your downstairs neighbors until it's overflowing."

"I was going to say that the Infermiterol—"

"Because of *leaks*," Dr. Tuttle clarified.

"I get it. But I think the Infermiterol—"

"Now just a moment while I pull your file." She shuffled papers on her desk. "I haven't seen you since December. Had a happy holiday?"

"It was all right."

"Did Santa bring you something nice this year?"

"This fur coat," I told her.

"Family time can put a strain on the mentally deranged." She clucked her tongue as though out of pity. Why? She licked a finger and leafed slowly through the pages in my folder, too slowly. Maddening. "The blind leading the blind," she said wistfully. "The expression has been misused for centuries. It isn't about ignorance at all. It's about *intuition*—the sixth sense, which is the *psychic* sense. How *else* could the blind lead? The answer to this question has more to do with science than you might think. Ever seen doctors try to revive someone whose heart has stopped? People don't understand electroshock. It's not like sitting in the electric chair. The *shocker*. Psychiatry has come a long way, into the spiritual realm. Into energies. There are deniers, certainly, but they all work for big oil. Now tell me about your most recent dreams."

"I don't know. I always forget them. And I'm not sleeping at all, I don't think."

"We don't forget things, OK? We just choose to ignore them. Can you accept responsibility for your memory lapse and move on?"

"Yes."

"Now let me ask you a technical question. Do you have any heroes?"

"I guess Whoopi Goldberg is my hero."

"A family friend?"

"She took care of me after my mother died," I said. Who hadn't heard of Whoopi Goldberg?

"And how did your mother die? Was it sudden? Was it violent?"

I had answered this question half a dozen times by now.

"I killed her," I said then.

Dr. Tuttle smirked and adjusted her glasses. "How did you achieve that, metaphorically speaking?"

I racked my mind. "I crushed oxycodone into her vodka."

"That would do it," Dr. Tuttle said, scribbling maniacally with a ballpoint pen to get the ink flowing. I couldn't watch. Dr. Tuttle had never been so irritating. I closed my eyes.

It was true that my father had kept a white marble mortar and pestle in his study—an antique. I tried to imagine taking a leftover bottle of his oxycodone and crushing the pills in there. I could see my hands grinding, then spooning the white powder into one of my mother's frosty bottles of Belvedere. I swirled it around.

"Now sit still for a minute," Dr. Tuttle said, dismissing my confession. I opened my eyes. "I'm going to assess your personality shift. I notice today that your face is slightly off center. Has anyone pointed that out to you? Your *whole face*," she held out her pen and squinted, measuring me, "is at approximately negative ten degrees. That's counterclockwise to me, but clockwise to you when you go home and look in the mirror. A very minor slant. Really only a trained eye could pick it up. But it's a significant deviation from when we started your treatment. So it makes sense that you're having extra trouble sleeping now. You're having to work *that* much harder just to hold your mind centered. It's effort wasted, I'm afraid. If you let your mind drift, you'd find you can adapt quite easily to the deviated reality. But the instinct for self-correction is powerful. Oh, is it *powerful*. Proper medication should soften the impulse. You had no idea about your facial deviation?"

"No," I answered, and raised my hands to touch my eyes.

She reached down into a paper shopping bag and pulled out four sample bottles of Infermiterol. "Double your dosage. These are ten milligram tablets. Take two," she said, and slid the boxes across her desk. "If vanity is going to keep you up at night, let me just say, it's a *very* minor slant."

IN THE CAB HOME, I looked at myself in the reflection of the tinted windows. My face was perfectly aligned: Dr. Tuttle was obviously crazy.

In the gold-tone doors of the elevator up to my apartment, I still looked good. I looked like a young Lauren Bacall the morning after. I'm a disheveled Joan Fontaine, I thought. Unlocking the door to my apartment, I was Kim Novak. "You're prettier than Sharon Stone," Reva would have said. She was right. I went to the sofa, clicked the TV on. George Walker Bush was taking his oath of office. I watched him squint and give his monologue. "Encouraging responsibility is not a search for scapegoats; it is a call to conscience." What the hell did that mean? That Americans should take the blame for all the ills of the world? Or just our own world? Who cared?

And then, as though I'd summoned her with my mundane cynicism, Reva was knocking on my door once again. I answered somewhat gratefully.

"Well, I scheduled the abortion," she said, rushing past me into the living room. "I need you to tell me I'm doing the *right thing*."

"I ask you to be citizens: Citizens, not spectators; citizens, not subjects; responsible citizens building communities of service and a nation of *character*."

"This Bush is so much cuter than the last. Isn't he? Like a rascal puppy."

"Reva, I'm not feeling well."

"Well, neither am I," she said. "I just want to wake up and it all be over, and I never have to think about this again. I'm not going to tell Ken. Unless I feel like I should. But only after. Do you think he'll feel bad? Oh, I feel sick. Oh, I feel terrible."

"Do you want something to take the edge off?"

"God, yes."

I pulled one of the Infermiterol samples Dr. Tuttle had given me from the pocket of my fur coat. I was curious if Reva would respond to it the same way I had.

"What are these?"

"Samples."

"Samples? Is that legal?"

"Yes, Reva, of course it's legal."

"But what *is* this, In-fer-mit-er-ol?" She looked at the box and tore it open.

"It's a numbing aid," I answered.

"Sounds good. I'll try anything. Do you think Ken still might love me?"

"No."

I watched her face flash with fury, then cool. She shook out a pill and held it in the palm of her hand. Was *her* face at a deviant angle? Was everyone's? Were my eyes crooked? Reva bent over and picked a hair elastic up off the floor.

"Can I borrow this?" I nodded. She put the pill down and fixed her hair. "Maybe I could look it up when I get home. In-fer-mit—"

"Jesus. It's fine, Reva. And you can't look it up," I said, although I'd never tried. "It's not on the market yet. Psychiatrists always have samples. The drug companies send them. That's how it works."

"Does she ever get Topamax samples? Skinny pills?"

"Reva, please."

"So you're saying it's safe."

"Of course it's safe. My *doctor* gave me it."

"What does it feel like?"

"I can't really say," I said, which was the truth.

"Hmmm."

I couldn't be honest with Reva. If I'd admitted to having blackouts, she would have wanted to discuss it endlessly. I couldn't stand the prospect of watching her shake her head in horrified awe, then try to hold my hand. "Tell me everything!" she'd cry, salivating. Poor Reva. She might actually have thought I was capable of sharing things. "Friends forever?" She'd want us to make some sacred pact. She always wanted to make pacts. "Let's make a pact to have brunch at least twice a month. Let's promise to go for a walk through Central Park every Saturday. Let's have a daily call-time. Will you swear to take a ski trip this year? It burns so many calories."

"Reva," I said. "It's a sleeping pill. Take it and go to sleep. Give yourself a break from your Ken obsession."

"It's not an obsession. It's a *medical* procedure. I've never had an abortion before. Have you?"

"Do you want to feel better or not?"

"Well, yeah."

"Don't leave the house after you take it. And don't tell anyone about it."

"Why? Because you think they're illegal? Because you think your doctor is some kind of drug dealer?"

"God, no. Because Dr. Tuttle gave the Infermiterol to *me,*

not you. People aren't supposed to share medications. If you have a heart attack, it would trace back to her. I don't want to mess up my relationship with her over some lawsuit. Maybe you shouldn't take it."

"Do you think it could hurt me to take it? Or hurt the baby?"

"You care about hurting the baby?"

"I don't want to kill it while it's still *inside* of me," she said.

I rolled my eyes, took the bottle from where she'd left it on the coffee table, shook one out. "I'll take one, too." I opened my mouth, threw the pill back. I swallowed.

"Fine," Reva said, and pulled a Diet 7UP from her purse. She placed the Infermiterol onto her tongue like Holy Communion and sucked down half the can.

"What do we do now?"

I didn't answer. I just sat down on the sofa and flipped through the channels until I found one that wasn't covering the inauguration. Reva moved from the armchair to sit next to me to watch TV.

"*Saved by the Bell!*" Reva said.

We sat and watched together, Reva chatting every now and then. "I don't feel anything, do you?" and then, "Why bother having a kid when the world's just going to hell anyway?" and then, "I hate Tiffani-Amber Thiessen. She's so trailer park. You know she's only five foot five? I knew a girl who looked like her in middle school. Jocelyn. She wore dangly earrings before anyone else." And then, "Can I ask you something? I've been sitting on it for a while. Just don't get angry. But I need to ask you. I wouldn't be a good friend otherwise."

"Go ahead, Reva. Ask me anything."

WHEN I WOKE UP three days later, I was still at home, on the sofa, in my fur coat. The TV was off and Reva was gone. I got up and drank water from the kitchen sink. Either Reva or I had taken out the trash. It was strangely quiet and clean in the apartment. And there was a yellow Post-it note left for me on the refrigerator.

"Today is the first day of the rest of your life! xoxo"

I had no idea what I'd said to inspire Reva to leave me such a patronizing note of encouragement. Maybe I'd made a pact with her in my blackout: "Let's be happy! Let's live every day like it's our last!" Barf. I got up and snatched the note off the fridge and crumpled it in my fist. That made me feel a little better. I ate a cup of vanilla Stonyfield yogurt that I hadn't remembered buying.

I decided to take a few Xanax, just to calm myself down. But when I opened the medicine cabinet in the bathroom, my pills were gone. Each and every bottle had disappeared.

My stomach dropped. I went slightly deaf.

"Hello?"

Reva had taken my pills, of course. I had no doubt. All she'd had left for me was a single dose of Benadryl in the foil blister, a one-inch square containing two measly antihistamines. I picked it up in disbelief and shut the door to the cabinet. My face in the mirror startled me. I leaned in and looked to see if it had shifted anymore since Dr. Tuttle's weird assessment. I *did* look different. I couldn't put my finger on how, but there was something that hadn't been there before. What was it? Had I entered the new dimension? Ridiculous. I opened the cabinet again. The pills had not magically reappeared.

I'd never known Reva to be so bold. Maybe I'd tried to hide the pills from myself, I thought. I started opening drawers and cabinets in the hallway, in the kitchen. I hoisted myself up and stood on the counter, looking into the back reaches of the shelves. There was nothing there. I looked in the bedroom, in the drawer of my bedside table, under my bed. I pulled everything out of the closet, found nothing, and piled everything back in. I sifted through my drawers. I went back into the living room and unzipped the cases of the sofa cushions. Maybe I'd stuffed the pills inside the frame, I thought. But why would I do that? I found my phone charging in the bedroom and called Reva. She didn't answer.

"Reva," I said into her voice mail. She was a coward, I thought. She was an idiot.

"Are you a medical doctor? Are you some kind of expert? If my shit isn't back in that medicine cabinet by tonight, we are done. Our friendship is over. I will never want to see you again. That is, if I'm even alive. Did it occur to you that you might not know the whole story behind my condition? And that there would be harmful consequences if I just all of a sudden stopped taking my medicine? If I don't take it, I could go into seizures, Reva. Aneurysms. Neurotic shock. OK? Total cellular collapse! You'd feel pretty sorry if I died because of you. I don't know how you'd live with yourself then. How much puke and StairMaster would it take to get over something like *that*, huh? You know that killing someone you love is the ultimate self-destructive act. Grow up, Reva. Is this a cry for help? It's pretty fucking pathetic, if it is. Anyway, call me back. I'm waiting. And honestly, I don't feel very well."

I took the two Benadryl, sat back down on the sofa and turned on the television.

"In a sweeping vote of one hundred to zero, the Senate has confirmed Mitch Daniels as director of the White House Office of Management and Budget for the freshly minted Bush administration. Fifty-one-year-old Daniels has been a senior vice president for Eli Lilly and Company, the Indianapolis-based pharmaceutical giant."

I turned the channel.

"Negotiations began this week between Hollywood's screenwriters and production executives, trying to head off a possible strike that could result in a TV-film shutdown and in thousands of writers having *no* business in show business. The tremendous impact of such a strike would be felt most profoundly in television, where viewers could be left watching virtually nothing with a script."

That didn't sound so bad. Was the Benadryl working?

Then I noticed that there was another Post-it note affixed to the top of the broken VCR. The horror of that thing! Probably another trite message from Reva encouraging me to "live life to the fullest," I expected. I got up and plucked it off. Trite it was: "Everything you can imagine is real.—Pablo Picasso." But it was not Reva's handwriting. It took me a moment to place it. It was Ping Xi's.

I ran to the toilet.

My puke came up as sour, milk-flavored syrup. A little splashed up into my face. I saw a swirl of neon pink as the two Benadryl I'd swallowed plunked down into the water. A few days earlier, I might have tried to fish them out, but they had mostly dissolved anyway. Let them go, I told myself. Besides, two Benadryl were a joke. Like blowing a snot rocket at a forest fire. Like trying to tame a lion by sending it a postcard. I flushed and sat down on the cold tile. The room spun for a moment, the floor bobbed up and down like the deck of a ship rising in a swell. I felt sick. I needed something. Without it, I'd go crazy. I'd die, I believed. I turned up the ringer on my phone so it would be as loud as possible when Reva called. I stood up slowly. I brushed my teeth. My face in the mirror was red and wet with sweat. This was anger. This was bitter fear.

I sat back down on the sofa and stared at the TV screen and put my feet up on the coffee table. I crumpled the idiotic Post-it Ping Xi had left me. Then I put it on my tongue and let it dissolve slowly as my mouth filled with spit. *Sybil* was playing on the Turner Classic Movies channel. I was determined to remain calm. I chewed and swallowed the soggy paper bit by bit. "Sally Field is bulimic," Reva would have told me had she been in the room. "She's been candid about it. Jane Fonda, too. But everybody knows that. Remember her thighs in those exercise videos? They were *not* natural."

"Oh, shut up, Reva."

"I *love* you."

Maybe she did, and that's why I hated her.

I wondered, would my mother have been better off if I had stolen all her pills, as Reva had stolen all of mine? Reva was lucky to be plagued only by the image of her mother's burning body. "Individual pans." At least her mother's body was ruined. It didn't exist anymore. My dead mother was lying in a coffin, a shriveled skeleton. I still felt like she was up to something down there, bitter and suffering as the flesh on her body withered and sank away from her bones. Did she blame me? We buried her in a carnation pink Thierry Mugler suit. Her hair was perfect. Her lipstick was perfect, blood red, Christian Dior 999. If I unearthed her now, would the lipstick have faded? Either way, she'd be a stiff husk, like the sloughed-off exoskeleton of a huge insect. That was what my mother was. What if I'd flushed away all those prescriptions before I went back to school, poured all her alcohol down the sink? Did she secretly want me to do that? Would that have made her happy for once? Or would it have pushed her further away? "My own daughter!" I sensed a bit of remorse in me. It smelled like pennies in the room, I thought. The air tasted like when you test a battery with your tongue. Cold and electric. "I'm not fit to occupy space. Excuse me for living." Maybe I was hallucinating. Maybe I was having a stroke. I wanted Xanax. I wanted Klonopin. Reva had even taken my empty bottle of chewable peppermint melatonin. How could she?

In my mind, I made a list of pills I wanted to take and then I imagined taking them. I cupped my hand and plucked the invisible pills out of my palm. I swallowed them one by one. It didn't work. I started sweating. I went back to the kitchen and drank water from the tap, then stuck my head in the freezer and found a bottle of Jose Cuervo wrapped in a crinkly white plastic bag. I was glad it wasn't a human head. I drank the tequila and glared at Reva's Polaroid picture. Then I remembered that I had a set of keys to her apartment.

I HADN'T BEEN TO the Upper West Side in several years, not since the last time I'd been over to Reva's. It felt safe in that part of town, sobering. The buildings were heavier. The streets were wider. Nothing there had really changed since I'd graduated from Columbia. Westside Market. Riverside Park. 1020. The West End. Cheap pizza by the slice. Maybe that's why Reva loved it, I thought. Cheap binges. Bulimia was pricey if you had fine taste. I always thought it was pathetic that Reva had chosen to stay in the area after graduation, but passing through it in the cab, in my frenzied state of despair, I understood: there was stability in living in the past.

I rang Reva's buzzer at her building on West Ninety-eighth a few times. Ativan would be nice, I thought. And strangely I was craving lithium, too. And Seroquel. A few hours of drooling and nausea sounded like cleansing torture before hitting the sleep hard—on Ambien, Percocet, one stray Vicodin I'd been sitting on. I was thinking I'd get my pills from Reva's, go home, and then I could hit the sleep for ten straight hours, get up, have a glass of water, a little snack, then ten straight more. Please!

I buzzed again and waited, imagining Reva trudging up
the block toward her building with a dozen bags of groceries
from D'Agostino's, shock and shame on her face when she
saw me waiting for her, arms laden with brownie mix and ice
cream and chips and cake or whatever it was Reva liked to eat
and vomit up so much. The nerve of her. The hypocrisy. I
paced in circles around her crummy little vestibule, punching
at her buzzer violently. I couldn't wait. I had her spare keys. I
let myself in.

Going up the stairs, I smelled vinegar. I smelled cleaning
detergent. I thought I smelled piss. A mauve-colored cat sat
on the second-floor railing like an owl. "Fussing with animals
in dreams can have primitive and violent consequences," Dr.
Tuttle had said to me once, petting her fat, snoring tabby. I
felt like pushing the cat down the stairwell when I reached
the landing. The look in its eye was so smug. I knocked on the
door to Reva's apartment. I heard no voices, just the wind
howling. I expected to find Reva in her apartment wearing
pink flannel pajamas with cartoon bunnies on them and furry
pink slippers, in some weird sugar coma, perhaps, or crying
hysterically because she was "at a loss for how to handle
reality," or whatever garbage she was feeling. The silver key
opened her apartment door. I walked inside.

"Hello?"

I could have sworn I smelled puke in the darkness.

"Reva, it's me," I said. "Your *best friend*."

I flicked up the light switch by the door, casting the place in a sweltering blush-hued glow. Pink lighting? The place was messy, silent, stuffy, just as I remembered it. "Reva? Are you in here?" A five-pound weight propped open the one window in the living room, but no air was coming through. A Thigh-Master hung from the curtain rod, a floral drape bunched and pinned to the side with a Chip Clip.

"I came for my shit," I said to the walls.

Stacks and stacks of *Cosmo* and *Marie Claire* and *Us Weekly*. The only movement in the living room was the swirling screensaver on Reva's enormous Dell, which sat on a little side table in the corner and was mostly obscured by a drying rack weighed down with Ann Taylor sweater sets and Banana Republic dress shirts, matching bras and panties. A half dozen discolored white sports bras. Pairs and pairs of flesh-colored nylons. "Reva!" I called out, kicking through a pile of brightly colored sneakers in the living room.

In the kitchen, a dried-out sheet cake with finger gouges in it sat on the counter next to a tub of I Can't Believe It's Not Butter and sugar-free maple syrup. There were stacks of dirty dishes in the sink. A small trash can overflowed with junk-food packaging and apple cores. Half a toaster waffle smeared with peanut butter, a murky bag of baby carrots. Crushed cans of Diet 7UP filled a cardboard box next to the trash can.

Diet 7UP cans everywhere. A glass of orange juice with fruit flies floating on the surface.

Her cabinets contained exactly what I'd expected. Herbal laxative teas, Metamucil, Sweet'N Low, stacks of canned Healthy Choice soups, stacks of canned tuna. Tostitos. Goldfish crackers. Reduced fat Skippy. Sugar-free jelly. Sugar-free Hershey's Syrup. Rice crackers. Low-fat microwave popcorn. Box after box of yellow cake mix. When I opened the freezer, smoke billowed out. The thick frosted inside was crowded with fat-free frozen yogurt. Sugar-free Popsicles. A cloudy bottle of Belvedere. Déjà vu. Reva's new favorite cocktail, she'd told me—had I been on Infermiterol?—was low-calorie Gatorade and vodka.

"You could drink this all day and never get dehydrated."

"Reva, if you're hiding from me, I will find you," I called out.

Her bedroom was hardly any bigger than her king-size mattress, which she'd told me she'd inherited from her parents when her mother got sick "and so they got two doubles because my dad couldn't sleep at night with all her fidgeting." Green numbers on a digital alarm clock glowed between cans of Diet 7UP on the bedside table. It was 4:37. I smelled peanut butter and again, the bitter tang of vomit. The comforter was Laura Ashley, folded back from the bed. Food stains on the sheets. I looked under the bed, found only shoes, more magazines, empty little yogurt containers, paper bags from Burger King punched flat like deflated footballs. In the drawer of her bedside table, a purple vibrator, a diary with a waxy green cover, a purple eye mask, a pack of cherry Lifesavers, a Polaroid of her mother wearing a Tigger costume, smiling shyly, her eyes caught midblink, sitting on that plastic-covered sofa in Farmingdale, a five-year-old Reva dressed as a tiny Winnie-the-Pooh on her knee, Reva's mother's hand cradling her fuzzy yellow potbelly. I picked up the diary and looked inside. It was just a daily log of numbers, mathematical sums and subtractions, the final results circled and annotated with either smiley or frowny faces. The last entry was marked December 23. Reva seemed to have abandoned her daily numbers game when her mother died.

I thought of Reva sleeping in that bed each night, probably drunk and full of Aspartame and Pepcid. In the mornings, she prepped and set out into the world, a mask of composure. And *I* had problems? Who's the real fuckup, Reva? I hated her more and more.

The bathroom looked like it belonged to a pair of adolescent twins preparing for a beauty pageant. I could smell the mildew and the puke and Lysol. A pink expanded toolbox burst with brushes and applicators of all shapes and sizes, drugstore makeup, nail polish, stolen testers, a dozen shades of Maybelline lip gloss. On the shelf, there were two hair dryers, a curling iron, a flat iron, a bowl of bejeweled barrettes and plastic headbands. Cutouts from fashion magazines were taped to the edges of the mirror over the low vanity and sink: Claudia Schiffer's Guess Jeans ad. Kate Moss in her Calvins. Runway stick figures. Linda Evangelista. Kate Moss. Kate Moss. Kate Moss. There was a bowl of cotton balls and swabs. A bowl of bobby pins. Two huge bottles of Listerine. Next to the cup that must have held a dozen toothbrushes, each head of bristles yellowed and frayed, a prescription bottle of Vicodin. Vicodin! From the dentist. There were twelve pills left in the bottle. I took one and pocketed the rest. I found more pills under the sink in a wicker box with a pink ribbon tying the lid shut—an Easter relic, I guessed. Maybe when Reva bought it, it was full of chocolate eggs. Clearance sale. Inside: Diurex, ibuprofen, Mylanta, Dulcolax, Dexatrim, Midol, aspirin, fenphen. A Victoria's Secret gift bag was tucked into the back corner of the cabinet. Inside, glory! My Ambien, my Rozerem, my Ativan, my Xanax, my trazodone, my lithium. Seroquel, Lunesta. Valium. I laughed. I teared up. Finally, my heart slowed. My hands started trembling a little, or maybe they'd been trembling all along. "Thank God," I said aloud. The draft sucked the bathroom door shut with a celebratory bang.

I counted out three lithium, two Ativan, five Ambien. That sounded like a nice mélange, a luxurious free fall into velvet blackness. And a couple of trazodone because trazodone weighed down the Ambien, so if I dreamt, I'd dream low to the ground. That would be stabilizing, I thought. And maybe one more Ativan. Ativan to me felt like fresh air. A cool breeze, slightly effervescent. This was good, I thought. A serious rest. My mouth watered. Good strong American sleep. Those pills would scrape out the sludge of Infermiterol left in my mind. Then I'd feel better. Then I'd be set. I'd live easy. I'd think easy. My brain would glide. I looked at the assortment of pills in my palm. Snapshot. Good-bye, bad dream. I wished I had my Polaroid camera to document the scene. "Forget me, Reva," I'd say, flapping the photos in her face. "You'll never see me again." But did I care? I didn't think so. If Reva's body was hanging by the neck behind the bath curtain, I might have just gone home. But this moment was ceremonious. I had my magic back. This is mine now, I told myself. I'm going to sleep.

The water in the tap was orange and tasted like blood. I didn't want to wash down my nice pills with Satan's sweat. I'd get water from the kitchen sink, I thought, so I went to the bathroom door and tried to open it. It did not open. I fiddled with the lock, turning the knob back and forth. "Reva?" Something was jammed or broken. I shoved the handful of pills into the pocket of my coat and twisted the knob again, pulling and wrenching. But it didn't work. I was locked inside. I pounded on the door.

"Reva!" I called again.

There was no answer. I sat on the fuzzy pink toilet lid and fiddled with the knob for what felt like twenty minutes. I would have to break the door down, or wait for Reva to come home from work, I thought. Either way, it would result in a confrontation. I already knew everything she'd say.

"I've stood by the sidelines long enough. You have a *problem*. I can't just look the other way while you kill yourself."

And what I'd say back.

"I appreciate your concern," me seething, me wanting to kill her. "I'm under a doctor's supervision, Reva. There's nothing to worry about with me. I wouldn't be allowed to do this if it wasn't kosher. It's all safe!"

Or maybe she'd go the heartbroken route.

"I buried my mother a few weeks ago. I'm not going to bury you, too."

"You didn't bury your mother."

"Cremated, whatever."

"I want a sea burial," I'd tell her. "Wrap me in a black cloth and throw me over. Like a pirate."

I pulled back the mildewed shower curtain, hung my coat on the towel rack, lay down in the tub, and waited. In the hours before Reva came home and let me out, I did not sleep. I knew I wouldn't. I needed a way out of this—the bathroom, the pills, the sleeplessness, the failed, stupid life.

When the solution to my problems came to me, it landed in my mind like a hawk on a cliff. It was as though it had been circling up there the whole time, studying every little thing in my life, putting all the pieces together. "This is the way." I knew exactly what I had to do: I needed to be locked up.

If one tablet of Infermiterol put me into a state of vacuous unconsciousness for three days, I had enough to keep me in the dark until June. All I needed was a jailkeeper, and I could live in constant sleep without fear of going out and getting involved in anything. This all seemed like a practical matter. The Infermiterol would work for me. I was relieved, almost happy. I didn't mind at all that when Reva finally came home and wrestled the bathroom door open, she shrieked, expressed her grave concern for my sanity, all while rushing me out the door, I guessed, because she had a stomach full of junk she wanted to puke up.

I left the pills with her, all but the Infermiterol.

At home, I called a locksmith, arranged a meeting with Ping Xi for the following afternoon, and called Dr. Tuttle to tell her I was going off the grid for the next four months.

"Hopefully I won't ever need to see you again," I told her.

"People say that to me all the time," she said.

That was the last time we spoke.

Seven

"ARE YOU SURE you won't wear this stuff? What if I stretch something out, and then you want it back?"

I had called Reva to say that I was cleaning out my closets. She brought over a collection of large paper shopping bags from various Manhattan department stores, bags she'd obviously saved in case she had to transport something and needed a vessel that would connote her good taste and affirm that she was respectable because she'd spent money. I'd seen housekeepers and nannies do the same thing, walking around the Upper East Side with their lunch in tiny, rumpled gift bags from Tiffany's or Saks Fifth Avenue.

"I never want to see any of these clothes again," I told Reva when she arrived. "I want to forget it all existed. Whatever you don't take, I'll donate or throw away."

"But *all* of it?"

She was like a kid in a candy store, methodically and

vampirically pulling out every dress, every skirt, every blouse, hangers and all. Every pair of designer jeans, every bit of packaged lingerie, every pair of shoes except for the filthy slippers I wore on my feet.

"They *kind* of fit," she said, trying on an unworn pair of Manolo Blahniks. "Good enough."

She packed everything into the shopping bags with the urgent efficiency of someone building a sand castle at sundown, as the tide comes in. Like a dream you know will end. If I move fast enough, I won't wake the gods. Most of the clothes still had the tags on them.

"This is good motivation to stick to my diet," Reva said, lugging the bags into the living room. "Atkins, I think. Bacon and eggs for the next six months. I think I can do it if I really set my mind to it. The doctor said the abortion won't cause any dramatic weight loss, but I'll take it. I'll take whatever I can get. Especially now. Size twos are a challenge for my hips, you know. You're *sure* you won't want any of this back?" She was gleeful and flushed.

"Take the jewelry, too," I said, and returned to the bedroom, which now felt hollowed and cool. Thank God for Reva. Her greed would unburden me of my own vanity. I started picking through my jewelry, then decided just to give her the whole box. She didn't ask why. Maybe she thought I was in a blackout, and if she questioned me, I'd wake up.

Don't disturb the sleeping beast. The white fox in the meat freezer.

I went down in the elevator with her, the bags in our fists heavy yet cloudlike, the air in the elevator shifting pressure as though we were flying through a storm. But I felt almost nothing. The doorman held the door for us as we walked out.

"Oh, thank you so much, that's so kind of you," Reva said, suddenly a lady, gracious and verbose. "That is just so sweet of you, Manuel. Thank you."

His name. I'd never bothered to learn it. I gave her forty dollars cash for the ride crosstown. The doorman whistled for a taxi.

"I'm going on a trip, Reva," I said.

"Rehab?"

"Something like that."

"For how long?" Just the slightest twitch in her eye, barely balking at the lie that was obvious in its vagueness. But what could she say? I'd paid her off in high fashion to leave me alone.

"I'll be back on June first," I said. "Or maybe I'll stay longer. They won't let me make phone calls. They told me it's best not to have contact with people from my past."

"Not even me?" She was being polite. I could tell she was already hatching plans, all the hunting for love and admiration she'd do with this new wardrobe, flashy armor, the brightest camouflage. She blew on her hands to warm them and craned her neck at the approaching cab.

"Good luck with the abortion."

Reva nodded sincerely. In that moment, I think our friendship ended. What would come later would be only airy remembrances of the thing called *love* she used to give me. I felt a kind of peace about Reva seeing her off that day. I'd cost her so much dignity, but the bounty she was now shoving into the trunk of the cab seemed to make up for it. I was absolved. She gave me a hug, kissed my cheek.

"I'm proud of you," she said. "I know you can get through this." When she pulled away, there were tears in her eyes, maybe just from the cold. "I feel like I won the lottery!" She was happy. I watched her through the tinted glass, smiling and waving as she drove off.

AT THE BODEGA, I got two coffees and a piece of pre-packaged carrot cake, bought all the garbage bags the Egyptians had in stock, then went back upstairs and packed everything up. Every book, every vase, every plate and bowl and fork and knife. All my videos, even the *Star Trek* collection. I knew I had to do it. The deep sleep I would soon enter required a completely blank canvas if I was to emerge from it renewed. I wanted nothing but white walls, bare floors, lukewarm tap water. I packed up all my tapes and CDs, my laptop, unmelted candles, all my pens and pencils, all my electric cords and rape whistles and Fodor's guides to places I never went.

I called the Jewish Women's Council Thrift Shop and told them my aunt had died. Two guys came with a van an hour later, lugging the garbage bags four at a time into the hallway and out of my life forever. They took most of the furniture, too, including the coffee table and the bed frame. I got them to carry out the sofa and the armchair and leave them on the curb. The only pieces of furniture I kept were the mattress, the dining table, and a single aluminum folding chair with a cushion whose stained gray linen cover I threw down the trash chute. Ta-ta.

What I kept for myself amounted to one set of towels, two sets of sheets, the duvet, three sets of pajamas, three pairs of cotton underpants, three bras, three pairs of socks, a comb for my hair, a box of Tide laundry detergent, a large bottle of Lubriderm moisturizing lotion. I bought a new toothbrush and four months' worth of toothpaste and Ivory soap and toilet paper at Rite Aid. A four months' supply of iron supplements, a women's daily vitamin, aspirin. I bought packages of plastic cups and plates, plastic cutlery.

I had instructed Ping Xi to bring me one large mushroom pepperoni pizza with extra cheese every Sunday afternoon.

Whenever I came to, I'd drink water, eat a slice of pizza, do some sit-ups and push-ups, some squats, some lunges, put the clothes I was wearing into the washer, transfer the washed set into the dryer, put on the clean set, then take another Infermiterol. In this way, I could stay in the black until my year of rest was up.

When the locksmith came, I told him to install the new lock on the outside of the door, so that anyone inside the apartment would need the key to get out. He didn't ask why. Locked inside, the only way out would be through the windows. I figured that if I jumped out while I was on the Infermiterol, it would be a painless death. A blackout death. I'd either wake up safe in the apartment, or I wouldn't. It was a risk I'd take forty times, every three days. If, when I woke up in June, life still wasn't worth the trouble, I would end it. I would jump. This was the deal I made.

BEFORE PING XI CAME over on January 31, I took a final walk outside. The sky was milky, the sounds of the city muted by the hard ruffling of wind hitting my ears. I wasn't nostalgic. But I was terrified. It was lunacy, this idea, that I could sleep myself into a new life. Preposterous. But there I was, approaching the depths of my journey. So far, I thought, I'd been wandering through the forest. But now I was approaching the mouth of the cave. I smelled the smoke of a fire burning deep inside. Something had to be burned and sacrificed. And then the fire would burn out and die. The smoke would clear. My eyes would adjust to the darkness, I thought. I'd find my footing. When I came out of the cave, back out into the light, when I woke up at last, everything—the whole world—would be new again.

I crossed East End Avenue and shuffled across the salted walkway through Carl Schurz Park toward the river, a wide channel of cracked obsidian. The collar of my fur coat tickled my chin. I remember that. A couple was taking pictures of each other by the railing.

"Can you take one of the two of us?"

I pulled my limp, pink hands from my pockets and held the camera numbly.

"Stand closer together," I said, teeth chattering. The girl rubbed the wetness from her top lip with her gloved finger. The man lurched forward in his stiff wool coat. I thought of Trevor. In the viewfinder, the light did not find their faces but illuminated the aura of the wind-whipped hair around their heads.

"Cheese," I said. They repeated it.

When they were gone, I threw my cell phone into the river and went back to my building, told the doorman that a short Asian man would be visiting me regularly. "He's not my boyfriend, but give him that kind of consideration. He has my keys. Full access," I said, then went upstairs and took a bath, put on the first set of pajamas, lay down on the mattress in the bedroom, and waited for a knock on the door.

"I BROUGHT A CONTRACT for you to sign," Ping Xi said, standing in the doorway, a handheld digital video camera in his hand. He switched it on and held it at chest level. "In case something goes wrong, or in case you change your mind. Mind if I tape this?"

"I'm not going to change my mind."

"I knew you'd say that."

He then encouraged me to burn my birth certificate so he could record the ritual on videotape. His interest in me was like his interest in those dogs. He was an opportunist and a stylist, a producer of entertainment more than an artist. Though, like an artist, he clearly believed that the situation we were in together—he the warden of my hibernation with full permission to use me in my blackout state as his "model"— was a projection of his own genius, as though the universe were orchestrated in such a way as to lead him toward projects that he'd unconsciously predicted for himself years earlier. The illusion of fateful realization. He wasn't interested in understanding himself or evolving. He just wanted to shock people. And he wanted people to love and despise him for it. His audience, of course, would never truly be shocked. People were only delighted at his concepts. He was an art-world hack. But he was successful. He knew how to operate. I noticed that his chin was greasy with something. I looked closer: under the smear of Vaseline was a tattoo of a cluster of big red zits.

"I think I'm going to be taking lots of footage," he said. "Handheld digital with this thing mostly. Comes out grainy. I like it."

"I don't care. As long as I'm on the drug, I won't remember."

He promised me that he would lock me up and keep my sleeping prison a secret, that he wouldn't allow anyone to accompany him into my apartment, not an assistant, not even a cleaning person. If he was going to bring in props or furniture or materials, he'd have to bring them in himself, and above all, each time he went away, no trace of his activities could be left. Not a scrap. When I came to on the third day of each Infermiterol blackout, there was to be no evidence of what had happened since my last awakening. There was to be no narrative that I could follow, no pieces for me to put together. Even a shade of curiosity could sabotage my mission to clear my mind, purge my associations, refresh and renew the cells in my brain, my eyes, my nerves, my heart.

"I wouldn't want you to know what I'm up to anyway. It would screw up my work. The creative incentive for me is that you'll be constantly . . . naive."

I think it disappointed him that I wasn't begging him to tell me what the work was going to be about. It didn't worry me that he could make sex tapes. He was obviously homosexual. I wasn't threatened.

"As long as the place is clean and empty and you're gone before I wake up every third day, and I don't starve to death or break any bones, I don't care about your artwork. You have carte blanche. Just don't let me out of here. I'm doing important work of my own. Tit for tat."

"Tit for tit makes more sense," he said. "What about just burning your passport or cutting up your driver's license," he suggested. I knew what he was thinking. He was imagining how the critics would describe the video. He needed fodder for analysis. But the project was beyond issues of "identity" and "society" and "institutions." Mine was a quest for a new spirit. I wasn't going to explain that to Ping Xi. He would think he understood me. But he couldn't understand me. He wasn't supposed to. And anyway, I needed my birth certificate and my passport and my driver's license. At the end of my hibernation, I'd wake up—I imagined—and see my past life as an inheritance. I'd need proof of the old identity to help me access my bank accounts, to go places. It wasn't as if I'd wake up with a different face and body and name. I'd appear to be the old me.

"But that's cheating," he said. "If you're planning to walk out of here and go back to being the same person you are now, what's the point?"

"It's personal," I said. "It's not about ID cards. It's an inside job. What do you want me to do? Walk out into the woods, build a fort, hunt squirrels?"

"Well, that would be a more authentic rebirth. Have you seen any Tarkovsky? Haven't you read Rousseau?"

"I was born into privilege," I told Ping Xi. "I am not going to squander that. I'm not a moron."

"I might have to, like, downgrade to Super 8 then. Can I take down the blinds in the bedroom?" He pulled a handwritten document from his messenger bag.

"Put the contract away," I said. "I won't sue you. Just don't fuck this up for me."

Ping Xi shrugged.

I gave him the key to the new lock.

"If I need anything, I'll stick a Post-it note here," I said, pointing to the dining table. "You see this red pen?"

Each time Ping Xi came over, he was to mark off the days on a calendar hanging on the door to my bedroom. Every three days, I'd wake up, look at the calendar, eat, drink, bathe, et cetera. I would only spend one hour awake each time. I did the math: for the next four months, 120 days total, I would spend only forty hours in a conscious state.

"Sweet dreams," said Ping Xi.

His face was wan, fleshy, something blurry about it—maybe it was the Vaseline on his chin—but his eyes were sharp, hooded, dark, clear, and although I understood that he was foolish, I trusted his resolve. He wouldn't let me out of there. He was too conceited to fail to keep his word, and too ambitious to give up the opportunity to take advantage of my offer. A woman out of her mind, locked in an apartment. I shut the door in his face. I heard him slide in the key and lock it.

I took the first of forty Infermiterol, went into the bedroom, fluffed the pillow, and lay down.

THREE NIGHTS LATER, I came to in pitch darkness, crawled off the mattress, turned on the lights, and went into the living room, expecting to find scratches at the door, evidence of a wild animal being held against her will. But I found nothing. Ping Xi hadn't even crossed out the days on the calendar. My apartment was almost unrecognizable in its blankness, clean and empty. I could imagine some well-dressed real estate agent bursting in—a floral scarf fluttering like a sail from her upheld arm as she extolled the virtues of the unit to a newly married couple: "High ceilings, hardwood, all the original molding, and quiet, quiet. From those windows, you can even see the East River." The agent's suit was canary yellow. The couple, I imagined, were the ones whose photo I'd taken a few days earlier on the Esplanade. My memory had blundered into my imagination, but I knew what was what. I understood that three days had passed without me, and there was a long way ahead.

I saw no trace of Ping Xi until I went to the kitchen: Pabst Blue Ribbon beer cans; tin foil smeared with the contents of what I could assume was a burrito; the *New York Times* from February 2. I wrote a list of things I desired on a Post-it and stuck it to the table: "Ginger ale, animal crackers, Pepto-Bismol." And then, "Remove all garbage after each visit! Cross out the days!" I guessed Ping Xi had been over to take measurements or talk or sketch plans for some video project, but had made no real work yet. I just had that feeling.

I pulled a slice of pizza from the fridge and ate it cold, with my eyes closed, swaying under the fluorescent light streaming down from overhead and reflecting back up off the kitchen floor. I should have bought a sunlamp. The thought occurred to me, then rang a bell that I'd left in a boring corner of my mind to remind myself to take my vitamins. I gulped grayish water from the tap. When I righted myself, I felt a little swoon of panic at the thought of that lock on the door. If something happened to Ping Xi, I could die in here, I thought. But the panic vanished as soon as I flicked off the kitchen lights.

I bathed quickly, put my laundry in, did a few exercises, brushed my teeth, took an Infermiterol, and went back to the bedroom. Nothing felt very deep yet. Everything was mundane and practical. In the moments waiting to lose consciousness, I imagined Trevor on one knee, proposing to his current lady friend. The self-satisfaction. The stupidity of wanting something "forever." I almost felt sorry for him, for her. I heard myself chuckle, then sigh, as I drifted away, back into the cold.

THE SECOND AWAKENING WAS at midday. I came to with my thumb in my mouth. When I pulled it out, it was white and wrinkled, and I had a kink in my jaw that reminded me of the cramp I used to get giving blow jobs. This didn't alarm me. I rose, alert and hungry, and went to the kitchen. Ping Xi had crossed six days off the calendar and stuck a Post-it note on the fridge that said, "Sorry!" I opened the fridge, chewed a slice of pizza, took my vitamins, and chugged a can of Schweppes. The trash can was empty this time, no liner. I left the empty soda can on the kitchen counter and thought only passingly of Reva and her Diet 7UPs full of tequila before I bathed, combed my hair, did some jumping jacks, et cetera. I made a mental note to change the sheets upon awakening, took an Infermiterol, lay down, massaged my jaw with my fingers, and lost consciousness.

THE THIRD AWAKENING MARKED nine days locked inside my apartment. I could feel it in my eyes when I got up, the atrophy of the muscles I'd use to focus on things at a distance, I guessed. I kept the lights low. In the shower, I read the shampoo label and got stuck on the words "sodium lauryl sulfate." Each word carried with it a seemingly endless string of associations. "Sodium": salt, white, clouds, gauze, silt, sand, sky, lark, string, kitten, claws, wound, iron, omega.

The fourth awakening, the words fixated me again. "Lauryl": Shakespeare, Ophelia, Millais, pain, stained glass, rectory, butt plug, feelings, pigpen, snake eyes, hot poker. I shut the water off, did my due diligence with the laundry, et cetera, took an Infermiterol, and lay back down on the mattress. "Sulfate": Satan, acid, Lyme, dunes, dwellings, hunchbacks, hybrids, samurais, suffragettes, mazes.

SO MY HOURS WENT by in three-day chunks. Ping Xi was dutiful about the calendar and the garbage. One time I wrote a Post-it note and asked for Canada Dry instead of Schweppes. Another time, I wrote a Post-it note and asked for dryer sheets. I paid minor attention to the dust on the windowsills, swirls of lint and hairs caught between the floorboards. I wrote a Post-it note: "Sweep or tell me to sweep when I'm blacked out." I forgot Ping Xi's name, then remembered it. I passed the hallway to the locked door of the apartment and vaguely nodded at the idea of the lock, as though it might be *just* an idea, the door itself, just the notion of a door. "Plato": chalk, chain, Hollywood, Hegel, *carte postale*, banana daiquiri, breezes, music, roads, horizons. I could feel the certainty of a reality leeching out of me like calcium from a bone. I was starving my mind into obliqueness. I felt less and less. Words came and I spoke them in my head, then nestled in on the sound of them, got lost in the music.

"Ginger": ale, smoke, China, satin, rose, blemish, treble, babka, fist.

ON FEBRUARY 19, I stared into the mirror. My lips were chapped but I was smiling. Two syllables chimed in my mind and I wrote them down on a Post-it for Ping Xi: "Lip balm."

"ChapStick": strawberry, linoleum, pay scale, sundae, poodle.

And then, another Post-it note: "Thank you."

· · ·

ON FEBRUARY 25, I could tell immediately that some-thing was different. I awoke not sprawled on the mattress in the bedroom, but curled up under a towel on the floor in the northeast corner of the living room, where my desk used to be.

I thought I smelled gas, and the association with fire alarmed me, so I got up and went to the stove before remem-bering that it was electric. Maybe, I thought, what I'd smelled was my own sweat. I relaxed.

I opened the fridge, stood in the yellow light, and chewed my piece of pizza. My salivary glands were hesitant at first, but then they acquiesced, and the pizza tasted better than I'd re-membered it. I pulled clean pajamas from the dryer and put them on in the hallway. I sniffed the air again and recognized the distinct tang of turpentine. It was coming from the bed-room. The bedroom door was locked.

I knocked.

"Hello?"

I listened with my ear pressed against the door, but all I heard was my own shallow breathing, the blink of my eyes, my mouth filling with spit, the echo in my throat swallowing it down.

I took my vitamins, but did not bathe.

When I took the Infermiterol that day, I pictured Ping Xi's paintings. They flashed into my mind like memories. They were all "sleeping nudes," mussed beds and tangles of pale limbs and blond hair, blue shadows in the folds of the white sheets, sunsets reflected on the white wall backgrounds. In every painting, my face was hidden. I saw them in my mind's eye—small oils on cheap prestretched canvases or smaller primed panels. They were innocent and not very good. It didn't matter. He could sell them for hundreds of thousands and say they were self-conscious critiques of the institutionalization of painting, maybe even about the objecti-fication of women's bodies through art history. "School is not for artists," I could hear him say. "Art history is fascism. These paintings are about what we sleep through while we're read-ing books our teachers give us. We're all asleep, brainwashed by a system that doesn't give a shit about who we really are. These paintings are *deliberately* boring." Did he think that was an original idea? I would never remember posing for the paintings, but I knew that if I was high on Infermiterol, I must have just been feigning sleep.

I took an Infermiterol, lay down on the living room floor, a fresh towel folded under my head as a pillow, and went back to sleep.

Over the next month, when I'd wake up, my mind was filled with colors. The apartment began to feel less cavernous to me. One time I awoke to find my hair had been cut off, like a boy's, and there were long blond hairs stuck to the inside of the toilet bowl. I imagined sitting on the toilet with a towel over my shoulders, Ping Xi standing above me, snipping away. In the mirror, I looked bold and sprightly. I thought I looked good. I wrote Post-it notes requesting fresh fruits, mineral water, grilled salmon from "a good Japanese restaurant." I asked for a candle to burn while I bathed. During this period, my waking hours were spent gently, lovingly, growing reaccustomed to a feeling of cozy extravagance. I put on a little weight, and so when I lay down on the living room floor, my bones didn't hurt. My face lost its mean edge. I asked for flowers. "Lilies." "Birds of paradise." "Daisies." "A branch of catkins." I jogged in place, did leg lifts, push-ups. It was easier and easier to pass the time between getting up and going down.

But by the end of May, I sensed that I was going to grow restless soon. A prediction. The sound of tires on the wet pavement. A window was open so I could hear it. The sweet smell of spring crept in. The world was out there still, but I hadn't looked at it in months. It was too much to consider it all, stretching out, a circular planet covered in creatures and things growing, all of it spinning slowly on an axis created by what—some freak accident? It seemed implausible. The world could be flat just as easily as it could be round. Who could prove anything? In time, I would understand, I told myself.

. . .

ON MAY 28, I came to, knowing this was the last time I would perform my habitual ablutions and take the Infermiterol. There was only one pill left. I swallowed it and prayed for mercy.

Light from passing cars slid through the blinds and flashed across the living room walls in yellow stripes, once, twice. I turned to face the ceiling. The floorboards gave a short screech, like the squelch of a boat turning suddenly in a storm. A hum in the air signaled the approaching wave. Sleep was coming for me. I knew the sound of it by now, the foghorn of dead space that put me on autopilot while my conscious self roamed like a goldfish. The sound got louder until it was almost deafening, and then it stopped. In that silence, I began to drift down into the darkness, descending at first so slowly and steadily, I felt I was being lowered on pulleys—by angels with gold-spun ropes around my body, I imagined, and then by the electric casket lowering device they used at both my parents' burials, and so my heart quickened at that thought, remembering that I'd had parents once, and that I'd taken the last of the pills, that this was the end of something, and then the ropes seemed to detach and I was falling faster. My stomach turned and I was cold with sweat, and I started writhing, first grasping at the towel under me to slow my fall, and then more wildly because that hadn't worked, tumbling like Alice down the rabbit hole or like Elsa Schneider disappearing down into the infinite abyss in *Indiana Jones and the Last Crusade.* The gray mist obscured my vision. Had I crossed the seal? Was the world crumbling? Calm, calm, I told myself. I could feel gravity sucking me deeper, time accelerating, the darkness around me, widening until I was somewhere else, somewhere with no horizon, an area of space that awed me in its foreverness, and I felt calm for just a moment. Then I recognized that I was floating without a tether. I tried to scream but I couldn't. I was afraid. The fear felt like desire: suddenly I wanted to go back and be in all the places I'd ever been, every street I'd walked down, every room I'd sat down in. I wanted to see it all again. I tried to remember my life, flipping through Polaroids in my mind. "It was so pretty there. It was interesting!" But I knew that even if I could go back, if such a thing were possible with exactitude, in life or in dreams, there was really no point. And then I felt desperately lonely. So I stuck my arm out and I grasped onto someone—maybe it was Ping Xi, maybe it was a wakefulness outside myself—and that other hand steadied me somehow as I fell past whole galaxies, mercurial waves of light strobing through my body, blinding me over and over, my brain throbbing from the pressure, my eyes leaking as though each teardrop shed a vision of my past. I felt the wetness trickle down my neck. I was crying. I knew that. I could hear myself gasp and whimper. I focused on the sound and then the universe narrowed into a fine line, and that felt better because there was a clearer trajectory, so I traveled more peacefully through outer space, listening to the rhythm of my respiration, each breath an echo of the breath before, softer and softer, until I was far enough away that there was no sound, there was no movement. There was no need for reassurance or directionality because I was nowhere, doing nothing. I was nothing. I was gone.

ON JUNE 1, 2001, I came to in a cross-legged seated position on the living room floor. Sunlight was needling through the blinds, illuminating crisscrossed planes of yellow dust that blurred and waned as I squinted. I heard a bird chirp.

I was alive.

AS I'D REQUESTED BACK in January, Ping Xi had laid out a set of clothes for me on the dining table: sneakers, track pants, T-shirt, zip-up hoodie. My credit cards and driver's license, passport, birth certificate, and a thousand dollars cash were in the envelope I'd sealed and given him to hold. There was a bottle of Evian, an apple in a plastic bag from the grocery store, and a sample-size tube of Neutrogena sunscreen—a thoughtful touch. The table had been cleared of all the Post-it notes, which I appreciated, but then I found the cluster in the trash, like a tossed-out bouquet of daisies. I picked one up and read it: "Don't forget: clothes, shoes, the envelope, keys. Buy me some sunscreen, please." And then on another one, "Thanks, good luck." A smiley face.

My old white fur coat hung on the hook by the front door. A Post-it note stuck to the wall read: "When I bought this for you, it was simply because I wanted you to have it. I'll really miss working with you. PX."

The door was unlocked.

I got dressed, put the coat on, went out and down the elevator to the lobby and made my way dizzily toward the light exploding through the glass doors onto the street.

"Miss?" I heard the doorman say. "Can you hear me?" Then the stiff rustle of his uniform pants as he squatted down and cradled my head in his hands. I hadn't realized that I'd hit the floor.

Someone brought me a glass of water. A woman held my hand and sat me in a leather armchair in the lobby. The doorman gave me the egg salad sandwich from his brown-bag lunch.

"Is there anyone we can call?"

People were so nice.

"No, there's nobody. Thank you. I just had a dizzy spell."

It took another week until I had the strength to make it outside and walk around the block. The next day I walked to Second Avenue. The next day, all the way to Lexington. I ate prepackaged egg salad sandwiches from a deli on East Eighty-seventh. I sat for hours on a bench in Carl Schurz Park and watched the lapdogs doddling around a tiled, fenced-in area, their owners dodging the sun and clicking at their cell phones. Someone left a collection of books out on the curb one day on East Seventy-seventh Street, and I brought them home and read them all cover to cover. A history of drunk driving in America. An Indian cookbook. *War and Peace. Mao II. Italian for Dummies.* A book of Mad Libs that I filled in myself using the simplest words I could think of. I passed the days like this for four or five weeks. I did not buy a cell phone. I got rid of the old mattress. Every night at nine I lay down on the smooth hardwood floor with a stretch and a yawn, and I had no trouble sleeping. I had no dreams. I was like a newborn animal. I rose with the sun. I did not walk south of Sixty-eighth Street.

By mid-June, it was too hot to wear the tracksuit Ping Xi had left me. I bought a pack of white cotton panties and plastic slip-on shoes from the 99 Cent Store on 108th Street. I liked it up there, almost Harlem. I paced slowly up and down Second Avenue in red or blue gym shorts and oversized athletic tees. I got in the habit of buying a box of Corn Flakes from the Egyptians each morning. I fed the Corn Flakes in gentle handfuls to the squirrels in the park. I drank no coffee.

I discovered the Goodwill store on 126th Street. I liked looking at things other people had let go of. Maybe the pillowcase I was sniffing had been used on an old man's deathbed. Maybe this lamp had sat on an end table in an apartment for fifty years. I could imagine all the scenes it had lit: a couple making love on the sofa, thousands of TV dinners, a baby's tantrums, the honeyed glow of whiskey in an Elks Lodge tumbler. Goodwill indeed. This was how I refurnished my apartment. One day, I brought the white fox fur coat with me to the Goodwill and handed it to the teenager taking donations through the door around the corner from the store entrance. He took it calmly, asked if I wanted a receipt. I watched his hands smooth the fur, as though he were assessing its value. Maybe he'd steal it and give it to his girlfriend, or his mother. I hoped he would. But then he just threw it in a huge blue bin.

In August I bought a battery-operated radio and carried it with me to the park each day. I listened to the jazz stations. I didn't know any names of the songs. The squirrels flocked to me as soon as I uncrumpled the bag of Corn Flakes. They ate straight from my palm, tiny black hands crunching into the cereal, cheeks ballooning. "You pigs!" I told them. They seemed perturbed by the music coming out of my little radio. I kept the volume low when I fed them.

I DIDN'T THINK MUCH of Ping Xi until I saw Reva. I called her on August 19 from the doorman's cell phone. Despite all the sleep and forgetting, I still knew her number by heart, and recognized the date on the calendar as her birthday.

She came over the following Sunday, nervous and smelling of a new perfume that reminded me of gummy worms, said nothing about the odd assortment of furniture and decorations in my apartment or my six-month disappearance, my lack of cell phone, the stacks of mildewed books lining the wall of the living room. She just said, "So, it's been a while, I guess," sat down where I pointed, at the Goodwill afghan that I'd spread out like a picnic blanket across the floor, and rattled on about her new position at her company. She described her boss as a "CIA tool," rolling her eyes and emphasizing certain technical terms in her description of her duties. At first I couldn't tell if they were aphorisms about sex positions. Everything about her seemed troublingly pornographic—her matte foundation, her darkly outlined lips, that perfume, the poised stillness of her hands. "Innovative solutions." "Anatomy of workplace violence." "Strong objectives." She wore her hair in a lose chignon, my tiny pearl earrings budding from her earlobes like drops of milk, simultaneously perverse and innocent, I thought. She also wore my white eyelet blouse and a pair of jeans I'd given her. I felt no longing or nostalgia for the clothes. The jeans had frayed at the cuffs, an inch too long on Reva's legs. I thought to suggest to her to have them professionally hemmed. There was a place on Eighty-third.

"I just read this story in the *New Yorker*," she said, and pulled the rolled-up issue out of her enormous purse. The story was called "Bad at Math." It was about an adolescent Chinese American in Cleveland who bombs the PSAT, jumps off his two-story junior high school, and breaks both his legs. After the school guidance counselor pressures the boy's family into group therapy, his parents tell him they love him in a supermarket parking lot and they all start to cry and wail and fall on their knees, while all the other shoppers wheel their carts past and pretend like nothing amazing is going on. "Listen to this opening," Reva said. "'For the first time, they said the words. I think it pained them more than the cracking of my shins and femurs.'"

"Go on," I said. The story was terribly written. Reva read aloud.

Ping Xi appeared in my mind as I listened. I imagined his small, dark eyes staring at me and squinting, one pinching shut as his paint-stained hand, outstretched with a brush, measured me for proportions. But that was all I could remember. He struck me as a reptilian, small-hearted being, someone placed on the planet to strike a chord with similar people, people who distracted themselves with money and conversation rather than sink their hands and teeth into the world around them. Shallow, I guess. But there were worse people on this Earth.

"I had studied for months for the PSAT." Reva read the story in its entirety. It took at least half an hour. I knew she was just trying to fill the air, take up the time until she could go and leave me forever. That's what it felt like at least. I can't say it didn't hurt me that she held herself at such a distance. But to confront her about it would have been cruel. I had no right to make any demands. I sensed she didn't really want to hear about my experiences in "rehab" or whatever it was she imagined I'd been through. I watched her mouth move, every little wrinkle in the skin of her lips, the vague dimple on her left cheek, the moon-shaped sadness of her eyes.

"'A black shred of bok choy had dried and attached itself to the rim of the garbage can,'" she read. I nodded along, hoping to make her feel at ease. When she was done, she sighed, and pulled a piece of gum from her purse.

"It's heartbreaking, isn't it, how certain cultures can be so cold?"

"It's heartbreaking, yes," I said.

"I really identify with the Chinese kid," Reva said, rolling the magazine back up.

I reached across her folded legs, tugged at the magazine in her tense clutch, like a tug-of-war. I didn't want her to leave. The white glare off the overhead light gleamed across her collarbones. She was beautiful, with all her nerves and all her complicated, circuitous feelings and contradictions and fears. This would be the last time I'd see her in person.

"I *love* you," I said.

"I love you, too."

PING XI'S VIDEOS and paintings went up at Ducat in late August. The show was called "Large-Headed Pictures of a Beautiful Woman." He or Natasha FedExed me tear-outs of the reviews. No note. The images from the show were not what I'd remembered imagining from my days with Ping Xi in my bedroom. I had expected a series of all sloppily painted nudes. Instead, Ping Xi had painted me in the style of Utamaro woodblock prints, wearing neon kimonos printed with tropical flowers and lipstick kisses and Coca-Cola and Pennzoil and Chanel and Absolut Vodka logos. In each piece, my head was huge. In a few portraits, Ping Xi had collaged my actual hair. In *Artforum,* Ronald Jones called me a "bloated nymph with dead man eyes." Phyllis Braff condemned the show as "a product of Oedipal lust" in the *New York Times*. *ArtReview* called the work "predictably disappointing." Otherwise, the reviews were positive. The videos described were of me talking into the camera, seeming to narrate some personal stories—I cry in one—but Ping Xi had dubbed everything over. Instead of my voice, you heard long, angry voice mails Ping Xi's mother had left him in Cantonese. No subtitles.

I FOUND MY WAY into the Met one afternoon in early September. I guess I wanted to see what other people had done with their lives, people who had made art alone, who had stared long and hard at bowls of fruit. I wondered if they'd watched the grapes wither and shrivel up, if they'd had to go to the market to replace them, and if, before they threw the shriveled strand of grapes away, they'd eaten a few. I hoped that they'd had some respect for the stuff they were immortalizing. Maybe, I thought, once the light had faded for the day, they dropped the rotted fruit out an open window, hoping it would save the life of a starving beggar passing below on the street. Then I imagined the beggar, a monster with worms crawling through his matted hair, the tattered rags on his body fluttering like the wings of a bird, his eyes ablaze with desperation, his heart a caged animal begging for slaughter, hands cupped in perpetual prayer as the townspeople milled around the city square. Picasso was right to start painting the dreary and dejected. The blues. He looked out the window at his own misery. I could respect that. But these painters of fruit thought only of their own mortality, as though the beauty of their work would somehow soothe their fear of death. There they all were, hanging feckless and candid and meaningless, paintings of things, objects, the paintings themselves just things, objects, withering toward their own inevitable demise.

I got the feeling that if I moved the frames to the side, I'd see the artists watching me, as though through a two-way mirror, cracking their arthritic knuckles and rubbing their stubbled chins, wondering what I was wondering about them, if I saw their brilliance, or if their lives had been pointless, if only God could judge them after all. Did they want more? Was there more genius to be wrung out of the turpentine rags at their feet? Could they have painted better? Could they have painted more generously? More clearly? Could they have dropped more fruit from their windows? Did they know that glory was mundane? Did they wish they'd crushed those withered grapes between their fingers and spent their days walking through fields of grass or being in love or confessing their delusions to a priest or starving like the hungry souls they were, begging for alms in the city square with some

honesty for once? Maybe they'd lived wrongly. Their great-
ness might have poisoned them. Did they wonder about
things like that? Maybe they couldn't sleep at night. Were
they plagued by nightmares? Maybe they understood, in fact,
that beauty and meaning had nothing to do with one another.
Maybe they lived as real artists knowing all along that there
were no pearly gates. Neither creation nor sacrifice could lead
a person to heaven. Or maybe not. Maybe, in the morning,
they were aloof and happy to distract themselves with their
brushes and oils, to mix their colors and smoke their pipes
and go back to their fresh still lifes without having to swat
away any more flies.

"Step back, please," I heard a guard say.

I was too close to the painting.

"Step away!"

The notion of my future suddenly snapped into focus: it
didn't exist yet. I was making it, standing there, breathing,
fixing the air around my body with stillness, trying to capture
something—a thought, I guess—as though such a thing were
possible, as though I believed in the delusion described in
those paintings—that time could be contained, held captive. I
didn't know what was true. So I did not step back. Instead, I
put my hand out. I touched the frame of the painting. And
then I placed my whole palm on the dry, rumbling surface of
the canvas, simply to prove to myself that there was no God

stalking my soul. Time was not immemorial. Things were just *things*. "Ma'am!" the guard yelled, and then there were hands gripping my shoulders, pulling me to the side. But that was all that happened.

"Sorry, I got dizzy," I explained.

That was it. I was free.

The real estate agent upstate sent a handwritten note the next day to say there'd been an offer on my parents' house. "Ten K below asking, but you might as well. We'll put it in stocks. Your phone seems to be out of order and has been for quite some time."

I took the letter with me on a walk in Central Park. The humidity carried in the warm wind mixed the sweat of the city and its dirt and grime with the heady fragrant lushness of the grass and trees. Things were alive. Life buzzed between each shade of green, from dark pines and supple ferns to lime green moss growing on a huge, dry gray rock. Honey locusts and ginkgos aflare in yellows. What was cowardly about the color yellow? Nothing.

"What kind of bird is that?" I heard a child ask his young mother, pointing to a bird that looked like a psychedelic crow. Its feathers were iridescent black, a rainbow reflected in the gleaming darkness, eyes bright white and alive, vigilant.

"A grackle," the woman replied.

I breathed and walked and sat on a bench and watched a

bee circle the heads of a flock of passing teenagers. There was majesty and grace in the pace of the swaying branches of the willows. There was kindness. Pain is not the only touchstone for growth, I said to myself. My sleep had worked. I was soft and calm and felt things. This was good. This was my life now. I could survive without the house. I understood that it would soon be someone else's store of memories, and that was beautiful. I could move on.

I found a pay phone on Second Avenue.

"OK," I said into the realtor's answering machine. "Sell it. And tell them to throw out whatever's in the attic. I don't need it. Just mail me whatever I have to sign."

Then I called Reva. She answered on the fourth ring, panting and tense.

"I'm at the gym," she said. "Can we talk later?"

We never did.

Eight

ON SEPTEMBER 11, I went out and bought a new TV/ VCR at Best Buy so I could record the news coverage of the planes crashing into the Twin Towers. Trevor was on a honeymoon in Barbados, I'd later learn, but Reva was lost. Reva was gone. I watched the videotape over and over to soothe myself that day. And I continue to watch it, usually on a lonely afternoon, or any other time I doubt that life is worth living, or when I need courage, or when I am bored. Each time I see the woman leap off the Seventy-eighth floor of the North Tower—one high-heeled shoe slipping off and hovering up over her, the other stuck on her foot as though it were too small, her blouse untucked, hair flailing, limbs stiff as she plummets down, one arm raised, like a dive into a summer lake—I am overcome by awe, not because she looks like Reva, and I think it's her, almost exactly her, and not because Reva and I had been friends, or because I'll never see her again, but because she is beautiful. There she is, a human being, diving into the unknown, and she is wide awake.